Amelia Lambe and the Search for the Light

Amelia Lambe and the Search for the Light

Carl Hubbard

Library of Congress Control Number: 2018907860

ISBN:	Hardcover	978-1-5434-9110-4
	Softcover	978-1-5434-9111-1
	eBook	978-1-5434-9112-8

Print information available on the last page.

Rev. date: 09/04/2018

To order additional copies of this book, contact:
Xlibris
800-056-3182
www.Xlibrispublishing.co.uk
Orders@Xlibrispublishing.co.uk
775345

CONTENTS

Chapter 1

The Creation of Villainous Intentions

Wednesday, October 16, 1918

It was a cold but sunny day in Northeast France, the air heavy with dread and fear as the dogs of war seemed ever closer. It had been a long, brutal war fought by once-friendly nations, fought in man-made burrows miles long and barely deep enough to ensure a scalp would not become an ashtray on the enemy's fireplace. A war which had seen boy soldiers, barely old enough to consume alcohol when they could get their hands on it, die merciless deaths, caked in slushy mud in the anonymous, monotonous fields onto which they stumbled from the trenches-tombs they had built with their nail-bitten fingers.

Major "Fast" Eddie Rickenbacker of the US Army Air Service, the "ace of aces", the most decorated flyer of the age, was despatched once more to the front line. His target was the silent enemy balloon observing the Allies' movements as it hung above the battlescape of one of the last unconquered frontiers of the Western Front near Remonville, in North-Eastern France. Silent from the outside, inside a bee's nest of buzzing circuitry and terrified, chattering *fliegertruppen*, the balloonmen's panic rose fast as the propellered nose of the SPAD XIII bore down on the vulnerable wicker cockpit dangling from the vast dirigible. The wind, a whistling cold easterly, mixed menacingly with the icy rain, adding to the sense of foreboding arising in the basket as the operators groped anxiously at its entry gate, screaming for help from the ants on the ground below. But it never came.

As ever, the major flew towards the enemy target with fear as his friend and one hand on the gun turret. He swooped towards the stationery balloon, firing a volley of gunfire at the hulking, hydrogen-filled tarpaulin. A flash of metal shoots out from the dangling basket, its anchoring line the target of a panic-filled bayonet as the crew desperately tried to fly above the marauding American. Successfully severing its target, the weapon freefalls towards the innocents below, bounced off a rooftop, only to be swallowed by a gutter on the butcher's roof. No-one could hear the roars of unspeakable terror from the radio operators careening westwards as they overshot the village of Remonville. Only Eddie saw the terror in the men, and like a red rag to a bull, he banked his nimble craft to swoop down and torment the enemy occupants. The balloon and its newly detached basket flew briskly on the cold easterly, momentum propelling them along, streaking low above the anxious Remonville villagers below.

The fast-deflating dirigible carried on towards Chateau Landreville on the edge of Remonville, sinking with the ear-piercing squeal and hiss of last week's punctured tyre on Bouchard's Boulangerie's new and ornately decorated delivery van. Rickenbacker guffawed at yet another kill as he steered *Number One* up and away. Smiling a satisfied smile, he looked down on the crumpling balloon flapping in the wind, freefalling towards the sycamores below.

While the cockpit went into freefall, and no longer sure of their fate on this most strange of days, its soldier-inhabitants clambered up the inside to time their jumps to safety. In their panic, all practice drills were forgotten. On the count of "*Drei, zwei, eins*", three two one, and at just the right moment, two of the three crew tipped over the edge of the basket and fell head first into the newly refilled moat. The pilot, rooted to his position in the cockpit, was paralysed by fear. He thought of his family as he faced uncertainty about his fate when the basket hit land.

Impact and Injury

On the fertile soil of Chateau Landreville, sixteen-year-old Michel Meixmoron tended the trees planted by his ancestors when they lived in the imposing manor house in the 1800s. All that was left of those glorious days of wealth and privilege was tenancy of a lodge on the estate, graciously granted by the current owner's father to his grandfather, in exchange for the upkeep of the nearly fifty acres of woods and gardens on the compact estate. There was also the payment of a small retainer for the smattering of paintings by a distant Meixmoron cousin, inherited by his father for safe keeping. They now adorned the flocked walls of the great houses of his cousin's old patrons, the Bourbons, throughout France.

As ever, Michel was daydreaming as he snipped the blades of his secateurs together, trimming the branches of the cascading yellow tea rose growing at the foot of this lone copse of chestnuts. The trees had recently shed their load of bristly green fruit. Year in, year out, broken starfish shapes mingled with the rotting petals of this season's roses, slowly decomposing and fertilising the verdant green lawns shaded by the branches. He suddenly wondered, *What would my ancestors think of me, of their young successor in the service of the newest occupier of the old family seat? Ashamed, perhaps? Perhaps proud – I am, after all, a Meixmoron playing an important role in preserving the fate of my family's heritage in the gardens?*

He was idling on this thought when his reverie was broken by the sudden unleashing of hell on his normally quiet working day. Suddenly, he could hear voices screaming, getting louder and closer as Michel - "Max" to family and friends, they liked the juxtaposition of "Max" with "Meix" in his surname – frantically scanned the landscape around him to see where the terrified yells were coming from.

At the last second, he looked upwards and he immediately saw the source of those unearthly sounds. The freefalling basket, still with one of its *truppen* on board, slammed into the side of the unprepared teenager's head. With two of the truppen having abandoned ship moments earlier to avail of a wet landing in the newly refilled moat, the impact was considerably softer than it would otherwise have been but he was still catapulted across the copse. His upper body caromed violently off the trunk of the chestnut tree behind the yellow rose. Clothes and skin were ripped by the thorns of the soon-to-flower rosebush. His head and thorax ricocheted violently off the immovable tree, and his knees buckled as he sank to the ground, deeply unconscious, but somehow, still alive.

Recovery and Revenge

Tuesday, 22rd October 1918, another bright, cold autumn day and Michel Meixmoron's miracle began on his hospital bed. His mother is the first to see it, an almost imperceptible twitch and suddenly the ward was filled with voices chanting, "Max, Max!!". Eyelids closed tightly for seven long days had finally begun to flutter and flicker as his body at last responded to the infusions of epinephrine to bring him back from his deep coma. Staff, his parents and his two closest friends, whispering words of encouragement throughout, had ignored their growing fears of the possibility of him not making it. Instinctively, they knew that their role was to bring him back to life. The doctors and the chaplain insisted that it was their duty to offer up encouraging words and prayers so that hope was not lost in those darkest of days.

On that seventh day, and through fluttering lashes, Max began to see the familiar faces of his young life, willing him to come back to them. Today was the day that brought an end to what had seemed to his loved ones an eternity in a living hell. The nurses and trainee surgeons milling around slowed to watch the unfolding miracle. Until now, all they could offer were platitudes at each heave of his unmarked body: "He may live, but who knows how he'll be affected", were not the most reassuring words the senior doctors could muster as it began to seem that, in fact, he was not going to wake. But now, with the resurrection underway, his aunt Enid reverently and solemnly returned the Splinter from The Cross to its ermine-lined sarcophagus, the move that confirmed its mission was over for now. She would have to return it to its rightful owner, Ms Weil. It was she who had loaned it to her as the ultimate comfort in this period of stress. Enid had laid it on her nephew's chest every day while she prayed the Holy

Rosary. It was the miracle she knew she had started and she was happy.

Blinking manically like a new-born kitten, Max reached out for his mama and papa. His friend and colleague, Pierre was there. And, of course, there was Walther Popov, his friend from across the Belgian border. His mother had gone to school with Maxine, Walther's mother, in Berne and it was a great joy to the women when they discovered how near to each other they were when the Popovs arrived in Belgium. Walther was not here, however, to offer platitudes to his oldest friend, he wanted to tell Max about the anger he felt about what had happened to his friend, and most of all about what was happening in Germany, to Germany.

"Some day, mark my words, Max, someone, some*thing* will emerge to help us get over it all, and there will be hell to pay!", he firmly stated. Max's father ushered Walther away from his uncomprehending son and heir with the words "Not now, Walther, can't you see he has only opened his eyes? He hardly even recognises us!"

Nurses and doctors, all with alarm writ large on furrowed brows, took his wrist to check for his pulse as he stretched out cold, sinewy fingers. There was awkwardness amongst some as they silently recalled how they had written off any chance of survival for young Meixmoron. For others, it was a joyous moment as "medicine" had been, for them, the victor. Max was destined never to remember what had happened. Nor did he know how it would change his life forever. The focus for now had to be on maintaining his breathing, keeping his heart beating. There was regular monitoring of blood pressure with the sphygmomanometer as he was still in mortal danger of passing away before his time.

Monday, November 11, 1918

Finally, the day of days had come. Patients and hospital staff had heard the rumours on the corridors and wards, now they could read it in the newspapers: today at 11am the War would officially end. At 11am on the Eleventh Day of the Eleventh Month, the Kaiser would surrender on behalf of the decimated and demoralised people of the Axis nations. It was a time and date deigned to be a fitting end to the war just ceded. Even though victory appeared to be theirs, the Allied soldiers on the ward – the Victors - sat dazed, unbelieving that all of their hard work here was either for nought or it was for everything – Victory! Men and boys, reeling from the shock of a war they had survived, cried openly as they woke on this, the most anticipated day of everyone's lives.

A bottomless nothingness gripped them now. There was little joy, just raw memories of friends lost, killed by bullet and explosion, by disease, by pestilence caused by the giant rats or dysentery caused by eating mud or uncooked rations. Perhaps some were wasted lives now, they thought, and victory did not taste so sweet. An eerie silence filled the wards, punctured only by the pained groans of the "newbies" and the sobs of the long-term injured. Coloured, stained-glass light burst from the arched window in the gable wall, projecting grotesque images of the saint of the sick, Camillus, ministering to the sick, onto the whitewashed walls above their beds.

A kaleidoscope of dazzling colours filtered across Michel Meixmoron's anxious stare again as he blinked repeatedly to clear his vision. His eyes scanned around the curtained ward, taking in the moaning cesspit of despair and yet, somehow, he sensed a bright beacon of hope burning right here, in this room. Max would have to get used to seeing legless men exercising shorn limbs as if this was something they had been doing all of their lives but he knew how wretched they must feel inside, fit trained bodies reduced to this. But it was the training and tough lives in the trenches that had hardened their resolve and that was why they never doubted that they would overcome all of this. There was no room for self-pity here, just determination to rise above the setbacks and get back to normal life again.

Renewal and Recovery

With the unequivocal agreement of his Lordship and the Meixmoron extended family (a few well-heeled cousins left scattered throughout the land), it was agreed quickly that his parents would use a share of the old Meixmoron family inheritance, the sale of a painting, to bring him to the American Hospital in Paris. And so it was that the quick sale of Port de Boulogne to a private buyer in Paris, an Englishman named Mendl, meant his parents had the money to pay for the best available treatment.

Arriving in Paris in late November with his father in His Lordship's Rolls Royce, the American Hospital was the place where he would recover from his injuries and, they were promised, be re-equipped for his future. He was fortunate: this hospital was one of the first in which the young neurosurgeon, Kurt Goldstein, had introduced his new model of "post-traumatic injury" treatment. Goldstein had seen, first-hand, the damage inflicted by this most ravaging of conflicts - he himself had seen too many of his peers return from the front line as broken men, former medical colleagues who only went to the front line to treat the wounded and the sick: some, though, had felt compelled to take up arms to help the cause. Goldstein worked with his friend Fritz on a plan to do something worthwhile for them, and the two worked tirelessly to develop a programme of services to help them: new exercise routines ("physical therapy", a new American idea that others had told him about); a process for speech recovery (he liked to call it "speech therapy"), and a new "therapie" he was devising to give the wounded a new set of skills to replace those recently acquired butchery skills of bayonet and artillery fire. It was called, for now, *beschäftigungstherapie*, occupational therapy. He had worked on it with American medical colleagues in Cologne, Goldstein saw the value of it and he wanted to use it in his programme.

Recovering allied soldiers filled this hospital, and the air was heavy with excited talk about the likelihood of returning to the soldier's life that had been all they had known since leaving school. Of course, it was an ideal that was, for so many of these infantrymen, little more than an impossible dream, most of them too mentally scarred and exhausted by their deeply oppressed lives in the trenches, and simply not fit enough to be discharged home. Others would leave with insurmountable problems - severest head injuries rendering many barely intelligible, others who would never fully recover from the shrapnel wounds in their legs, others who woke in terror in the middle of the night, shattered by what they had seen and experienced. In truth, few had little hope of ever regaining the fit bodies that had been a pre-requisite on signing up to a life on the front line. Still others would never recover having been blinded by the shrapnel from explosions, others deafened by the blasts going off all around them. Many, too many, had been reduced to quivering wrecks, never again able to cope with the gore and grime they had been trained to confront.

Renewal

For the next five months, Goldstein's staff cajoled and trained Max with a daily routine of hard work, unlike anything he had experienced before and, perhaps, would ever again. Throughout this part of his ordeal, Max would have to listen to Walther complaining about his country's situation on his weekly visit. Walther would even encourage his friend to reek vengeance on the American airman who had done this to him. In the here and now of his situation, Max had a sense, deep down, like the horribly injured and broken men still lining the bleach-laced corridors of this old, airy military hospital, that this was his best chance for a return to the life from which he had been so cruelly torn away.

For the young Max though, all of the daily tasks were tough work. "Therapies", Goldstein called them. He saw Eva for therapy in the morning, consisting of physical exercises and limb-stretching; Timothie in the afternoon for therapy which would help him to, ultimately, regain control of his secateurs, his tree-cutters and his pen. He didn't understand why there were painting classes and why he constructed mechanical toys with worn Meccano sets in his workshop, but he did it happily, and Tim would praise his efforts. Averse as he was to jigsaws, it was not long before Tim had him eagerly completing two hundred piece, then five hundred piece, puzzles.

In another part of the workshop, there was Terése who helped him to re-find and refine words he had lost and to gain some he had never known before. From the moment that he was wakened from his deep sleep, he had refound his speech and Goldstein assigned Terése straight away to help him recover the rest of his speech. With her, he found himself pleasantly absorbed in games of concentration like chess and crosswords. He learned, much to his annoyance really, that he could actually enjoy what had always been to him such boring pursuits. Hovering always in the background was Dr. Goldstein, overseeing and motivating his patient at every turn in order to get past this, as he would say, "temporary little setback in life".

Every day was filled with the same routine but it was this repetition that was actually making him better and more determined to find his way back. Alone in his ward at night and before he would cry himself to sleep, he would look at his reflection in the shaving mirror and wonder if his life had, in fact, ended? Sure, he knew he was getting better, certainly stronger, certainly more like his old self. He was gradually coming to an acceptance that, well, the old Max is dead, the new Max will be much better.

Physically, his recovery was quick: at the start, a rickety wheelchair was used to get him to Eva in the gymnasium and he had to be shown how to stand and walk again. It was not long before he could shave himself and there was a short-lived necessity of daily exercises performed with Eva in Dr. Jahn's gymnasium. This helped him to speed up his physical recovery. He had to relearn how to feed himself again, yes, but his brain responded to everything that Eva required of him. That was the part of the day he enjoyed most of all – the pretty Eva would demonstrate what needed to be done, he would watch her lithe frame bend and dip as she demonstrated the gentle exercises and his face would redden when she caught him watching her breasts strain against the buttons of her tight chemise.

Eva's work with him was indeed short-lived as his young body repaired itself quickly: there were no broken bones, no permanent marks, no physical signs which would tell the world of what he had lived through in the darkest period of his life. He was getting through this part of his recovery with ease and Eva's frequent praise confirmed that he was indeed getting better. Eva was kind, but he knew he had a long way to go before he would be useful again amongst the sycamores and cypresses and chestnuts of Landreville. Inside, though, he was determined not to deviate from his goal to resume work at the chateau as soon as possible.

Fermenting along with these seeds of restoration, was the seed of hatred: Walther it was who had planted it and Walther it was who fertilised it at every opportunity. Walther would travel across from Belgium with his father on his father's weekly journey to Paris to collect the French silk he preferred to use in making shirts for his wealthier clients. Walther had been quick to tell Max that an American airman had been responsible for his incarceration in "this American hell-hole" in Paris, a fact that he reminded his friend of over and over again. The war was well over but it was not long before Max felt an all-consuming resentment for the anonymous airman. Slowly, his thoughts were turning to revenge and retribution.

March 1919

The day had come at last when Michel "Max" Meixmoron could return to his family on the Landreville estate after almost five long months of therapy in the American Hospital. He was dying to get back to his work in Landreville on the agreed date in mid-April, as he continued to be the grateful recipient of his Lordship's patronage, patience and loyality.

Initially, he was sent back out to tend to the groves of sycamore and ash on the boundary of the estate. He was also back to pruning and tending the copses of chestnuts again with Pierre, the soon-to-retire head gardener. Inexplicably, his nerves got the better of him on the first day and he refused, point blank, to return to the chestnut copse alone. Although he had no memory of the incident - the actual moment of impact – he found himself continually glancing skywards and all around, his anxiety such that he had to get back out onto the lawn so that he could lie down on the grass and calm himself.

He was pleased to know that "Topiary" was one of the subjects he would be studying in the Agricultural College in Nancy soon enough so, with Pierre close at hand, he continued to develop his skills in topiary on the evergreens and fruit bushes of the estate. The work was not stressful and that would allow for his recovery to continue unchallenged. Despite being so close to death, his plan to progress to Head Gardener was still alive. Nancy was just around the corner now, with all fees and lodging paid for by the Lord of the Manor. It was proof that all of his hard work in Paris would bear fruit sooner than he might have reasonably expected.

September 1919

By September, Max was now fully five months back on the land, his hatred for the American undiminished since his discharge. His mind was never too far from a plan to avenge that brush with a violent death, yet his parents had told him to focus on his work and to do his job "to the best of his ability". "After all, Max, you will never see or hear of that criminal ever again!", they would say. The phrase "best of your ability" always angered Max: he felt that it was designed to placate him, designed to put down his ambition to exact revenge for what had happened in the chestnut grove on that day before his birthday. He was starting to notice that he was beginning to feel invincible again.

CHAPTER 2

Walther Popov, the Committee of Independent Workers and Other Political Awakenings

Michel Meixmoron's friendship with Walther Popov, the young, nervous Russo-German, whose father was the local tailor in Bouillon across the border in Belgium, was well established. The arrival of the Popovs to Belgium brought this well-connnected Prussian family to the lands of the victors of the '14-'18 war. The well-to-do Natascha Popov was a descendant of a Russian prince, a Gallitzin, and she had attended finishing school in Lausanne where the future Mme De Meixmoron, Michel's mother, also attended. Back then, Meixmoron's mother was known as Nathalie de Rivarol and she too came from an old and well-to-do family with Franco-Italian origins. Both women had married well, Nathalie marrying an heir of the diminished de Meixmoron family fortune and Natascha marrying the rather grey Prussian, Franz Popov, an immediate relation to the scientist the Russians claimed was the inventor of radio, Alexander Popov. Franz, Walther's father, was a first cousin of the Russian, his father arriving in East Prussia as part of a wave of middle-class Russian migrants who left their homeland to secure new landholdings in the friendly eastern regions of Poland and in German East Prussia.

Lately, Walther had delighted in telling Max all about an anti-Treaty of Versailles movement calling itself the 'Committee of Independent Workers', informing his friend that he had read about its founders late last year in a German army newspaper, published in Belgium, which he had bought in Coneg's newsagents. Walther encouraged his friend to read the article and he brought the propaganda pamphlets that had fallen out of that same newspaper. Max took everything his friend gave him, more out of courtesy to his friend than out of any real interest or desire to get involved. After all, this would indeed be a strange organisation for him to be interested in: the Axis Powers had surrendered, so he was on the side of the winners. He would be considered somewhat middle-class and, therefore, hardly a "worker". Most of all, of course, he was *not* German. Max knew nothing about politics or communism and this he had stridently pointed out to Walther on more than one occasion but still Walther thrust pamphlets into Max's hands so that he felt obliged to leaf through his friend's material. Even when Walther read them to him, he could sense that just handling them would be dangerous but he wanted to be polite to his friend and so he indulged Walther's appetite for news of his fatherland.

In fact, Max was quite fascinated by his friend's new-found interests and he was starting to piece together an interpretation of what this Committee's goals might be - anti-government, yes, anti-Imperial powers, unquestionably. Max was surprised that Walther found any connection with this but decided that perhaps his friend had wanted to be seen as a slightly unpredictable sort, the opposite of what his parents had brought him up to be. Overall though, Max was happy in the knowledge that, if Walther was involved, it must be good, and he needed all of the stimulation he could get in order to maintain his recovery from his horrible injury.

Max was used to Walther waxing lyrical about the night the German general Count Von Bothmer - head of the German Army campaign in Lorraine - had spoken at a meeting in Popperinghe. Walther had been fascinated by the German occupiers of the town during the brief time his family had spent there and he had heard about this meeting in the church hall. It was about a new German nationalistic, socialist, ideal, an attempt to mobilise every citizen to devote themselves to "the nation", the nation being the German people themselves. This 'Committee of Independent Workers' would copy the "tireless rise of the people to rule over themselves" as had happened to the east in Russia. The committee, limited to Munich in Bavaria at present, would soon overthrow the Wittelsbachs and would join Munich up with Lenin's mighty Union of Soviet Socialist Republics across the Urals. Germany would soon fall under Communist control, and Munich was going to be the stronghold for this monumental power grab by the people. Walther had been enthralled by the charismatic and rousing speech of the Count and felt he must join this new movement. Very soon, his wishes were to come true but not quite in the way he had envisioned.

Journey to Munich

Time was moving onwards and April found Popov arriving early one morning at Landreville, on his bicycle as always and on fire with excitement as he was arriving to remind Max that he had invited his friend to a meeting of the newly formed

German Worker's Party, "Deutsche Arbeiterpartei", the DAP, tonight. He had invited Max to attend just as an "observer".

At this point in time, Walther had already abandoned his notions around the Committee of Independent Workers as it continued to be harangued and crushed by the anti-Communist Freikorps. The Committee had been finding it difficult to garner support among the populace and the Freikorps were swiftly and cruelly crushing any desire among the Munchner for people power. The major problem facing the boys today was that the Deutsche ArbeiterPartei meeting was to be held in Munich that very evening, a massive eight hundred kilometres away. Max was pessimistic that they could make this meeting: "I mean, Walther, how the devil are we going to get there?", he had asked his friend. He had decided that he should try to excuse himself from the trip but Walther was unperturbed and insisted that he had "a plan". What Walther was joining, however, as well as a committed group of Germans, was a party which was committing itself to battling against "international Jewry". Walther, although vaguely aware of this when applying to be one of the first wave of members, had decided to say nothing about his background to Drexler, the leader, but found that he was increasingly uncomfortable and nervous that his identity would indeed be unmasked. For the time being at least, the party leadership accepted that he would be an upstanding member, never afraid to be counted as a true German, and that was all that mattered.

Back in their Belgian hometown however, Walther's father worried that his teenage boy had been fatally distracted by the rhetoric and nonsense of Drexler and had taken to regularly berating Walther, telling him: "No good will come of this, no good at all, that man is no friend of the Jew!" "Or of the Russians", Walther would wearily reply. To be fair, Walther usually listened to his father and would nod in agreement but he continued to be drawn to this exciting new movement. With its ideology drawn from the "volkisch spirit" and a moral compass derived from the odd belief that "pure Germans" had come from some mythological land in the high north of the world, Walther was convinced that this new movement was destined to be the greatest thing to ever hit Germany.

His zeal had led him to ask a visiting textile seller, Schubert, in town to deliver and sell rolls of new suiting fabric and assorted monogrammed handkerchiefs to his father, if he could hitch a lift to Munich in the open back of his smart Unic van. Herr Schubert's factory was in Saxony, in the east of Germany and, bearing in mind that Walther would some day be his customer, he had somewhat reluctantly agreed to allow the Popov boy to travel incognito with him. He only agreed on condition that Popov travel in the open hold under the tarpaulin protecting his valuable cargo, much of which had been salvaged and cut from old military uniforms and parachute materials gathered up during the Great War.

Schubert was bemused and thought that Walther simply wanted to go on a teenage boy's adventure to a big city and experience life beyond the stifling austerity, which was now the currency in occupied Belgium. He was all in favour of giving the youth back their freedom – after all, so many had lost their lives, and, indeed, their fathers, and for what? Neither was he perturbed when Walther turned up on that Friday morning in the company of his friend, the carefully-spoken and slightly reticent Michel ("Max, for short", as he would be told): "I want you to meet my best friend, Herr Schubert. This is Michel Meixmoron, sir. We are like brothers. He was injured by an American at the end of 1918 and he is hoping to meet again the special doctor from his Paris hospital, in Munich", said Walther. "German doctor in Paris? Well, well! Interesting. Okay, hello Max", said Herr Schubert, unperturbed to find his Unic's cargo now would have two live ones, not just the Popov boy. Suddenly anxious about the extra cargo, he quickly said: "I haven't seen you around the Popov's shop, do you live in Bouillon? I hope you checked with your parents? Walther is going on a long trip here with me today, you know!?". "Yes, I know, Herr Schubert", said Max. "But I do intend to find Dr Goldstein's surgery, it's off the Marienplatz. I will look for the other doctor in Cologne some other time", continued Max, before allowing himself to let his anger take hold, growling through gritted teeth: "I want people to be angry at the American who nearly destroyed my life!" Startled, Schubert could only say: "That's fine, Max, I won't press you on that", surprised at how animated the young man had become. "Delighted to be of assistance", he said, pleasantly. "Welcome aboard! Make sure you keep out of sight too, don't want the enemy to see you boys, do we?" Neither of the boys was sure what he meant as surely there was no enemy now, just the Allied troops marshalling the roads and towns, so they let the comment pass.

Munching to Munich

The boys settled into the open hold of the Unic, gripped with excitement at the start of what would turn into the journey that would change their lives forever. They pulled the tarpaulin across their heads and munched greedily on their provisions of water biscuits and rocquefort and camembert cheeses. Walther had also smuggled a large slab of homemade chocolate torte from his kitchen. They had two flasks of water each to slake their thirsts.

For the next few hours, they whispered entertaining anecdotes from home. Walther whispered about how he had learned about this new party from his Uncle Fritz who had served in the Wehrmacht on the Russian Front. He had encouraged his nephew to acquire secret membership of the "German Worker's Party", a new political movement he had heard about in Bavaria before he returned to his home in Augsburg. He saw it as a way of keeping German traditions alive, he told Walther. The van careered south-eastwards across Belgium, and once they had passed through Luxembourg, it was not long before the van reached the border with Germany.

Schubert had immunity from the newly-installed Nazi border guards in his French-made van, and had papers to prove he was a company owner, going about his business in occupied territories. Only one guard stopped him to inspect his cargo of fabric with a cursory glance under the tarpaulin, the boys having shimmied up towards the driver's cabin. It was a little too close for comfort though and the three of them heaved a sigh of relief as the van was waved on to continue its shaky trundle across the hills south-east into Bavaria.

During a break for the driver in Dachau, the "live cargo" took a few minutes to get their bearings. Schubert told them that they were getting close to Munich (Dachau was "a stone's throw from Munich", he said, and, hopefully, "some large orders for suiting cloth and kerchiefs"). He explained: "Sorry, Walther, business in Belgium is a bit slow, there doesn't seem to be much money around but I'm fond of your father, you understand? He works hard to bring in the business around your hometown", he said, "and you should learn as much as you can from him".

Schubert was filled with trepidation when he thought about the long trundle facing him from Munich homewards to his Saxony base – strangely, having two clandestine passengers had given him a sense of purpose about his joumey and, now that they were gone, he found that his desire to slog his way home this evening was fading which was why he had decided that he would find accommodation near Nuremberg.

Left on the outskirts of Munich, the charged up young men knew that they had to head in towards the city's centre. Hitching a lift on Lorenz's butcher's van, which was heading back to the now scaled-down meat markets of the Marienplatz, they glanced around nervously as they drank in the bubbling excitement on the streets of Munich. They inhaled the exotic smells of the restaurants as they waited outside, while the driver made his deliveries. The van pulled up on Tal, close to the Marienplatz, to make its delivery at the Sterneckerbrau and it was here where Walther's new hybrid party had booked its first meeting.

The German Worker's Party

It was a new party with, in reality, very few members, fifty perhaps, plus at least one new one, the disaffected German son of an emigrant German family called Popov, now living in Belgium. Walther and Max shook hands nervously with Drexler and Harrer of what the two men proudly called the "German Worker's Party" and the boys signed the registration book. Max was somewhat more reserved in his enthusiasm and it seemed that Walther's presence was little more than an initiation ceremony towards his induction into the fledgling party's membership: Drexler told Walther that he would be member 541, although it was clear that the party numbered little more than fifty members, now just a shade more than fifty.

There was nothing advertising this event but Walther had been told that someone by the name of Feder was to address the initial gathering. He turned out to be, oddly, "just" a civil engineer with fairly radical views on economics and the young men were awe-struck by his extraordinary rant against the capitalist system which controlled all of their lives. Herr Feder saw no reason for German people to pay interest on money they were borrowing from the banks: if that money helped a business to earn money, then why should ordinary working folk, the ones who had built the business, have to pay extra money back to the lender? Let everyone share in the earnings, and the common good of all Germans would be achieved! It was during this speech that Walther got a distinctly cold shiver down his spine when Feder named "these wealthy Jewish bankers" for their "anti-German" practices. Feder's animosity was ill-concealed and Walther began to realise that he would have a difficult time concealing his true background in this company, but he was determined that "conceal" was what he would do for now.

There was shock too at the reaction in the audience about these Jewish people - at the applause ringing out - so much so that he wished the floor would open and swallow him. It brought him to ponder if this trip had been such a great idea after all. Max saw the startled look of his great friend and realised that this was not what either of them had expected. He motioned to Walther to move towards the back of the room as a Bavarian nationalist took to the podium, unleashing a remarkable rant in favour of Bavaria joining up with Austria in a new state. Thankfully, this was cut short when a small, neatly besuited and moustachioed man with carefully parted chestnut brown hair stood up and harangued the speaker, labelling him a "fool" and giving a startling counter-argument against the whole "preposterous notion" of such a "romantic ideal". The little man spoke with purpose, the cadence in his voice rising and falling with each counter-argument. It was nothing short of hypnotic, and his arguments were made in a clearly well-rehearsed manner. He smirked and bowed graciously to the low ripple of applause when he abruptly concluded his rebuttal of the Bavarian's argument.

The boys watched him as he sat down, his face shining with perspiration as he made notes in his little moleskin notebook. Later, they watched as Drexler pressed a leaflet into the flint-eyed man's hand. How Walther wished that he was that little man, whoever he was. The boys caught Drexler's eye and he approached them promptly: "Boys, come over here with me, I want you to meet Herr Feder, we hope he will become a key member of our new party, the man who will present our counter-arguments against the further enslavement of our great people by the invaders". Then, motioning to the small faced and neatly dressed man who had just quietened the room, he said "And this is Herr Hitler, Corporal Hitler". Turning to the little man, Drexler said "It strikes me, sir, that you now have a flavour of what we want to do for our country, from what I know of you, we are on the same line. I trust that you will wish to join with us in reclaiming our land from the west's latest Crusaders?" The little man gave a non-committal "We shall see."

As he shook the boys' proffered hands, he asked them if they had come to Munich especially for this meeting. Walther saw his chance to make an impression: "My family was forced to leave our home near Frankfurt when the French arrived. They started to harass my father and steal his goods – "we will pay you later!", they would say. We have ended up in Bouillon in Belgium but I don't like it there, it's full of British soldiers. I want to help my people, the common and good

German people, to get back what is rightfully theirs! My best friend Max here came to see what this is all about; our mothers are old school friends and we live half an hour away from each other, by bicycle."

Walther continued talking to Herr Hitler, telling him that he was enrolling in a Munich tailoring college, as his father had planned for him. He said that one day he would take over his father's business. "Isn't he a sensible young fellow?", said the older man to nobody in particular. "It's great to hear of someone so young planning for a life of commerce", he said brusquely, somehow beginning to sense that perhaps there was a Jewish link here somewhere (it was a well known fact that tailoring was a particularly Jewish occupation). "Thank you sir, that makes me very happy to hear. I hope I will be able to help our comrades in some practical way when I come to Munich for my training", Walther replied, not missing an opportunity to stake his claim well in advance.

Walther's early return to Munich

Max had been so unimpressed with that September meeting, he had decided that he would not revisit Munich with his friend anytime soon. But, out of loyalty to Walther, he arranged for him to accompany his boss on one of his regular business trips to the Bavarian capital. So after introducing Walther to his employer and owner of Chateau Landreville, the Monseigneur de Manoir himself, Max followed them into Bayonville on his bicycle to see them off on the train: first, they would have to journey to Paris for the Orient Express, the only and fastest train, which would leave them in Munich. First though, the Monseigneur had arranged for one of the local gendarmerie to drive them to Bayonville in his 1914 Rolls

Royce "Continental", the "Alpine Eagle", an imposing white Silver Ghost limousine, named in honour of the first race the car had won. Max had tried in vain to get Walther to enrol him in the party too so that he could join his friend on his trips to party meetings but, at his friend's insistence, he had come to the realisation that the "German Worker's Party" was really something he could not be a part of, although he could always attend as an observer. The best he could hope for was that if perhaps a similar movement was to form in France, a French Worker's Party perhaps, he may be enrolled. If he was honest, he hadn't really liked the atmosphere at that meeting back in September anyway but, for the moment, he wanted to help his friend and encouraged his fascination with his "homeland", as Walther was now referring to Germany.

Stationary

Meixmoron cycled vigorously and, even on his bicycle, arrived at the station just minutes after the Rolls. Always fascinated by the silent power of the six-litre giant which his Lordship maintained with great love and devotion, he watched the elegant motor silently disappear around the corner into the town square. He had watched his boss enviously many times from the edge of the estate as the big car floated over the roadway up to the chateau and gracefully draw to a silent halt on the apron at the side of the manor house.

As always, the gleaming car turned heads in the little hamlet of Bayonville: it distracted the elderly ladies sipping their café au laits as they stopped mid-dunk with their chocolate–coated waffles, dropped jaws hanging in mid-air, chocolate as bitter as the words they exchanged about the oncoming ghostly automobile and its owner: “Oh! Regarde! Voici ce fluage dans sa voiture tape-á-l’oeil!” and other insults were bandied openly.

Gliding to a halt on the gravel in the village square, the only gendarme visible in the village that day, replete with lovingly waxed handlebar moustache, took over driving duties from his Lordship. Immediately, immaculate white gloves clutched the polished walnut of the steering wheel and he eased the silver beast (it was more a “beast” than a “ghost”) forward onto the road, taking Walther on the latest leg of his foray into this gripping new future to which he so passionately wanted to belong.

His Lordship sat in the rear-facing seat on the opposite side of the car, his back comfortable against the back of the driver’s seat. Walther grinned to himself as he contemplated the dandruff-dusted shoulders of the eager policeman immediately behind his Lordship and presumed that his Lordship was blissfully unaware that he too was sharing in his driver’s snowstorm. Max bid farewell to Walther and his master through the open window with a wave, and he reflected on the contrast between Walther’s first trip to Munich and the luxury at the start of this new adventure. He had made Walther promise to bring back some fresh weisswurt and brazen, the delicacies the boys had feasted on in Munich back in September at that strange meeting.

“Don’t forget the prinzregententorte for our mamas!”, called Max, having passed the remainder of his Reichsmarks to his friend the night before.

The Tailor's Son and the Leadership

It was two days later when Walther reappeared at the estate cottage of the Meixmoron family, very much subdued and not a little bit tearful. He had returned somewhat rudderless as his earlier enthusiasm had been dampened by the thrust of what this Hitler fellow was bringing to what had been, after all, Walther's party. It was fair to conclude that this trip to Munich had been a huge disappointment as, and perhaps Max had wisely foreseen in signs back at that September meeting, it had become clear for Walther that, for his continued involvement in the renewal of his "homeland", he would be required to behave in a traitorous manner towards his own kind. But Walther, convinced that he could become indispensible to the leadership, had decided to pin his colours to this small group of ambitious men and had chosen to play along with the anti-Jewish chanting and raucousness that had become the frightening norm at the meetings.

The Popov's Arrival in Belgium

Walther's father, Franz, had served at the end of the last of the most recent Franco-Prussian Wars and had surprisingly received two call-up notices to serve again with the Prussian Army at the end of 1915. He was somewhat relieved to learn that he could recuse himself from duty by virtue of the fact that he had been released in the summer of 1871, aged only fifteen, with a land mine injury to his left foot. On his return to the family home in the dry summer of 1871, Franz's father, increasingly irritated by the attention from the authorities (brought about by the fame of that aforementioned first cousin in St Petersburg), had decided that the family would leave Konigsberg to get away from the near-constant intimidation. By early 1872, Grandpappy Popov had decided on Belgium as an acceptable staging post for the young Popov family as it would bring them westwards and closer to the more peaceful and prosperous powers in the west, Britain and France. He had lost patience with the intimidation from the local government officials and he had always felt conscious about that understated threat of violence from beyond the Eastern borders, from the Bolsheviks.

Having arrived initially in Bastogne, the Popovs discovered that they were very much on their own. There was no community of Germans in this town, and Walther's grandfather felt there was very little reason to stay there. There was no preferential treatment from the banks as could normally be enjoyed if someone happened to have some ties with the German Jewish community and, oft times, Walther's father would be confronted in the alleys of Bastogne by boys a year or two older poking fun at him because they knew he was different, partly Russian, partly Jewish. This upset him but he delighted in annoying them by telling them that "no", he was "not Jewish" but was, "in fact, a Buddhist" (a peace-loving Asian religion he had read about in the local library), so that they would look at him as if he were an idiot. Unable to make an intelligible response, they would run away, intellects frayed and roundly beaten.

Ultimately, Walther's grandfather was happy with the move to Belgium but the family, on not settling well in Bastogne, were soon on the move again before the year was out. They moved further west, to Bouillon, although Walther's young father was perturbed by, and questioned, the choice of destination. But Franz Popol soon fell into line as he saw his father's new tailoring business attracting the patronage of the local Belgian royal Prince Alois, along with his acolytes.

Walther's Arrival and the NSDAP

After an uneventful train journey, travelling in first class with his Lordship, Walther had arrived at that meeting in Platzl's Hofbrauhaus, in what had been the headquarters of a short-lived Communist outpost in Bavaria. Drexler continued to remain oblivious to Walther's Jewry as, to him, it was sufficient that the Popov boy had the necessary revolutionary nationalist streak which would serve the party well in its plan to overthrow the government of the "November Criminals". He had it noted that Popov had stridently joined in the racist chanting and the drunken cheers of approval for the party's spokesman, the strange ex-corporal with the cartoon moustache.

The very raison d'ètre for the movement, "the advancement of all of the German people", Walther Popov's reason for being captivated by it, was challenged frequently in the little man's regular maelstrom of anger against "foreigners". For Walther, it was regrettable that this xenophobia had now become enshrined in the party manifesto and it made Walther nervous. He remained in reflective silence for much of the meeting, as this Hitler character vascillated from grey, prim and neatly groomed office worker to demonic, red-faced volcano, denouncing foreigners, foreign banks, Communists, Jews, religion, even all non-Germans.

He was seducing the members with his claims that Germany's destiny was to rule over all of the races, that the "blond German male was the ideal man" for the new Aryan world Germany was going to lead. To do this, he stormed, Germany – and this is where it became entirely sinister to Walther – must be "Judenfrei", free of the Jews. Walther could not understand why the Jews had been singled out like this and was most surprised when Hitler said the country needed to dispense with this "detritus of society, the Jews!", the phrase that made Walther's heart sink as he remembered the oath of allegiance taken at his Bar Mitzvah. He was not a diligent member of the religion – his mother had simply pushed him to confirm his ancestry by going through with the ceremony – and he could barely recite two lines from the Torah. But here he was now, suddenly faced with the possibility that he could be thrown out of the party he had come to regard as his destiny.

All Walther had simply wanted to do was express his comradeship with his fellow German, be they Jew, Gentile, Lutheran, Roman Catholic, Orthodox, since he had decided that he wanted to get into commune with his homeland once more. He longed to be a part of the gathering pace of this "Völkisch" movement sweeping the nation again and he was embarrassed by the enthusiasm with which his fellow countrymen appeared to endorse this anti-Jewish feeling at the meeting.

Sadly, and in spite of himself, his confusion led him to join the raucous xenophobia as sure as the lemming happily launches itself over the precipice to certain oblivion, not quite knowing why he was doing it but better to do it than remain on the edge, looking in. The rule that said "Only Germans can be citizens, no Jew can be a German citizen" would prove to be the hardest pill to swallow.

He was mortified to realise that, in the heat of the moment, he himself had cheered this duplicitous and crude insult to his family and the many thousands of Jews who had fought shoulder to shoulder with their fellow German citizens in the recently ceded "War to End All Wars". How could that "rule" sit with the other one promoting "freedom of religion" for all citizens, he wondered? However, it was not in Walther's nature to question authority, and he innocently expected that this was something he would be able to raise when he was a bonafide party member. Now was not the time to bring it up, so for the moment, he bit his lip and went with the quickening flow.

Walther and the Leadership

Walther told Max all about his trip without taking breath and Max wondered aloud as to where his friend had stayed on those two lost nights? It turned out he had no reason to worry, confirmed Walther, for he had stayed in the as-yet-unofficial offices of the new party on the first floor of the Sterneckerbrau Inn. After that formative September gathering, it seems the Hitler chap had set up an office of sorts in the Inn and, on this occasion, he had allowed a few of the over-zealous drinkers to bunk down on both nights. Walther, too young to be a drinker, had planned to stay just one night but Haller and Drexler had convinced him to act as "Personal Assistant" to the leadership team of Haller, Drexler, Feder and Hitler. It was quite the most responsible job Walther had ever been given and he told Max how he had proudly pressed the jackets, knotted the ties and even shaved the men (Max would later recount how Walther had marvelled that, in assiduously wielding Drexler's cut-throat razor in stroking away the stubble on the throats of those four men, he perhaps more than any Allied Commander had come closest to preventing the maelstrom of terror and inhumanity that was to be unleashed on his homeland.)

"Well, I'm still not too impressed, old pal. I mean what would your father say about this? Couldn't Drexler have treated you better? Look at how far you had to travel!! Shame on him! On them!", stuttered Max, with surprising force. He was, of course, doing his best to conceal his envy at the freedom his friend enjoyed, obliged as he was to abide by the small changes in his life brought about on that fateful day at the chestnut grove. Feeling like a bird in a gilded cage as always, and still too low in self-confidence to assert his deepest wish to accompany his friend on his adventures, his family was always there to remind him how the doctors at the hospital had implored him to read, read, read. He did not want to disappoint his family, so read was what he would do. Taking the advice of his boss, he determined to struggle through the great classics of literature in some sort of chronological order.

His lordship had a reputation as a man of letters, as well as being an all-round bon viveur and a mean shot with a hunting rifle. Possessing a majestic library crammed with antique editions of "The Great Works" of literature on it's seventeenth century mahogany bookcases, Le Seigneur prompted Max to start with Aristotle and Homer, then Plato and Ovid: in fact, all of these classics should be the first to be tackled, he said. Having decided for the dubious young Max, his Lordship insisted they would be a welcome distraction for him when he went off to start his studies at Nancy's Agricultural College. Max was less than convinced as he thumbed through the heavy leather-bound tomes, reeking of the Guardsman's polish keeping the bookcases dust-free. But he ploughed through them cheerlessly, unsure how these ancient texts would make him a better person

Walther delighted in telling Max that the new party leadership was very interested to hear that he would finally be moving to Munich to pursue his studies in tailoring, with Herr Hitler jokingly suggesting that the student could make suits for him as he believed he would be making many more speeches for the party. Although Walther had felt a little uncomfortable at that suggestion, he said to Max "give the little man his due, he does seem supportive of my studies so perhaps I am over-reacting". Truth to tell, Walther so desperately wanted to be accepted by the leading players, he would have polished the little man's shoes and tied his laces had he been asked.

This pattern of devotion to his new cause continued on throughout that year. Fervour for the cause – "Walther's cause" - was continually raised only to be snuffed out by the little man with each bombastic speech. Meanwhile, Walther's father was desperate to ensure that the family tradition would continue with Walther, and nothing would make him happier than to establish his son's career in the inoffensive trade and continue on in the family tradition as a tailor. To that end, he continued to organise prized visits for his son to the many shirt factories and cloth weavers across Switzerland and Bavaria. Oft-times, to save time and money, his son would travel with the salesmen who came to visit his father's shop and there were other times his father would drive him up to Paris and see him off on the Orient Express. Of course, and his father suspected it, these visits also presented Walther with easy opportunities to both do his duty by day, in visiting the factories, and then, by evening, attend one of the flurry of party meetings in the city. Following Drexler's short-lived attempt to convert Munich into a Soviet playground, the city had quickly become the centre of a gaggle of new socialist movements and it was not long before party membership would be opened up across the country. After that, the NSDAP quickly grew in influence and size across the country and beyond Bavaria.

Walther had had to admit to himself that he found it increasingly hard to listen to the continuous condemnation of the Jewish role in the German capitulation of 1918; the rants at unproven "Jewish interference" in the fledgling "Soviet Union" (as that huge collection of communist states was now called), as well as in Britain, France and America"; and still the Popov boy so wanted to be a leading light. Craving the affirmation of his peers in the Partei, he had become unswervingly loyal to it. Yet this was causing him to question his disloyalty to his Jewish lineage, acknowledged now by much reduced secret religious practices and his seeming participation in the slandering of his kind.

Suddenly one evening at home, and with an untypical flourish, a proud and relieved Herr Popov was able to tell his family, at the usual family dinner table, that he had succeeded in securing an apprenticeship for Walther in the "highly reputable Lodenfrei's" in Munich. It was exactly the diversion Père Popov had wanted for Walther as he believed that his son should focus on his studies now that he had a clear career mapped out for him. Popov's father had grown weary of his son's preoccupation with this new German movement and would say at the dinner table, when Walther had become too animated: "But Walther, I left Prussia with your grandfather because he wanted a new, better life, why this hankering after a "New Germany", do we not have a happy, successful life in Belgium?" Walther knew that this was not a question but a statement of fact aimed at shooting down his new passion for what his father called "this myth of homeland". As far as his father was concerned, Belgium was their homeland and that was the end of it. It was a comment also aimed at his wife, who he felt indulged Walther's fantasy by not disagreeing firmly with their son's preoccupations. In fairness, Walther correctly sensed that he should not disagree with his father, and decided not to mention his ideals again, lest it cause his father's weak heart more distress than was possibly acceptable.

Naturally, relocation to Munich would simply give Walther the perfect opportunity to attend party meetings, and it was at these meetings that he would find himself disparaging his father's innocent intentions for his career to the party leaders. In this way, he believed that he was proving he was a genuinely keen party member, even if so very young.

Chapter 3

The Nazis Grow and Walther Grows Too

The government of the so-called November Criminals had fallen after the short revolution of 1919, and chaos quickly became the new norm in 1920. The Freikorps, swelled by the ranks of the unemployed, had become a forceful band made up of the original disaffected veterans, a thoroughly right-wing rabble, which the government nevertheless allowed to exist, fully armed, alongside the Reichswehr. The government owed them a debt of gratitude, it seemed, as their military nous had not only suppressed, at first, an uprising in Berlin, but they had also infiltrated and disrupted other rebel meetings in Munich and other cities. Even though they had quelled one uprising, their bold attempt to seize their moment in Berlin saw the ordinary workers standing firm to not let it happen: rebuffed firmly and decisively, rudderless, they were forced to abandon their notions. But they were a loose cannon and were becoming as notorious as the NSDAP leadership's bodyguard, the Sturmabteilung, into which many of the Freikorps' veterans were being recruited. The "Brownshirts", as they were christened by the citizens, acted out their barbaric fantasies of torture and violent slaying, terror and intimidation, on whoever stood in their way and quickly became the most-feared suppressors of the people's will. But the door had been unwittingly opened for a group of ambitious misfits, and this group, styling themselves the Nationalist Socialist Deutsche Arbeiter Partei, the NSDAP (quickly becoming the "Nazi Party", for short), was drawn together by their mutual hunger for power and influence: the former corporal Hitler was hungriest of all.

All the while, Max Meixmoron had regarded his friend's departure to Munich as perhaps Walther's opportunity to become a leading player in this new party. Having attended that first meeting, he was wary of the party's position on Jews but was unaware of the change of policy now being promoted to exclude Jews from German life, even denying them their nationality. Of course he missed his friend, and their happy times carving names and swear words into the trees around the Landreville estate now seemed so long ago. They had learned and played lawn tennis against each other since they were five years old and the twice-weekly teas in the Popov's home in Bouillon had become distant memories. The cycle to his friend's house across the Belgian border might take a half an hour or longer if he was avoiding the heavily guarded main road to Bouillon in taking the dirt tracks so beloved of the local Resistance. More dangerous, certainly, but then he would think of the day ahead: "Ah yes", pondered Max, "Frau Popov was such a kind lady, she always treated me like her own. I always enjoyed the strudel and Pere Popov's tales of his training days in Saxony". In return, he would recount how his cousin in St Petersburg had come to invent the radio and how that had caused so much anguish for his grandfather, as the authorities had looked on him with the suspicion of him being a Communist. Max also thought Mrs Popov must be very worried for Walther now that he was living so far away from home. Walther's sister Katrin had always seemed like such a pest when he went to tea but he missed the gentle ribbing she would give her brother for his political ambitions: "When are you going to take over Belgium, Walther?", she would tease, "the country needs you, you are the man for the job!". He was worried that, as his friend lived so far away now, Walther would also be anxious for his family, which that may mean he would not be able to give so much of himself to the new party's cause.

Walther Popov: Tailor to the Top Table

By the end of 1920, however, Drexler's notions of a "Party of the People", was turning into the hate-filled vision of Nationalist Socialism espoused by the party spokesman, the Chaplin-esque Hitler. Drexler had lost much of his interest now; even his friend and co-founder Harrer had gained an edge over him as his journalistic skills had started to influence the direction of the new party's newspaper and, thus, the tenor of the message they were communicating. This was often xenophobic and was certainly nothing that Drexler wanted to be party to.

Just months into '21, Drexler made the momentous decision to appoint Hitler to lead the party that he had dreamt of since his first encounter with Madame Blavatsky and her fawning devotee, Harrer. The inexorable rise of the party spokesman – "this bit player!" thought Drexler at first - had been little short of catastrophic for him. However, it was a defining moment for Walther, for although he did not instinctively trust the little man, he took the pragmatic view that he would anchor his future near to Herr Hitler for surely his own boat would rise with this irresistible new leader?

In Munich, Walther immersed himself in his two apprenticeship roles: the most important of these, he was not slow to realise, was his real reason for being in Munich – the menswear department of Lodenfrei's Department Store, where he would learn the necessary cutting, design and tailoring skills to, first and foremost, assist his father back home in Belgium. This was his mission and his newly-developing allegiance to the Volkisch movement in his homeland must remain in the background for now.

However, his new friends were keen to utilise his skills as well as his enthusiasm. By way of recognition for his loyalty and dedication to the new party, and to help him advance his tailoring skills, Walther was selected for the daunting task of fitting shirts to each new member of the StormAbteilung. Nobody knew the exact circumstances, but Commandant Rosbach had come upon a large supply of Austrian-made heavy brown denim shirts and it had been decided that these tunics would serve as some sort of uniform.

Alterations were to be paid for by a textiles magnate in Bissingen, and Walther was asked to sew and stitch the white and black swastika armbands that the leadership had decided would be a requirement for every member to wear. This task had been presented to him as some sort of sign that the tasks was guaranteed to him, after he produced a sample from a bale of white linen from one of his father's suppliers in Normandy. Using black silk thread, he had meticulously stitched the symbol onto each armband, before finally working out a template he could use on the twenty-year-old Veritas he had been given by Lodenfrei's to practice stitching in his room at the Sterneckerbrau. His father's contacts in the textiles trade were coming in useful too and he was using them judiciously to impress the Party leaders: he brought them houndstooth cloth from Saville Row in London; white linen and Caudry lace from Normandy and the north-east, taken from manufacturers in regions conquered in France's fall; there was rare Sea Island Cotton secured by German agents in the Caribbean, travelling ever eastwards to be eventually sold on to the Fascists in Italy at great profit; and there were bales of silk salvaged from parachutes and hot-air balloons over the course of the last conflict, restored, delicately dyed and recut into the finest shirts, officer's caps, and lanyards.

Popov Dresses the Troops

For the party's Sturmabteillung, the "Stormtroopers", from their beginning, Walther was tasked with making the necessary alterations to those brown military shirts in individual fitting sessions, and he did this with each new member in Munich. Growing from an initially limited number in those early years, it had become a time-consuming process as the numbers of new recruits in all regions was rising, year on year. As the decade wore on and the cult of the leader became stronger, Hitler also charged him with training volunteers in the regions, hand-picked by the local leaders (frequently their own sons and daughters) from the Party's youth arm. Walther started off by training a core group of volunteers, then he succeeded in having the party leaders back his plan for those volunteers to become the core group of trainers who would then train another select group of volunteers with the required sewing skills and pattern-cutting techniques. Despite his ingenuity, and the backing of the Nazi party leaders, this clever "school of tailoring" would carry the

Fuhrer's name and eagle crest, and was to be known as "De Fuhrer Schneiderschule", The Fuhrer's Tailoring School.

The SA were adept at securing droves of the broken, unemployed young men of Germany to join the nascent Nazi Party and the recruitment campaign was simple: the message was that the Allied nations had left Germany destitute and that the people were on their way to reclaim their birthright. They had fast become a "party within a party" and had quickly become skilful and ruthless at disrupting the affairs and meetings of the other militant groups which had begun to form after 1919's revolution. Initially, the intolerant behaviour towards Jews, blacks, even Asians and the disabled and the cruel intolerance even for god-based religions, had seemed completely wrong to Walther and he regularly found himself biting his tongue so as not to seem weak. "What harm could these people be to me or Germany?", were his deepest thoughts on it. The party leaders thought differently, however, with, increasingly, those views being shared by the swelling ranks of party members, thoughts that were most certainly starting to be influenced by the party's "Rules".

Chapter 4

The Madness of Michel Meixmoron

Back at the gate lodge of Chateau Landreville, the Meixmoron family pride was being restored by the rapidly improving outlook of Michel/ Max. Thanks to the Lord of Landreville, a genuinely caring man, Max, much to his surprise, quickly saw his ambitions were back on track when he was promoted to Assistant Head Gardener. That promotion came before he had even opened a textbook in Nancy's Institut Colonial et Agricole, as his boss saw it as a motivator for his young charge to do well in his studies. By the mid-1920s, Meixmoron had qualified as an Agricultural Scientist, with specialist knowledge in soil and plant science, and a solid understanding of horticulture principles and science. He had majored in topiary and, at weekends during term, he practised his newly-learned skills on the flora throughout the estate.

Meixmoron thought often on his friend's activities in Munich, with a definite mixture of admiration and trepidation. He felt that he himself would find it too difficult to relocate so far from home. Of course, he had indeed relocated to study over in Nancy, a straight car journey of two hours from his home: his father would drive him up there at the start of the week in his old Delahaye 135 and, although the accommodation at the university was spartan, Meixmoron compared it favourably with the bed and ward he had had to endure during his sojourn in the Paris hospital. After all, anything had to be better than the "American hospital", as the idea that anything American could be an improvement on what he was used to in Landreville was preposterous.

Having lost contact with each other - unsurprisingly because they had both been very preoccupied with their studies and were some distance travel from each other - Max was not to know that Walther had continued to make an impression on the party elite with his eye for detail for improving design and cut and had effectively been promoted to the important, if modestly salaried, position of "Tailor to the SA". The leadership had a vision of how they wanted their military to appear to the world - no more awkward helmets and shapeless lederhosen, they wanted sharp, utilitarian cuts, matching caps and coded epaulets. They had also seen an opportunity to develop Walther as their own private tailor and, naturally, Walther was only too delighted to be so feted, and he so far from home. In the early days, Walther's role had even seen him become something of a shared butler between Hitler, Himmler, Goebbels and occasionally the dour Speer, especially when the four of them were staying in their chosen beerhallen in and around Munich.

Quick Rise to Power and Walther Moves to Berlin

With the party's quick ascension to power in '33, Walther found himself transferred to Berlin, acting as chief "Dresser" to the Fuhrer himself and essentially continuing to act as personal tailor to the leaders, as before. In the following years, Walther would often travel down to Munich and then, after the invasion of Poland and much of Europe, he would travel on the secret train to Neuchwanstein, to visit the Himmler's home at Tagernsee. It was here that he would take measurements and make alterations to the latest suits for Hitler's great friend, even on occasion indulging in some dressmaking for the elegant Marga and her less than elegant daughter, Gudrun, who lived essentially alone and far from the former Deputy Gauleiter's work commitments (indeed, they barely knew of his elevation to Reichsfuhrer in 1929 and the extent of his power across Germany).

Walther sensed that this train was special because there would always be a platoon of SS soldiers packing crates and large packages onto it and, for the journey, he would always be accompanied by a group of silent, intense-looking men and women in brown uniforms and funny armbands, not the usual emblems at all. These weren't SA members and, from the little conversation Max understood, it appeared that they had been sent to keep watch on the assorted packages and boxes. Walther was largely ignored by them, indeed easy conversation was not in their gift, even amongst themselves, and it was clear that these grey people were "experts" of some description. Sometimes a soldier would bring a small package to one of the party and Walther would watch discretely as the package was opened and then, perhaps, the object would be raised up for inspection by the group: it could be an old ceramic jug, a small painting or any other objet d'art. It never mattered, because it would always spark a passionate discussion in the group before the SS commander would retrieve the source of the argument and return it to the hold from whence it came. Even on these journeys, every movement of every piece was carefully annotated by the same young SS troop in the same aisle seat near the adjoining carriage door, as he peered nervously over his old-fashioned nuremburgs.

Walther had long since decided on his future, having completed his apprenticeship with the patronage of Herr Hitler and the NSDAP leadership. On completion of this training, he found that he was held in high regard as an indispensable and highly skilled tailor. Despite that, the Nazi leadership decreed that he should give life to the plainer designs of the Waffen-SS uniforms and, disappointed, he set about focussing his mind on producing those dull uniforms.

Thanks to his early close association with the leaders though, and the fact that they never forgot him, they saw to it that he be set up in business. Gifted a substantial Berlin premises in an effort to recompense him for his many years of unswerving loyalty to the leadership, he was assigned the contract to make the rugged battlefield uniforms, a contract that came with an exceptional remuneration package and the patronage of the top table in the Nazi party: this would give him all of the exposure he would need to become ever more respected in his party role.

He would reflect contentedly that all of this was a long way from his early years in the party in Munich, covering the short journey from the Burgerbraukeller to the Sterneckerbrau to dance attendance on the tight-knit group of leaders, while the new party was building its support across the city and throughout Bavaria.

Chapter 5

March 1941 - A Light Goes On.

On what should have been a painless visit to the Luxembourg Gardens on Paris's Left Bank with his boss, in pursuit of garden design inspiration, Max endured not one but three air-raid warnings. The third air-raid had proven to be particularly stressful for the men when they found themselves trapped in the Orangerie, having rushed into it from the rose garden for cover: the German warplanes were flying overhead at the start of another mission to bomb London and the sirens were wailing all along the Seine as, yet again, the Germans cheekily took this shortcut through French airspace to the English south coast.

Looking skywards through Monet's glass-panelled ceiling, Max was enthralled by the efficiency of the anti-aircraft defences along the Seine. In the Orangerie, tourist faces were lit up by the dazzling display of white light above the Palais de Luxembourg as the searchlights criss-crossed the Parisian skyline in time with the half-hearted bullet traces, as the warplanes' drone deafened the city en route to their target in south-eastern England. Perversely, he would get excited whenever he saw one of those buzzing wasps pirouette like a drunken ballet dancer before sinking in flames in its death-spiral to the ground below – he felt guilty to celebrate these rare macabre dances but he still had not forgotten the trauma visited on him by the American pilot days before the Allies had been handed victory by the Kaiser.

Now a new thought was percolating in his brain: if the searchlights were so effective in Paris at detecting the overflying fighter planes from Germany, then the searchlights across the English Channel must be just as adept at tracking those same incoming German attacks. It was clear that fewer aircraft were returning to the Fatherland each time which meant that the English defences must be highly effective.

He wondered if he could help his old friend in Munich (he was unaware of his transfer to Berlin) and his chosen comrades in their aim to conquer France's ally and, in so doing, disable once and for all the hated American warplanes. He started thinking about how he could somehow find a way to destroy these searchlights in Britain - would it be through the kind of aerial bombardment so recently inflicted at Billancourt? No, he decided, he would have to find a way to infiltrate the British mainland, perhaps with some of the SA troops disguised as ordinary Britons. Yes, that was it, he would find a way to sabotage searchlight stations and then he got to wondering how many German sympathisers there could be amongst the British people, could he target them? He had read about a Scottish woman who married a German and had spied for Germany before being caught and executed: he was sure there were lots of people like her and he wanted to find a way to reach them. Always looking to ingratiate himself with whoever was in charge of the "next big thing", he wondered too if his idea would appeal to the ever-more-powerful German leadership, an idea born out of his still-burning ambition for revenge on the Americans?

It had been inevitable that he and Walther should have lost touch all those years ago - they had both had to settle into their studies, he aiming to consolidate that early return to his role at Landreville, and Walther embarking on his apprenticeship role at Lodenfrei's, which may lead to, perhaps, a senior role with the Nazi party, or, indeed, a return to Bouillon to take over the family business.

Struggling initially in his studies in Nancy, Max emerged like a butterfly after three years and had enjoyed the feeling of independence his relocation to Nancy had brought. When Pierre, the Head Gardener, decided to retire suddenly due to ill health in the winter of '38, His Lordhip had no hesitation in appointing his protégé at the same time as he told him the sad news about Pierre's sudden decision. The new head gardener did not immediately feel under any obligation to make changes as to how the gardens should be managed – the planting out of the usual varieties continued as normal in the early years of his tenure, with his newly developed topiary skills helping to turn the chateau's gardens into some of the most desirable in all-France. So desirable, in fact, that at the end of 1940, the duke himself had decided that the gardens should be opened all year round to the public at large and this was why they had found themselves in Paris in the spring of 1941.

Having just spent Christmas with his cousin in Blickling Hall in England, the Duke was intrigued at the way in which this cousin was going about making his own huge estate pay for itself: he had spotted a way to earn extra revenue from the gradual opening up of the estate to public patronage, charging a small entrance fee to view the magnificent walled gardens and letting the public tour a wing of the grand house. Of course, his cousin's family remained in the house even as visitors walked around the estate but, despite the inconvenience, his cousin revealed that at the end of the previous year, he had collected enough in entrance fees to renovate the old Orangery, and to repair the neo-classical Icehouse. The Duke realised that the good work he had done on renovating the chateau and on re-laying the well-established gardens and moat had helped to grow the reputation of the gardens. Now, with Meixmoron's development as the estate's head gardener, and with the chateau now described as a "perfect example of a French baronial style manor" in the newest edition of the Michelin Green Guide, he felt that with some added works, he could turn the chateau into quite the tourist attraction. He decided that he would commission three new buildings on the grounds: an icehouse to surround the old well; a botanical greenhouse; and a folly, in classical Roman style, at the eastern edge of the estate, beside the cypress trees.

The seeds of Meixmoron's plan were also planted this day in the Orangerie in Paris: the plan to attack the Allied searchlight stations across Britain and Europe was a viable one and, rather than waste his free time re-reading the great Greek and Roman classics (as was his wont these days) he decided that he would try to develop a network of saboteurs, all the better if they already lived and worked in Britain. But first he needed to contact his old friend and try to get an audience with Walther's old comrades in the government in Berlin.

Popov's fate?

On returning to Landreville from their expedition to Paris, Max knew he must get to the Popovs in Bouillon to find out about where he could find Walther now. He was quite sure that Walther would no longer be working in and around Munich and, if he was honest, he hoped that his friend would actually be back home in Bouillon. His apprenticeship was well finished, and he was either at work in the family business in Bouillon or he was forging a career in Germany.

Two days later, Max retrieved his bicycle from the small outhouse behind the family cottage and set forth once more for his old friend's home across the border. After forty minutes of intense pedalling, he arrived on the outskirts of Bouillon and lied politely in broken Flemish, when challenged by the border police, telling them that he was on the way to visit his aunt's house in Rue de Hautes-Voies. The gendarme, a native of Charleroi, had no idea where that was but, on looking the boy up and down, decided to let him through. Ten minutes later, Max was sitting down to tea and tomato sandwiches in the Popov's house, followed by three slices of Frau Popov's battenburg cake.

It almost felt like old times, except that now there was no Katrin – she had married her first boyfriend and had left for Nice some years ago. Disappointingly, there was no Walther either. In fact, and Max was rather sad to hear it from his friend's mother, Walther remained in Germany, apparently now working for the Nazis and earning a living making uniforms for the German army's foot-soldiers in the Waffen SS. He was surprised also to learn that his friend was now living in Berlin but glad also to know that he was no longer living in yet another grimy beerhalle's guestrooms. Apparently, he was now living in a smart hotel in Unter den Linden in central Berlin, with running hot and cold water, a laundry service, and even its own barbershop. Frau Popov was sad because she could not speak to her son often as he was forbidden to take calls so she would have to wait for him to telephone her: the good news was that his once-weekly call was due this very afternoon.

At the appointed time of 2.30pm, the telephone rang and he watched his friend's mother rush into the hallway to answer. After the usual exchange of pleasantries and her usual questions about how well he was eating and looking after himself, she turned to look back in to the kitchen at Max and told her son that his old friend had called this afternoon to see how he was doing: "Here he is, Walther, speak to him yourself!", she said, handing the mouthpiece over to Meixmoron. "Hi there, Walther, long time no speak!", said Max awkwardly, "How are you getting on? Your mama tells me you are in Berlin now? How is that?", he finished. "Max!! Great to hear your voice after all this time! Sorry, yes, we kind of lost contact, didn't we? Life sort of got in the way a bit, not to mention the distance!", the answer came back. "How is life in Landreville, are you even still there?", asked Walther. "Yes, yes, still there, Walther! Afraid I went a bit "safe", he continued. "Having done my studies in Nancy, no sooner was I back when suddenly I was Head Gardener: poor old Pierre had to retire – he had a lung condition, was a terrible smoker, you know – and I got his job. It's been very busy ever since, the estate is running tours of the grounds and the house now, making plenty of money for his lordship. Achh, its easy work, Walther, no great stresses for me. How come you're in Berlin now? You working for the Nazis?", the conversation flowed from Max as if his friend was standing in the hall in front of him. "I'm still involved if that's what you mean, old pal", Walther carefully replied. "Sorry I never got in touch before my visits home, I even forgot your home address. Sounds like you've got a nice set-up there in Landreville, delighted for you after all you went through, nice work!", was Walther's generous reply to his old friend. Max thought Walther's tone was quite stilted, as if perhaps someone was listening in on the call and he could not say very much.

"Tell you what, Walther, I have an idea for how your guys might be able to have a few good wins against the British! I wonder could I come and talk to someone there about it, we could just say I'm coming to Berlin on holidays? I hear you're staying in a hotel in the middle of Berlin, maybe I could get in there for a night or two?", said Max. "Yeah, great! What's your idea? I could see if the Reichsfuhrer is available to meet you too? He's very high up - have you heard of Himmler? - and he likes to hear ideas that might help us crush the enemy! I'll mention it to him... so what's the idea?", replied an excited Popov, amazed to hear his friend talk like he really wanted to be a part of the world he had joined. "My idea is to hit the searchlights, make it difficult for them to defend against the bombers and fighter 'planes! It will need men or women on the ground in Britain and careful co-ordination with the Luftwaffe, but I think it can be done. Hopefully, your guys will think the same. That's roughly the plan I'll be telling Mr Himmler", was Meixmoron's careful response.

"Reichsfuhrer!", insisted Walther, "make sure you call him that. You know, I'm absolutely sure you have hit on an excellent idea! As far as I'm aware, there are a lot of undercover agents working in Britain, even their "upper classes" are supporting us, apparently. It would be great to have them make a bigger contribution to the war effort. When are you thinking of presenting this idea? I'd say sooner rather than later. Actually, leave it with me, I will talk to the Reichsfuhrer later and try to get his agreement. It would be great to see you!"

"I was thinking before the end of this week, Max, I have a day off on Friday – what day is today? Wednesday – I could go on Friday? I'll leave it with you . . . the telephone number in Landreville is 324 30001", were Max's parting words.

CHAPTER 6

The Reichsfuhrer Visits Nancy

The following day, Meixmoron was in his office in the manor house discussing and reviewing the Seigneur's plans to build three new structures on his lands. As the duke explained in finer detail his plan to build the finest Orangerie outside Paris, the excited conversation was interrupted by the footman carrying the telephone – "Excuse me, my lord, there is a telephone call for M. Meixmoron". It was Popov: "Great news, old pal!", he said immediately, "I mentioned your idea to the Reichsfuhrer and he was quite impressed that a Frenchman would have the audacity to actually come up with a plan to attack a French ally! I told him you were no ordinary Frenchman, that you had survived an act of utter terrorism by that American at the end of 1918. I told him your story as I know it, Max, and do you know what? The Reichsfuhrer is going to go see you in Nancy! Actually taking a regular train to Nancy!" Walther was positively bubbling with glee on telling his friend. He was impressed that someone as senior as Himmler himself would actually take the time to make the journey and he left Max in no doubt that it was indeed a privilege for the Reichsfuhrer to take time out of his busy schedule to make this visit. "He's getting the first train out of Spandau, tomorrow morning at 4.30, and should be pulling into Nancy at around 1pm. Now, he will be travelling as a private citizen, Max, he has to, it has become too dangerous for him with what's going on, but I imagine he will be in his usual black leather great-coat. He has slicked-back black hair and wears black-rimmed glasses, and he told me he will be carrying a copy of the latest "Fehrberlinner Zeitung" newspaper. To be sure it is him when you meet, you are to ask him, "On what page is the crossword, Mein Herr?". En français. He will answer, also in French, "Page 22" – that is the signal, then, that you have identified each other!", Walther concluded, warning Max to remember these exact words. "Wow! That's like something from a Gaston Leroux! Very exciting! I don't suppose you will be with him?", said Max, surprised at the idea that Himmler – Himmler! – was making this journey to talk to him. "No. I have not been asked, Max", came Walther's answer, "it probably would not go down too well. Besides, my day is very busy these days, I have to keep a close check on the production lines for the uniforms, I have to make sure each one is up to standard and that there is no slacking off by anyone. That's not the part of the job I like, Max – sometimes we have to take these layabouts off the line and have them shot, there is no room for shoddy workmanship!" Meixmoron was shocked to hear his friend talk about shooting fellow workers but he decided that he would make no comment on it, it was not his place to do so.

The Best Laid Plan

By ten o'clock on Friday morning, Max was ready to make the journey and, like old times, he retrieved his bicycle once more to head down to Nancy. He had had to refuse the offer of a lift from his father because he did not want his father to know that he was meeting a senior Nazi, and also because he was embarrassed by his father's conspicuous old car, that old Delahaye. It was a long journey by bicycle but, after a brief stop in Metz to eat the pork sandwiches his mother had made for him (he had told her, much to her delight, that Walther was taking the train from Berlin to Nancy to meet him today), he reached Gare de Nancy at fifteen minutes before one.

He remembered the old station well as he used to drink coffee in its lone café, when he was in the university around the corner. Today, he bought a café au lait and a croissant and sat at what had been his usual table outside the coffee shop, waiting for the Berlin train to arrive. It would be quite a shock for the citizens if they knew that Hitler's right-hand man was visiting today, so he knew he had to watch out very carefully for him on it's arrival and make sure that as few people as possible saw him. The Reichsfuhrer's train, just the regular passenger train that plied the route, duly pulled into platform two at seven minutes past one and everyone disembarked.

There was no sign of the German until a bespectacled figure, wearing a full length, black leather coat, stepped off the train when all other passengers had alighted: this arrival was too dramatic in Max's view and he got up swiftly from his chair and walked towards his contact. He had only taken a few paces when one of the SS uniforms stepped across his path and quietly told him, in French, to make sure he kept his hands visible.

Sure enough, the Reichsfuhrer was carrying the prescribed newspaper and Max asked him the question he had been told to ask: "Sur quelle page est les mots croissés, mein herr?" "Vingt-deux!", exclaimed the Reichsfuhrer confidently. Max's heart jumped and he was nervous with excitement as Himmler shook his hand briefly and gestured for him to join him on the train. "We should not be seen here, you understand?", he said brusquely, as they stepped off the platform and up into the rear carriage of the commuter train. Himmler motioned to Max to sit and, once settled into his seat opposite the famous German face, Max straightaway took out some draft-paper with his written notes transcribed in some detail. He tried to launch into what his plan would entail but Himmler raised his hand to stop him and said, in faultless English: "Popov has told me about your previous encounter with the Americans – shocking arrogance! Yes, I can see why you want to hurt the enemies of Germany today, he tells me that you have a "proposal" for us?", he asked, stroking his chin quizzically. "Yes, that's right", Max replied quickly, and made ready to discuss his plans. But Himmler was not finished and he raised his gloved hand to halt any flow from Max: "Yes, this plan to destroy searchlight stations, we like it and were actually thinking of a similar plan. I have brought a list of names of possible British traitors who could be targeted. There is also a list of strategic air bases which should be destroyed before we launch our major attacks. Now, let me hear your ideas, maybe we can work out a plan?".

The Reichsfuhrer's use of the word "we" concerned Max – was this a Nazi leadership "we" or the "Royal We", as in it being just Himmler's idea? He suspected the latter and he proceeded to outline his ideas:

"Essentially, we would be taking a three-pronged approach:

Number one, the main thrust would be mobile co-ordinators of sabotage teams the length and breadth of Britain. Now that the Americans are getting involved, and coming in through Northern Ireland, any plans will have to include attacks on their bases there, especially if they have any headquarters in Belfast or even Dublin. It's absolutely essential to not let them get a foothold in Britain beyond Northern Ireland and it is vital that an attack on Belfast should happen as soon as possible".

Himmler sat, listening intently and nodding sagely at the notion of attacking Belfast and said, agreeing: "Excellent! Yes, that city has a lot of important manufacturing facilities, especially naval ships being built there and now, of course, the American scum are using it as their headquarters! I will make contact with our two supporters in the University there, the McGarrys – the names are in this list – they will be useful contacts. Yes, I think this plan will be good! Anything else?"

"Absolutely, yes, Reichsfuhrer! I do not think this plan will be enough on its own, do you want to hear parts two and three?", Meixmoron continued, excited and relieved that the first stage of his plan had met with such agreement. As he spoke, he was growing in confidence as he scanned down the list of names of known sympathisers. Fixing his eyes on the powerful man opposite him, he said: "If we know where your warplanes are targeting next, we will have a better chance of co-ordinating an attack on the nearest searchlight base". His face coloured slightly as he realised that he too had used the word "we", only this time his use of it really meant just "I", himself. Himmler noticed Meixmoron's discomfort and he realised that the Frenchman was, in fact, really just talking about himself, he still had not created their web of saboteurs. He noted that this collaborator was quite fluent in English, slipping, as he was, into English when he could not interpret French into German, and he assumed that Popov's friend simply wanted a piece of the action his friend was enjoying in Berlin. "Was he also proposing to relocate to Britain to help the cause?", Himmler wondered.

The Reichsfuhrer reflected: so, Meixmoron had proposed three courses of action to assist German domination in the air and a way for Germany to annihilate enemy cities – (he would) establish sabotage groups, targetting known Nazi sympathisers to help in the sabotage of bases; and, cleverly, Himmler thought, to weaken British defences, co-ordinate Luftwaffe attacks with these searchlight sabotages. In fact, Himmler had already weighed up the plans as had been told to him by Popov and he had become convinced that all three acts, combined together carefully and thoughtfully, could be the key to glory for the Third Reich. He was quietly impressed that this Frenchman's ideas may just unlock the victory that had thus far eluded the Luftwaffe. He must commend Popov on his return to Berlin for his choice of friend – another equally excellent young man, devising ways, unprompted, to build Germany's attack.

The German waxed lyrical about Walther's ingenuity in creating the Fuhrer's Tailoring School and about his tailoring skills, so much so that it seemed to Max that his old friend could do no wrong in the eyes of Hitler and his leadership team. In fact, Himmler referred to Walther so frequently, Max felt his face getting very hot indeed as it went varying shades of red: so, Walther had *arrived* in Berlin, thought Max, and had grown in standing as a trusted gofer and outstanding tailor to the leadership. *Well done, Walther*, thought Max, *so good to see you are doing so well.* But Max was jealous too – Walther's role had become a highly visible and important job with the Reich and he was going to be world famous for his artistry. Whereas he, Max, might only be known in France for his pruning and topiary skills – if the American had not caused his near-death in 1918, he believed he would be feted in whatever other role he might have taken on.

He was thinking these things when suddenly he heard himself say to the man opposite him: "Of course, it's wonderful for Walther that you gentlemen have chosen to overlook his Jewish grandmother, it seems to me that your policy of getting the Jews out is well thought out and long overdue". He was being mischievous with his comments and the Reichsfuhrer expressed "disappointment" with this information about "our dear friend, Walther – I am not sure how much longer he can serve our Fuhrer after hearing this information, M. Meixmoron", he said. "You are quite sure?" "I was at his bar-mitzvah!", replied the grinning Max, confirming it to the German by his easy treachery towards his friend.

"If this is so, Herr Meixmoron, the rewards for you shall be great indeed!", was the Reichsfuhrer's measured response. "You will need to be available to us at a moment's notice if your friend is unable to explain himself", he said, menacingly. "But, why is that, Mein Herr?", said Max quietly, knowing he had perhaps made an error in revealing Walther's secret. "We will need someone trustworthy, of course!", he hissed. "You have demonstrated that you are the natural choice! To run the factory making our uniforms, plus you will have to carry through with the promise of this covert action in Britain!", Himmler continued swiftly when he saw the doubtful look materialising on his young companion's face. "But, but, my work in Landreville?", was Meixmoron's muffled reply. Suddenly, Max realised that he had indeed bitten off more than he could chew, as the German continued: "Do not worry about salary, young man, we will take care of everything: you will be paid well and live in luxury in Berlin, you will never have to worry about anything again!" But Max *was* worried and he knew he had made a serious error in revealing Walther's true identity. There was no going back now though, and he knew it.

Chapter 7

Introducing Amelia Lambe

Sad news was delivered by telegram to Amelia Lamb, on March 1st, 1942: her lover of 1934, for that was how she remembered the ones who had made an impression - in date order - had met a watery end in Belfast Lough. She had been staying in London, as she had for the last three Christmases, with her Scotch-soaked brother, Geoffrey, and, somehow she had drifted into the New Year, still pottering around his apartment (*Why*, she had often thought to herself, *do we English need to refer to cramped bedsits in London as "apartments"? Is it our inherent snobbery, our need to elevate ourselves into something we are not? Or where we are not, perhaps . . .? And do we always have to take the lead from America? Their movies with "apartments" and all of those other diabolical subversions of the English language, like "technicolor", not "technicolour"; "tomay-to" instead of "to-mah-to", and all of that nonsense, it all just seemed so, so, very... lazy.* She alarmed herself when she realised just how often that question played on her mind and it never usually resolved itself. She would vex herself in her verbal sparring with American friends, so passionate was she about it. And then she would find herself retreating, realising that, "Oh dear, there she goes again!", her cheeks gently colouring into a healthy crimson glow, as her eyelids shuttered her off momentarily from her astonished friends.

She read the message and a poignant tear trickled to the tip of her patrician nose, her tongue flicking upwards to lick the damp residue from her top lip. "Poor Gordon. Do you remember him, Geoffrey, you met him when I was in London around the time of the Games?", she said to her brother. "He had everything going for him back then, big civil service job, think he was under-secretary to some minister at the time. I believe he went on to a super job in the Lord Lieutenant's Office in Northern Ireland, had a stunning wife Clarissa, I met her once. Poor girl. Last time I heard, two fabulous kids as well. Absolutely crazy, what must he have been thinking?"

"Drinking?", was Geoffrey's dry response, pretending to have misheard the final word. "Looks like suicide", she exclaimed, her eyes damp with sorrow. "Which reminds me", said Amelia, slyly bringing the topic right back on her brother, "is there ever a chance that you might actually sever the near-constant drip, drip of alcohol into your system? Your editor is a saint, you have not submitted one single article on time in the time I have been here this year, not one. How he puts up with you, I just do not know!", she finished.

"Oh, really? Is that so?", was Geoffrey's sarcastic retort. "Well, I'm not bothered, to be honest! Stupid sod is still paying me, is he not? And he hasn't complained, as of yet!". He liked to bait her into these confrontations and it perversely served to remind him of how much better off he was in his bachelor's paradise. He was never "Geoff", not to Amelia or his friends – their parents always told anyone who was bothered to listen that they had made a mistake in naming him thus as they couldn't bear the thought that his name could be shortened for the convenience of others.

"Achh, he's so wrapped up in this damn war stuff - says the readers want "real-time war news" – he can't be bothered with my arts and literary stuff, the "airy-fairy stuff", he calls it. The "icing on the cake", I say! Bloody nerve! Given a choice between a damned "shaggy dog saves German airman" story and one of my finer critiques on Orwell's flights of fancy in Spain or what-have-you, that idiot will go for the dog! There may be a drip-drip alright but it's where I get MY inspiration, dear! That guy has no imagination, thinks the readers only want to read printed versions of those damned "newsreels" – you know something, I positively *refuse* to go to the cinema now!", Geoffrey said, feigning an imaginary bad smell had permeated the air around his face, his right hand gesturing as if fanning the whiff away, emphasising "re-fuse" like it was some sort of Doomsday threat that was sure to drain the lifeblood from the entire movie industry.

The reason for his venom was that he (uniquely) believed that, if he had his way, newsreels ought to be consigned to the vaults of the BBC to be looked at in years to come by historians to show them how ridiculous, as he often thought, was the over-reaction to the little Groucho Marx-character's antagonistic, malevolent assault on those far away shores. "How could an attack on an "ally", a "friendly" nation (and what makes it *friendly*?, he often enquired), usually "hundreds of miles away, justify, once again, sending all of these young lads to their deaths in the King's name? Who asked us to "guarantee the borders" of our "friends", were WE consulted? You know, "the people"? Did we not learn anything from that ill-begotten battle in which we lost a generation of good men? All of those fields strewn with sacrificial lambs, sons and fathers who knew nothing of Franz-Ferdinand or Serbia or the assassin, who had no clue – how could they – about those worlds?"

Her brother's politics were simple – let the British defend what was British and let the other nations in Europe, the *actual* neighbours, police the ambitions of those who seek to conquer them and to dissuade their accomplices. It was none of our bloody business, surely? Now it ought to be recorded, in the interest of fairness, that Geoffrey had indeed seen action as a war reporter of sorts, albeit a late start in June 1917, his assignments never actually from the theatre of war in Europe. His disdain for the "shaggy dog" story had been well and truly ignited back then for that was the kind of story which the press seemed to manipulate in order to endear itself to the conscience of the nation. The people needed a morale boost, was the pervasive editorial view, so "human interest" stories were the order of the day. As a cub reporter himself in his first real journalist's job, Geoffrey had to, after all, cut his teeth.

When he thought back on those days of his youth, to his mind his talents had been wasted in the mechanics of this peripheral trivia: he could never ascribe to the notion that what he was doing was *for the morale of the nation.* Indeed when he cashed his paycheque, he came to accept that it bankrolled his *jolly good way of life when all of those poor blighters were stuck in the dark, dank, rat-infested hell-holes in the fields of France and Belgium, while the generals and - pah! - "military advisers", stayed warm and cosy in south east England, cosseted by the maids and footmen of the regiment headquarters in dear ol' Blighty.* These same men, for they were indeed men, had planned hell-for-leather to send thousands on an extended suicide mission. But that would be to give the lie that he regretted his spectator's view. In fact, he relished the opportunity to reflect back the vanities of the gentry, who comprised the commanding classes, with his particular brand of sardonic wit and pointed, mocking sarcasm.

In the meantime, he felt vaguely ashamed to admit that his greatest contribution to the war effort was the first-hand reporting of the recruitment campaigns and speeches of Kitchener, who seemed to him to be some sort of sphinx-like character, his imperious, knowing gaze looking down the range finder of his index finger in that infamous poster. To Geoffrey, the ghastly rhetoric seemed as asinine as that loaded finger and, by God, had this reporter been relieved to find that, in fact, he was immune from that new blight of "conscription", due to his, betimes, suffocating asthma. Now, it may seem to you, reader, that the poor Lambe delighted in his inability to contribute more than his pen and bon mots, however it is true that not alone was the asthma a hindrance but he was also certified unfit for duty due to "chronic flatfootedness", a condition that had been a source of cringe-making embarrassment to him as a child on the rugby field and now, he felt humbled to admit it, as an otherwise battle-fit adult. He was incredulous to have this diagnosis confirmed in the recruitment office. "Surely I could man a stationary Tommy gun, for pity's sake!", he protested to the smirking army doctor, but he was refused entry flatly, on grounds of his flatfootedness.

"So does that mean you will finally be moving on?", enquired Geoffrey, suddenly conscious that he was letting his normally gruff form desert him. That would not do, he had to remain firm with his sister as that was what she expected of him and he with her. "Not that I want you to think I'm sending you back to Europe, even I know how you always hate this time of year, since poor old Alan…", he let the air fill the void, finish the sentence, instead of the more innocently vacant words she had heard too many times before.

"Eventually", she drawled back in her gently husk voice, pronouncing each syllable as if she was a foreigner in an English lesson, for she still had not given much thought to a return to her Paris flat. She ran her fingers through her bobbed hair – not for her the shoulder length, coiffed look so beloved of this era of Hollywood glamour – and said: "First, though, I must get to Belfast for dear Gordon's funeral. He was a gentle, gentle man", she whispered, remembering again his soft kisses and deep passion for her. And she for him.

That happy time in London would always seem to have been an implausible affair, with anyone other than Gordon: he was as discrete as the party in Mayfair, thrown by her old acquaintance Elsie Carlisle - she it was, in fact, who had introduced Amelia and Gordon at the King's garden party in White City before the Games began. She had seen a raw chemistry between them, and even the matchmaker, had mischievously organised her own private "Empire Games Night" in her swanky Henrietta Street home. Now, it was undeniable that Amelia Lamb was betrothed back then to the American arms dealer, Chester Strong - she had a discrete diamond and sapphire ring on her engagement finger as proof, but, though madly in love with her fiancé, Elsie immediately recognised the animal attraction with the dapper Gordon and thought she would have a little fun at her friend's expense.

The hot, smoky living room reeked of Pimms, Hendrick's and vodka Martinis mixed with the vapours of assorted panatelas. Just for this special night, it had been converted into a two hundred square foot ballroom, replete with jazz ensemble of three dinner-suited virtuosos. Her old friend Ambrose was returning a favour and he had brought some of the Embassy with him, famed as the house band for Elsie in her concerts. They hammered out a cacophony of jaunty melodies and recognisable dancefloor hits by Elsie, George Webb, Duke Ellington and their ilk. The hostess bowed, redfaced, to chants from the assembly to sing and, with a nod across to Ambrose, she broke into "Smoke Gets In Your Eyes", a recent hit for her dear friend, Paul, closely followed by her own hit, "A Nightingale Sang in Berkeley Square". When the applause had faded, and she had slipped from centre-stage, she floated between couples, clutching her goblet of London Dry and tonic, discussing the next leg in her nervous tour of the army bases in the North-east. She reintroduced Amelia and Gordon and it was not long before the two found their bodies pressed against each other in a mock demonstration of an exaggerated paso doble. They amused, unquestionably aroused, the other furtive dancers in the room, who were positively itching to demonstrate their own expertise in this kind of close contact dance. The chemistry between the two was palpable and her engagement ring did not go unnoticed as it glinted in the band's spotlights whenever they got close to the musicians. Amelia found herself admiring her dance partner's dedication to achieving as exacting a performance as these two strangers could manage – it was as if they were competing with her dear friends, the Chapouls, in the World Championship in Paris! She gasped when he swung her out onto the sprung maple, her ermine court shoes bouncing sweetly and gently squeaking as she gaily enjoyed herself in the company of this most dashing of men: tall and elegant in his highly polished spats and ivory tuxedo, he was the perfect foil for the exotically grey-eyed and perfectly proportioned – oh, and betrothed - Amelia.

Her mauve shift dress accentuated her every twist and sway and, as he bowled her away on his fingertips, they each knew they were smitten. It all seemed a little disappointing to her that Gordon had gone on to marry his childhood sweetheart, Clarissa Dwight-Shelby, daughter of a Belfast shipping industrialist, which, she would have to admit, had come as a bit of a shock. But why should it have been a shock when, she thought, she herself had moved away from England to the Continent almost at the drop of a hat after Alan Mendl turned up in her favourite tavern, Lamb's on Conduit Street? He had proposed within two hours of meeting her and asked her to travel to Europe with him, "as that is where we shall be based".

The ceiling fans in the room turned slowly overhead, a decadent American invention which attempted to generate fresh air as the revellers laughed and danced and stole knowing glances across the room. He was quite the find, Gordon, she thought to herself, as their arms pulled and pushed each other to and fro, their hot alcohol-tinged breath reflecting back into each other's open mouths as their heads drew close in mock-passionate embraces. He liked the bitter-sweet scent of Hendrick's and quinine tonic on her breath, masking the malodorous cigarillo-tainted funk which he had grown accustomed to as they chatted between numbers. It subverted her tremulous feminity as he drank in her shapely body which was, he was to discover, encased in a blue and gold satin bustier beneath the stylish mauve ensemble, taut bosom spilling towards his chin as they pulled each other close for their mock "finale". He winced slightly when that most masculine mingling of fragrances invaded his nostrils again and he unleashed her lithe frame back out onto the dancefloor before they swept across the room. It did her little favour, he thought, that funk, and he wondered what sort of woman would let herself down by such a concoction of fragrances? "No matter", he thought, "she is the most ravishing woman in the room and, by God, I am dancing with *her!*"

Smothered in his aroma - she thought "Acqua di Parma", perhaps "Russian Leather" - which was hitting her in waves as they danced at arm's length one minute, then staring into each other's pupils the next, neutralised her as if being drugged with chloroform. He had politely shunned her offer of a Bock from her freshly opened pack of twelve and she wondered if he thought any less of her because she smoked. She daydreamed too: he could take me, take me right here, right now. He cradled her head in his splayed fingers, ridiculously, shamefully perhaps, noticing the hairs at the base of her neck were a darker shade than the studied unruliness of her light brunette bob. Suddenly, and without warning, he was compelled to kiss her, gently at first, as if greeting an old friend, and, when she responded favourably, they kissed again, this time one long passionate kiss, closed-lip softness giving way to a more urgent firmness, as if they may never have this moment again. For all his concern, he found her mouth tasted mostly of tonic water and that was not a bad thing.

Of course, this was Amelia, and yes, they would have many more moments like it that evening and for much of the next week while Chester remained in Egypt with his father on munitions business. Amelia wondered frequently, however, throughout her dalliance with Gordon Anderson, (which lasted a week and a day) how ever was she going to remain true to Chester?

An Atlantic on the Irish Sea

"How shall I get to Belfast?", she suddenly enquired of Geoffrey. "Same way the Irish get to our pleasant green land, I should think, Amelia: the mailboat to Dublin and drive yourself to Belfast, I believe it is a mere one hundred miles or so", came Geoffrey's gruff reply. "Of course", he suddenly recalled, "you could always drive up past Liverpool, think you can get a boat from Heysham, yes that's right - it's near Morecambe - straight to Belfast. You won't be able to get your car over with you, of course - I think that boat is mostly for lorries and their drivers, so it might be a bit, shall we say, "rough"?". "Hrrumph! Whatever about 'rough', if anyone knows nothing about "man-things", it is you, Geoffrey Lambe! I think Heysham it shall have to be", decided Amelia, having instantly taken a dislike to the notion of having to drive from Dublin to Belfast after eight hours spent on a boat. Much more preferable, she decided, would be a murky four hours with a bunch of Irishmen (she supposed) with their full cargo-loads of customs-approved war rations, their lorries parked neatly on the deck of the ship. "Sure, it might be a bit of fun in these desperate times and there is bound to be a drinking session!", Amelia said out loud, mischievously. Strangely, it was exactly what Geoffrey was thinking and, he thought, heaven knows how very long it had been since he and his sister had come to think in synchronicity about the world.

Even if Amelia had been the least attractive woman to ever have graced the haute couture shows of London and Paris, there was one thing that was guaranteed to bag her licentious proposals from jealous gentlemen: she possessed that 1937 Bugatti SC57 Atlantic, acquired through a Bonham's car auction in London. Some said it had been in Lord Rothschild's fleet of expensive cars and Amelia believed that she had wisely used some of the proceeds from the sale of one of Alan's family heirlooms, the Abyssinian Imperial Mace. Alan's grandfather, Viscount Slim, had been gifted the jewel-encrusted golden staff by the Officer Commanding of the British Indian Army as a memento of gratitude for his leading role in the expedition to Abysinnia in 1868. It was rumoured that the Koh-i-Noor diamond had once rested in it (although a good story for the auctioneer, it was unlikely as the stone had been presented to Queen Victoria by a maharajah's son at the end of the Sikh War).

The black Bugatti had rested silently and quite anonymously beside the footpath outside her brother's apartment for much of the yuletide, it's roar only making the patent leather beetle's presence obvious when, on Christmas Eve morning, the siblings exited the city south-south-westwards, to spend Christmas Eve and Day with their beloved maiden aunt, Gertrude, at the family pile in Hurstpierpoint, a stone's throw from Brighton.

The Atlantic was as extraordinary to drive as it was to look at – Gulliver might have picked it up and opened it as if pulling open a peanut and Amelia loved the lion's roar of its six exhaust fingers as it eased its way down the Cromwell Road. It never failed to turn heads as the extraordinary shape was unlike any other car yet seen: tear-drop-shaped, to many it looked like a black, metallic beetle, its roof having the appearance of a walnut which had been riveted together with the precision of one of Hardy Amies's seamstresses. For the technically minded, it was driven by a purring 3.3 litre engine producing a massive 170 break horse power. Amelia had shared the Bonham representative's worries that perhaps it was too powerful a car for her to own.

Even though Geoffrey and Amelia had been brought up in Brighton, they both still loved to return to the "Olde English" atmosphere of the village with its cut stone houses, shops and churches, emerging like a stone oasis from the lush greenery of Sayers Common just a few minutes beyond Hassocks. Gertrude had lived here all of her life, her brother - their father - and her sister Elizabeth, had both found love beyond the boundaries of the little village and had moved away to Brighton and Eastbourne respectively to start new lives with their well-to-do spouses. Amelia's father, Edmund, had travelled widely in his various diplomatic roles, mostly as First or Second Secretary in central and Eastern European embassies but the children's education always took precedence and there was never any question of uprooting the family to live the nomadic life he had chosen for himself.

As they sat in the car, she and Geoffrey looked like escapees from the reels of a Buck Rogers science fiction adventure as the sleek black aluminium car, it's unique "seam" holding it together, burst forth onto the road to Brighton, en route to Hurst. They had only, in the last five years or so, hit upon the idea of spending time with Gertrude again, as had been the ritual from when Amelia was four years old. Their maiden aunt was the last link with their father, Edmund, and they enjoyed her spicy stories of their father's courtship with their dearest mother, Nathalie. Their father had come from Serbia and was descended from Peter, one of the last kings of Serbia. They had met at the British Ambassador's party in Belgrade when Edmund had been Acting Second Secretary; it was a tempestuous affair and they had many stand-offs before settling into a marriage that worked, despite her reluctance to travel and his requirement to travel widely. It worked so well that both Amelia and Geoffrey were afforded comfortable and cosseted lifestyles that, had anyone known, would have been seen to put them on a par with members of the House of Windsor.

What a racy pair Edmund and Nathalie had been, and dear old Queen Victoria still warm in her grave! Edmund had had a "terrible tongue, that man! Profanity? I think he wrote the manual!", Gertrude often said. Unfortunately, she would recount, it begat tirades in equal measure of colourful language from Nathalie but "it was their way", her sister-in-law would sigh, in fudging some kind of mock excuse for it. Their aunt would forget that, for the most part, Edmund was completely unaware of the meaning of his wife's outburst and she of his - he spoke no Serbian and she had had great difficulty learning a proficient level of English, although she knew enough to know the thrust of Edmund's arguments.

Amelia's husband had gone one year with them, all three of them travelling there in Alan's luxurious Wolseley, which he proudly told Aunt Gerty was "part of the spoils of war": she had never approved of his chosen career and would roll her eyes heavenward as she tut-tutted her disapproval. Despite her criticism of him, Alan had enjoyed her company and her hospitality and he was wont to say that "she secretly adores me really, all of that mock irritation is just her way". He was not to know that that was, in fact, a fair assessment of her view of him, all part of the shield she hid behind all of her life to keep men at arms length. In fact, she was comfortable in Alan's company and she thought him witty and charming to a fault, which, Amelia had to admit, he most certainly was.

Amelia was unsure of this drive to Heysham – Liverpool was manageable but this port was unheard of to her, and so she had to check the directions to get there. The best thing, to Geoffrey's mind, was that at least when she got back to Heysham, her car would be available to her and she could head straight to Dover and back to Paris. She would just have a final stop with her brother to gather her belongings together before the ferry to Calais and onwards to Paris. How she hoped Paris would be agreeable to her, now that the Germans were in charge and in view of her simmering resentment for what had happened to Alan, her late husband. He had often said that his line of business was rife with danger and that it could be a fatal move to offend a customer, that the "customer is always right", "customer is king", etc. Except in this particular incidence, the customer had been fatally *wrong,* and she felt sure Alan had paid with his life.

"Okay, m'dear", said Geofrrey, settling a generous measure of whisky in front of himself before he launched into what he seemed to consider to be some sort of co-piloting job for his sister, even though he himself was not accompanying her on her trip. He had laid out his 1935 OS map as if in a battle command room and, flexing his fingers and waving a fountain pen, said: "You need to high-tail it to High Wycombe" – he patted himself on the back for the alliteration and his dry wit. She was not amused and he quickly said: "In other words get on the A40 in the direction of Oxford, that will bring you up towards Birmingham" - here he hammed up the accent, pronouncing the 'g' heavily, as if a native of that city. "Then you should start seeing signs for Liverpool and the A6", he continued. "Just follow that road, it will take you out past the metropolis of Blackpool, and Heysham is just this side of Lancaster. In that machine of yours, three hours should do it. Well, that's if you put the foot down. When is the last post?", he grinned. "The third, the day after tomorrow. I spoke to Daphne, Gordon's mother, on the telephone earlier, she is happy to put me up for a night or two so I really ought to make my way up there now, don't you think?", she replied. "Rather quick funeral, must be the Irish way. Yes, well, over two hundred miles ahead of you so best unleash the horses sooner rather than later", prompted a relieved, never a curmudgeonly, Geoffrey.

Geoffrey Lambe

Truth to tell, he really just wanted his sister to move on as he felt he had exhausted this year's, as well as last year's, supply of conversation in entertaining her since early December, give or take her absences at the nefarious soireés she had been invited to on her now-annual Christmas sojourn. And, of course, they had together broken forth from the neat two-bedroom apartment near Olympia to sojourn with Aunt Gertie over Christmas. G. Lambe simply was not the kind of fellow who could ever have been the marrying kind - he was, he decided, the quintessential bachelor boy, but "more for women than agin them", he would confirm when pressed, and he "most definitely was not a regular at the Turkish Baths on Jermyn Street", which was how he deflected any curved balls regarding his unmarried status. More than that he would not say, so that not even Amelia was aware of his unrequited love for Penny, a sub-editor with whom he had worked for the last six barren years. She sat at the largest mahogany desk on the mezzanine floor in the Black Lubyanka, the nickname that had been coined for the headquarters of his employers, because of its resemblance to a grandiose monstrosity of a Russian government building on Lubyanka Street in Moscow. Despite its rather inelegant moniker, it was one of the most elegant and inspirational art-deco buildings ever built in Central London, let alone grey Fleet Street. It's otherworldly, black vitroline-and-glass exterior, shone smooth and bright in the shards of bright sunshine that occasionally flashed through Fleet Street, the light reflecting and dancing on its gently angular construct, giving only the merest hint of its grandiose and expensive interior of aluminium-leafed ceilings and futuristic lanterns and frescoes. It was said by some that Fritz Lang had taken inspiration from it and that it had even inspired the backdrops in "Metropolis", his most impressive movie to date. The deep lustre of the solid mahogany wall panelling and furnishings, oozing the odour of French polish and human elbow grease, were a comfort to Geoffrey, reminding him, as it did, of the spick and span, red-bricked Victorian villa he had holidayed in as a child with Amelia and their parents in Marylebone nearby. And it was in this highly polished creative cocoon that his career had waxed and waned over the last fifteen years.

Their colleagues knew that Penny and Geoffrey regularly shared a Chesterfield over a coffee in nearby Anderton's and that, frequently, after work, they would retire to The Tipperary - The Tipp - London's best known Irish pub, for a draught of Guinness. They were both unsure as to why they were drawn so particularly to The Tipp, perhaps it was the fact that it was a favourite haunt of rivals in The Times and Telegraph and that there was always that possibility that they just might come by a story through selective hearing. Sometimes, if there was a leaving do for a staff member in any of the neighbouring newspaper offices, a sizeable throng would invade the Tipp late in the evening, making it hard to avoid friendships and the nods these acquaintances would entail. More likely, of course, was that perhaps it was because Geoffrey liked the creamy texture and the bitter taste of the Guinness: as he would say, "there's enough eatin' and drinkin' on four pints of that stuff!", in his mock, and quite poor, "Oirish" accent. Penny would have her usual ladylike glass or three of Guinness and blackcurrant cordial, so that it would all make a visit to the Gavroche an expensive and unnecessary diversion from the task in hand, that task being drinking and having a pleasant time together. Not to say that they were not, on occasion, to be found eating the best available sirloin of beef and gratinée potatoes in that afore-mentioned noble institution, washed down by an exhilarating bottle of 1918 Pronutto Barbera d'Asti', their favourite. In fact, maybe that was the main reason for making The Tipp the number one choice – it was a discrete place for their enjoyable interludes and, although Penny was a feisty bachelorette and quite capable of drinking Lambe under the table, they mostly spent their time discussing the day's political developments and copy deadlines. They would laugh out loud at their colleagues' penchants for fastidiousness and tidiness around their desks and they would critique their own writings in that week's different editions. The drinking was merely the glue which held their strands of shop-talk together. There were times too when they would brush fingertips and knock knuckles clumsily against one another, as they nested cosily on the tartan-covered seating in the snug, just to the right of the entrance. Then, they would both look startled into each other's eyes, cheeks glowing pink in the mottled lamp-light, and occasionally Geoffrey's lips would form to ask the question that always hung in the air that they shared in that confined space. But Geoffrey would always think better of it, and Penny would carry on as if she had not noticed her companion's pinking cheeks as all thoughts of inviting her on a "proper date" was forced into the back of his mind. Of course, he knew that at the end of the evening, he would rue yet another missed opportunity but what he never knew was that Penny would also feel cheated out of what she just knew would undoubtedly have been a most splendid encounter. He always, in his mind, concluded that it was, as she would crudely say, "better not to shit on your own doorstep": after all, they shared an office, intimacy greater than the kind they enjoyed in The Tipp would probably make work unbearable for them both. Or not, he would ponder . . . or not.

Amelia en route

As Amelia made her way westward along the A4 from the apartment which she had made her home, she reflected on her life. Coming away from London this time, she surprisingly felt that London had indeed seemed much more like "her home" since Geoffrey had returned to his work-desk in early January. This was a new experience for her as, for so long, she had felt nothing for Geoffrey's adopted home-town. She had found herself wandering around the bookshops on Charing Cross Road most days, just soaking up the atmosphere and revelling in that sense of referred knowledge she had always felt in bookshops since she was a child. It was because of that very same feeling Geoffrey had taken the path he had taken in life as he too had always found that there was something uplifting about bookshops and he liked the sense that simply by visiting one, one could also walk away with that sense of "referred knowledge". This time, for Amelia, she would drift off into a dreamlike detachment from the brutality of life, the life that was being enacted once more in England and in Europe, a life now of air raid sirens and constant vigilance, which was just so wearing. On one bright afternoon in early January, she had decided that she would visit places most Londoners probably would never even dream of visiting in their lifetimes – she would visit the National Library in it's home at the Museum; visit the Natural History Museum; she would visit that great bastion of Protestantism, Westminster Abbey, and that redbrick Cathedral in Whitehall, a regular haunt for the Paulina's when they traipsed the five miles or so across the city to it every Friday; St Paul's Cathedral; the Victoria and Albert; the Tower of London! There was just so much to see and she decided that she had better see it all just in case the bombs started to fall on it all.

She had been a widow now for two years, having been married to Alan for three and she reflected that they had had a good marriage, if tempestuous. The good times had almost been wiped from her memory, however, as the shock of his disappearance still reverberated around her life: he had only wanted the best life for her, for them both, and for a brief shining time, they had had it all together: a magnificent gated mansion in Paris Ouest; a winter residence on Rue le Corbusier in Geneva; a holiday chalet in exclusive St Moritz; they had wanted for nothing. But now, for sad Amelia, there was something she did want and that was a return to the life she had known with her husband, the life of travel and adventure and, she had to admit, luxury.

Chapter 8

Alan and Amelia Present Arms

Long before Alan Mendl had inherited the family fortune, he had inherited his German father's knack for identifying a business niche to exploit. His particular niche became arms procurement and arms dealing and with a huge loan of £1500 from the Bank of England, using his family's good name as security, Alan pursued a business deal with the Finns who, he had discovered, had a secret pact with the Lenin government to buy its overstocks of home-made artillery - rifles, machine guns, mortars, canon.

Originally, his plan was to sell this equipment on to the shattered British forces but what he had not banked on was that thanks to better production methods developed during that earlier conflict, Britain could now produce enough of its own weaponry to adequately arm its troops, and then some. Of course, its victory in that battle of wills also meant that it was less inclined to look beyond its own shores for munitions and in that regard, it sought to be as self-sufficient as possible. This had come as a bitter blow to Alan's business plans and he found himself driving across Europe to find likely buyers for his surplus arms.

From the earliest days, Amelia had accompanied him at some of his meetings with military and government representatives. It was really only after that meeting with the Italians that Alan had noticed how much easier it was for him to secure orders when accompanied by his beautiful wife. Amelia's intellect was never challenged by the technologically-advanced weapons her husband dealt in, indeed her curiosity to learn more about them meant that she quickly became very knowledgeable in the usefulness of each weapon in different situations. He had initially been surprised when her enthusiasm about the firepower and capability of his inventory prompted her to suggest that she could be a useful sidekick to him when he met with potential customers: he also realised that he needed to have something that would give him an edge in his sales presentations, something memorable.

Amelia was insistent, with her looks and charisma, she could surprise his potential clients with her schpeil on the weapons specification that he would normally give, and she could answer the sometimes awkward questions. She just had to rehearse with him the answers to the questions that were most frequently asked at his presentations and she did this with remarkable aplomb.

For his part, Alan was not particularly scrupulous in his targeting of likely clients: one of his best clients lately had been the unpredictable fascist Benito Mussolini, to whom he had made his first truly large arms sale. Mussolini was anxious to ensure that his opponents were discouraged from challenging his leadership and simply by having the hypnotic power of Amelia in the room, Alan secured the deal with the Italians with minimal effort.

Now, with Amelia beside him, Alan felt invincible as he stood there with his cache of nearly-obsolete DP26s and the new MP34s, which he had pre-ordered from the Austrian

Steyr company two years ago and which were only now on the way to his secret location in neutral St Moritz. And so it had come to pass, in the winter of 1938, on Mussolini's recommendation, Deputy Fuhrer Hess sent a courier with an official document expressing interest in and requesting to see Mendl's weaponry stock-holding, and that the Germans wanted particularly to see the MP34 as their friends in Italy were already putting their purchase to effective use. Alan, encouraged by the success he had enjoyed with the Italians, agreed to meet the Germans on condition that his fragrant wife could accompany him to the Kehlsteinhaus in Berchtesgarden in the Bavarian Alps as "she would explain the technology built into some of these weapons more expertly than me", an odd request but one the Germans had been expecting as their Italian friend had mentioned Mendl's "unique sales technique".

Setting out from their Geneva residence at 8am on a cold early March day, they arrived at the Eagle's Nest just before 4pm that afternoon. They approached the entrance tunnel to the lift up into the Kehlsteinhaus, the Eagle's Nest, and were flagged down by two guards in SS uniform. They nodded understandingly when Alan told them that they were here to meet with the Auswahlkomitee, the selection committee, and that they were expected. They were allowed to drive on up through the tunnel with the guards following in their Type 87. When they got to the lift gates, the guards helped Mendl to unload the sample cases from the Wolsely and the three men stacked them on one of the green leather seats in the lift. The lift made its journey without conversation, and, having arrived at its destination, one of the guards accompanied the Mendls to the interior of the house, while the other returned to his position at the tunnel entrance.

On exiting the lift, Mendl and the guard removed the sample cases, placing them carefully to the right of the lift door. Alan and Amelia followed him through a long, high-vaulted banqueting hall, complete with domestic staff dressed in grey uniforms, quietly resetting the table for dinner. They barely looked up to take in what was going on as the three walked through the hall, with the guard opening the door at the end of the room. It was late in the day now, sun dipping and it near 5pm, and as they walked through the door into the next room, they could see six men in the room, some in SS uniform, others in smart civilian suits. The selection committee had been gathering since mid-morning and had already seen their way through a dozen bottles of Domaine de Pégau Chateau Neuf-du-Pape, with the remnants of their lunch and residue-stained crystal goblets still strewn across two of the six card-tables in the room. There were shot glasses with varying measures of liquor in them as they were half way through the half dozen bottles of Chivas Reserve sitting on another one of the tables near the baby grand piano in the centre of the room. At the other side of the room and coming into focus in the room's gloomy light, Mendl was taken aback to realise that he was looking at the Fuhrer himself standing in front of the red fireplace, with his back to the room. One of the uniformed men moved swiftly across the room and Oberst Huffmeier exclaimed his name and rank in, what was for him, an unguarded moment, as he scuttled across the room to greet Amelia. Glancing across the room, he nodded a silent greeting to her husband but Alan missed it as his gaze was firmly fixed on the man at the fireplace.

He watched as the figure in the grey-green Donegal suit slowly turned to face the room, and Alan tensed when he saw it was indeed the Fuhrer himself: "Guten tag, Herr Mendl. Good afternoon, Frau Mendl, it is a pleasure to meet with you, we have heard so many good things from our friends in Italy about you", he said. Alan was unimpressed that he had almost been completely ignored, when the fact was that it was actually Alan that the leadership had asked to see: surely they knew that Amelia was merely there as a pleasant distraction, albeit one with an important role in his presentation that day. As the couple moved to shake hands with the Fuhrer, the tunnel guard from the lift arrived with the cache of sample cases stacked precariously on a rickety brass and teak tea-trolley. On seeing the couple reach out towards the Fuhrer, the guard stopped the trolley instantly and lunged across the room to get in the way of their handshakes: nobody could touch the Fuhrer without the agreed clearances and the guard had failed to ask for the required papers to confirm the couple's credentials. The Fuhrer waved the guard away immediately and the three shook hands swiftly and stiffly.

With the help of Huffmeier, Mendl and the guard carefully placed the cases on another one of the tables in the room. His duty complete for now (especially after his intercession on the handshakes), the guard proudly and ceremoniously clicked his heels and saluted the room with a "Heil Hitler!". He went straight to the lift so that he could return to his mate in the tunnel guardbox.

Presenting Arms

After that latest success with the Italians, they decided that future presentations would be that simple - Alan would unpack the samples, demonstrate the correct way to handle each weapon and give a brief outline of its firepower. If it needed assembly or the addition of accessories, that too would be part of his presentation. The technical specifications were

Amelia's "department", as he would tell the committee. This Nazi committee was a disparate collection of party members: Oberst Otto Huffmeier of the infantry; Deputy Fuhrer Rudolf Hess; weapons expert and civilian, Fritz Walther; SS Quartermaster Hermann Goering; General Von Epp from the Armed Forces; and, quite unexpectedly, the Fuhrer himself. As Alan showed and silently demonstrated each weapon, Amelia recited the specifications for each with cowed eyes and a breathtaking assuredness that seemed as natural to her as making love. Alan instantly knew that the addition of Amelia in his presentation was, indeed, the coup de grace. She answered the Germans' questions expertly and graciously took the compliments for her proficiency and her beauty.

However, the pièce de resistance of this particular sales presentation quickly became legendary: after the last piece of artillery had been shown and discussed, and without Alan's prior knowledge, she had decided to perform a seductive striptease to "seal the deal". Alan watched bemused as his wife surprised him when she silently rose from her chair, unbuttoning the top button of her cream blouse. She continued to rise up and step up onto her chair, the Germans shifting in theirs to get a better view of her purple lace stocking tops as she stood up on the table that had been between them. To compound their curiosity, she wore loose purple French knickers which offered her audience a glimpse of heaven with every move of her comely hips.

Her head lolled back as she swayed those hips seductively from side to side, as if in a trance. In her head, she was listening to Billie Holiday's "Summertime" as she slowly unbuttoned her wide shouldered, biscuit-coloured Lachasse jacket. With a deft sleight of hand and a discrete unzipping, her matching-coloured skirt fell to the floor. The reddening cheeks of the Germans were outdone only by Amelia's scarlet suspender belt, her shapely legs encased in the latest fully fashioned, finest denier Wolford stockings, seams diligently drawn by the hand of their owner.

She dismounted the table as she had dismounted the gymnastics beam when she was an Olympics prospect in the two years before her teenage years began. She worked the room, tantalisingly leaning across the backs of chairs and daringly revealing the pleasing contents of her lingerie, her excited nipples straining the satin cups of her brassiere. Her right thumb and index finger delineated her carefully shaven assets as she arched her back across the backs of the highly polished and upholstered chairs, and her hands moved across her groin, causing the married men to gaze longingly at her crotch. She pushed her left breast over the top of its retainer and circled a sucked finger around the excited nipple with great care and exaggeration before releasing its matching breast with a well-practiced undoing of the front brassiere clasp. She cupped her generous breasts in her hands and jiggled them together gently and provocatively, tossing the relieved brassiere towards the Fuhrer, who drank in its Chanel No.5 perfume thirstily. She dismounted the table and, in a deft one-handed move, pulled a chair between her legs and wiggled her lightly-covered backside onto the front edge of it. For her next move, she lifted her right leg a little off the seat just in front of her groin and, dangling her black patent stiletto on the toetips of her foot, she slowly detached her lilac stocking top from her red garter belt, one stay at a time. She rolled the expensive stocking slowly down her leg, offering occasional glimpses of her tightly groomed sex to the squirming Germans. Once again, she mounted the table and, as the finale in her impromptu show, bent forward into a crab position and slowly gyrated her backside invitingly in front of the Fuhrer. With her derrière thrusting up and down just in front of his sun-pocked face, he lurched forward and helped to ease off her satin knickers with surprisingly trembling stubby fingers. The striptease idea had been hers entirely as she had wanted "a bit of diversion to beat the boredom after my turn" at these sales demonstrations, she would later inform her husband, and after this first performance in front of the Germans, they had agreed it would be an innovative, if risky, way to help sales. Her husband's only interest was in securing business in whatever way possible and he reckoned that the Germans would be sane enough to know that they would never be able to advance their real agenda. He said to Amelia, "No harm in going to see these fellows" and "the Italians will be pleased these boys listened to their leader's suggestion".

Amelia had not been so sure about meeting the German contingent as she was deeply disturbed at the reports about the way in which people had been disappearing all over Germany, Jew and non-Jew. Amelia had heard rumours of these "miscreants", as it had been reported in the British media (although they seemed to be just quoting German news reports), who were being sent to labour camps for no apparent reason and she was very uneasy with the notion that her husband was contemplating business with such a two-faced government. Her role at these meetings had become much more vocal as they toured the various presidential and royal palaces of central Europe together and, of course, she had become very knowledgeable on the battle-readiness of the equipment. She was destined to play an increasing role - the combination of her beauty, her easy conversational style, and her obvious enthusiasm for her husband's business dealings was, indeed, a winning one and she got a lot of pleasure, maybe even sexual pleasure, from the fact that they were being invited to meet generals and presidents and crown princes to show Alan's holdings of pistols, submachine guns and Alan's new line, mortar launchers. The onerous task for Alan of making these sales appointments had been overcome by the smart introduction of his wife into the sales presentations: of course, Amelia's willingness to perform a highly charged strip show at this meeting with the Nazi hierarchy, meant that their teamwork immediately became noteworthy to the upper echelons of the military and to state officialdom. Doubtless the strip would now be seen as an official part of the sales presentation. It would be no surprise then, Alan thought, if they secured the biggest prize of all, the sale of his cache of MP34s, to the faltering Germans at this meeting here today.

Happily for Mendl, it was indeed the Steyr MP34 that was the singular item that roused most interest from Goring, Hess, Himmler and their weapons expert, Fritz Walther, and they had encouraged their leader to buy up the entire available stock from Mendl. Amelia sat quietly now, after her performance, studying the Fuhrer's reactions, and concluded that there was something other-worldly about him, a terrible scarifying something which was not attractive, at least not to her. By the end of this visit to the remote tea-house, Amelia had seen enough to be convinced that this group of Germans was bad news, that they had designs on a bigger prize and she was not at all happy that she had, perhaps, aided and abetted their plans. Worse still, she had noticed a look of disdain on the Fuhrer's face when it was suggested by her husband, somewhat meekly, that if this deal got past the Allies (and thereby the hated terms of the "Treaty"), perhaps he could become the regime's chief supplier? Hitler's curt reply was a menacing "Why, I should think we will take over the manufacturer, after all the German people own Austria now!" To Amelia, there was a madness in Hitler's voice and it chilled her to the bones.

"That was a disappointing end to the meeting", Mendl quietly conceded to Amelia in the lift back down to the car. "Why did you not tell me that you were planning your little show too? I thought we were guaranteed to sell all of the MP34s after you buttered them up with that performance: you must repeat it for me soon! In private . . .", he slyly said, pulling her close to kiss him and fondle her breasts as he spoke. True, they had come away with a modest order for the MP34 alright, nothing on the 26s, and Amelia did not feel she could tell her husband that she was concerned when she noticed the Fuhrer whispering to Goring and glaring across at Alan. Sure enough, it was the last time they would visit the German leadership with goods to sell, but not the last time they would take the Nazi's American dollars.

Chapter 9

The End of Mendl

At the end of March 1942, more than two years into this latest battle between the remnants of the Axis and the Allies of the previous war, and nearly twice as long after that visit to the Eagle's Nest, Alan got a surprise invitation to meet the leadership again. This time it would be just himself to meet the man who had replaced Hess as the Deputy Fuhrer, Martin Borrman, Hess having been taken prisoner the previous year in what one of the few German media reports had noted was "a crazed mission" to negotiate peace. Alan, of course was delighted at the prospect of once more doing business with the leadership, as it looked like he might finally offload his remaining stock of Soviet-made DP26s, which had long been superseded by the 28s, in use now with the Soviet army. He had placed a purchase option with the Finns for the more efficient, easy-clean, 28, and the Germans thought they would like to use the DP26 as well as the 28, with their own Mausers, on the Eastern front against the Soviets: they could not allow the Russians to get their hands on the technology behind their home-made weapons and so it had been decided to buy up and use the Soviet surplus from "Mendl the Jew" and limit the use of Mausers as much as possible, so as to ensure as few of the Mausers could be retrieved and added to the Russian arsenal.

"Mendl the Jew" - this was how his name had come up in conversations between Hitler and Bormann: Hitler had "had a bad feeling about our friend Mendl" and had charged Hess, after that meeting in the Kehlsteinhaus, with tracing "the Englishman's background". It was with little difficulty that Hess had uncovered Mendl's marginal Jewish heritage and it had come as no surprise to the Fuhrer that another one of his arms suppliers was indeed part-Jewish. "Do I not have a talent for sniffing those dogs out?", he shouted at Bormann. Now, the somewhat aristocratic Alan Mendl, whose aforementioned grandfather had fought in the Abyssinian war of 1868 and was rewarded with a vacant viscount title, was vaguely aware of his infinitesimal Jewish ancestry – his maternal great-great grandmother was a Samuelson from Dresden but that was pretty much all he knew about that share of his lineage. Even though he was agnostic, by Nazi definition he was indeed a Jew due to his great-great grandmother's ethnicity. This time, just Mendl was to be collected from his and Amelia's winter residence in Geneva, and by a Nazi staff car – Bormann believed this would be "men's work" and, ominously, he "had plans for our friend", in other words Amelia was not welcome. He was to be transported to Castle Vaduz in Liechtenstein to meet Bormann to discuss the latest purchase of his wares.

Call and Collect

On May 18, 1942 – the date was etched in Amelia's mind forever - a ruby-coloured Horch 853, its eight-cylinder engine buzzing like the engines of the Messerschmidts and Spitfires heard so often overhead in Germany and Britain, drew up outside the apartment block in Geneva to which Alan and Amelia retreated in the winter months. They had stayed longer than usual this year as Alan had been suffering with severe back pain and his doctor had noted that the air off Lake Geneva seemed to be beneficial in easing his breathing difficulties. Of course, it was also a highly dangerous time to be travelling up to Paris as it necessitated the negotiation of German-occupied roads and an unpredictable Resistance, staging roadblocks and occupying roadside sniper positions. Far preferable to remain in neutral Geneva a bit longer, decided Alan.

Much to Amelia's disappointment, she would miss the Paris fashion show season, although they could continue to enjoy the trappings of their luxurious lifestyle in their Geneva bolthole, far away from the rationing and begging and bombing that would doubtless be the experience in the much-changed, German-occupied Paris.

The SS-uniformed chauffeur held the kerbside door of the Horsch open for Mendl as he clambered into the luxurious interior of chestnut leather upholstery and mahogany sills, its roof folded back, secured and buckled into a concertina by two tan leather straps. Amelia held Alan's face between her carefully manicured and rose-scented hands as she kissed him goodbye across the door of the Horsch, wishing him well in his business dealings with the deputy Fuhrer. "Take care, my love", she sighed, as the guard unbuckled the soft-top and pulled the roof forward. This was a relief to Mendl as he had no desire to be a sitting duck in the back of this conspicuous vehicle, even if he *was* to be driven at breakneck speed through neutral Switzerland, en route to the seat of the Princes of Liechtenstein, Castle Vaduz, as had been the venue stated in that original invitation. The car eased away from the roadside as Mendl thought how impressed he was with the Germans – *Good Lord*, he thought, *they are driving me to meet them!* He wondered why the tiny neutral principality had been chosen to be the meeting place but no matter, it was far preferable to the thousand plus kilometres to Berlin.

Now Mendl had an, at best, reasonable understanding and fluency of German, learned and spoken with his half-German mother as a child, but it was put to the test on this short journey from his winter residence to Vaduz. He tried to make light conversation with the driver initially, asking him if he knew why Bormann had set up their meeting in Vaduz. The driver, so far as Mendl could decipher, indicated that he had simply been asked to perform this task and that, really, was a question for the Reichsminister, the Head of the Party Organisation, himself. That reply truncated any further banter between them and Mendl sat back on the deep leather back seat, contemplating Amelia's neatly fastened sample cases containing a full size and, new DP28, ammunition magazines and a steadying bipod stand.

He thought of her beautiful hands handling such lethal equipment, her delicate, manicured fingers packing these conveyors of equal parts death and horror into their respective display cases, she all the while trying to ensure that not one perfectly shaped and painted nail got chipped or broken. He was excited as he sat contemplating the promising sale of four thousand units of MP24s and the two hundred and fifty thousand magazine rounds he had bought from the Finns. He wondered now if he should have bought the million rounds that were on offer.

Of course, his goal would be the sale of his remaining horde of twelve thousand DP26s – he had no further intention of buying more of this older model, it took longer to clean and had smaller capacity than the MP24. He had not wanted to stretch his finances when he was aware that the regime was taking over arms manufacturers - his business associates - with each new territory it was invading all across Europe. Indeed, he reflected sadly, most of those associates had been either shot summarily by the Nazis or been taken prisoner for their "un-German work practices". Perhaps his goods would not be good enough, too outdated, he thought, and he was still reeling from the freeze in his earnings caused by the Italians who had decided not to buy up the larger quantity of newer MP28s, yet another promise they had broken.

Fantasy and reality

Castle Vaduz came into view barely two and a half hours later, famously perched atop the mountain overlooking the picturesque town named after it. Untroubled by the slings and arrows of "this little war" (as the sullen chauffeur had referred to it), the Horsch had hurtled across picturesque northern Switzerland, around the northern shore of Lake Geneva, through Lausanne, on to Zurich, and then into little Liechtenstein. Although Mendl had passed through the principality's unguarded, pleasant terrain many times on his way to armaments trade shows in Austria and Poland, the sight of Castle Vaduz in the dazzling sunlight of the eastern sky was a truly magnificent sight. It's famous lettercard-friendly silhouette of high, castellated walls and medieval tower once again cast his mind back to his youthful obsessions with European myth and medieval history. Today, the line between fantasy and reality seemed blurred, so awestruck was he at this awe-inspiring vista before him.

If he was honest too, a strange, unnerving anxiety had been creeping up on him about this meeting, not helped by his driver's enigmatic silence. The terse silence was not something he was used to: his exemplary salesmanship and normally jovial demeanour usually combined like a dream to break down even the most difficult customer but, on this occasion, it all failed miserably. The car entered the castle courtyard and Mendl balked slightly when he saw the fleet of robust German staff cars parked in an orderly line along the Eastern wing of the castle, the headlight of each one brandishing an ensign. Those little swastikas were fluttering cheerily like summer butterflies in the warm westerly that had helped propel his elegant chariot up and down the undulating jagged mountain climbs to this spectacular rendezvous point. Mendl was growing uneasy and not so sure that this was it after all, that he was going to sell on his final cache of twelve thousand DP26s. He felt sure that the new deputy would be easy to convince about the MP28s, once he saw the sample and learned that he had an option to buy twenty thousand, with enough ammunition to slaughter the population of Liechtenstein in one day, but the obsolete DPs . . .?

The Horsch crunched its way to a halt after it had gently swerved to its parking position close to the Deputy Fuhrer's vehicle (his car had eagle ensigns to denote his senior status). The driver hopped out and he moved swiftly down the side of the metal hulk to open Mendl's door. He ushered Mendl towards the castle door, a medieval monster of heavy bronze, decorated with the Liechtenstein coat of arms in the top panel and studded with rounded flower details on the lower panels. Held open by the SS uniform, the arms dealer strode into the room stiffly as he stretched his body from the seated position he had been in. He paused in the doorway, the pupils of his eyes once again adjusting to the electrical light in what appeared to be another large dining hall. After a few seconds of intense blinking, he focussed on the far end of the room, where three SS-uniformed officials stood: Bormann was immediately recognisable – he was a familiar fixture in Nazi newspaper photographs, the corners of his black eyes creasing under the black peak of his blue-grey Nazi cap. His thin voice greeted Alan Mendl as he crossed the room: "Good afternoon, Herr Mendl, thank you for joining us at such short notice", the voice simultaneously menacing and well-mannered. "Our Fuhrer sends his apologies, he is detained in Berlin on pressing matters of state (it was well documented in the English press that the Soviet Union was exerting much pressure on German forces to the East and he guessed that this was the "pressing matters of state" to which Bormann was referring.) He nodded an acknowledgement to Bormann's explanation for his master's absence and hoped that Bormann did not detect him breathing a sigh of relief that Hitler was absent today.

"Let us get straight to business, shall we?" said Bormann brusquely, clearly not here to waste time on pleasantries. "I have no wish to overstay our welcome in Vaduz and to compromise my dear old friend, the Prince. The DP26s – you have more of this weapon, I believe, the Fuhrer wishes for us to purchase them from you immediately. How many can you deliver and how quickly? Perhaps I can send a vehicle back with you to collect them, time is of the essence and we have no desire to wait your usual delay," said Bormann, his snide jibe jarring with his arms dealer. Mendl was taken off guard, that last cache of 26s was locked away in steel trunks in his chalet in St Moritz. It was to there that he had organised delivery from his Russian contact last year when he and Amelia had taken their winter skiing holiday. "Twelve thousand in six chests of two thousand", he replied, "with twenty thousand rounds in each trunk", he concluded.

This was going to be a difficult meeting, he thought, and his thoughts immediately turned to how he was going to broach the subject of the MP28s – he felt suddenly deflated as the unexpected mood he was feeling in the room was one of urgency and that, really, he was little more than an impediment. He had seen the way in which some of his associates in the trade had been swept aside by the hardnosed Nazis. Some had had there entire inventories commandeered by them and still some had disappeared mysteriously. He began to feel that perhaps this time, he should adjust his expectations for this meeting, cut his losses, and lead them to his chalet and offload that final cache. If they bought them, it was going to be a profitable deal, so perhaps he would leave the sample and offer a bigger discount on the MP28s? For the first time in his career as an arms dealer, he felt horribly exposed and his instinct was to get the hell out of Vaduz.

Sensing the Englishman's discomfort, Bormann suggested they sit down at the heavy banqueting table, and he called for a bottle of Armagnac and two balloons. The younger-looking of the other two officers in the room did his master's bidding and seconds later had removed the black cork and poured two full measures of a Delord 1914 for Bormann and the arms dealer. Mendl seized the moment and brandished his sample case with the MP28 cheekily, reluctantly offering his stock at cost price to the deputy Fuhrer. "A most generous offer, Herr Mendl, but as I am no expert on armaments, I will have to pass it to our artillery experts. Hoffman, bring me my case and take this one away!", he ordered the young officer, who disappeared with the sample case.

Ninety seconds later, he reappeared with a hard leather attaché case, engraved with a swastika, from which Bormann extracted ten bales of one hundred twenty dollar bills,

US$20,000 and passed it across the table to a relieved Mendl. "Thank you, Obergruppenfuher!", he said, perspiring heavily. Bormann immediately and impatiently replied: "Now where will we get this equipment, it is needed on the front line as soon as possible. I don't want to hear that it will be in two weeks, you will take us to them today", demanded Bormann, as they all moved back towards the entrance. "Of course", was Mendl's instant reply, even though he had sworn to himself that he would never let the Germans know the location of his residence in St. Moritz. "My dear man, you seem to be perspiring quite heavily", Mendl thought Bormann's comment sneering, and he refused the proffered lace-edged kerchief (surely rather too feminine for such a high-ranking Nazi) with which he was expected to wipe his brow. That simply served to make him feel even more nervous and not at all inclined to sit back comfortably into the heavy Horsch. Before he could answer, Bormann exclaimed: "What am I doing, Hoffman? Surely we should ALL toast our business deal?", he said as he waved his dealer back out of the car. "Hoffman, the Krug! And bring five flutes, we will all celebrate our work here! And our Fuhrer!" "Heil Hitler!", all of the Germans chanted in unison, taking the arms dealer by surprise. The animation in Bormann's voice and his eye movements seemed somehow insincere to Mendl but what of it, he thought, I have my money, what harm could it be to get rid of those weapons today, perhaps they will want the 28s next?

The men left the room once more together, their glasses of champagne drained. Once in the courtyard, the Horsch's door was held open for the Englishman. He clambered in, and to his surprise, he was closely followed by Hitler's deputy: "Oh no", thought Mendl, "what on earth can we possibly talk about on the way to the chalet?". He knew that the journey should only take a little more than an hour, at most, but in the stately and powerful Horsch, it may take considerably longer especially over the undulating mountains as they travelled through ancient Rhaetia down through Liechtenstein into Switzerland. Bormann made light conversation about the terrain and the weather, until he asked pointedly:

"And how is the fragrant Mrs. Mendl, she is quite extraordinary, how long did she take to learn all about the weapons? She is indeed a find for any man, brains as well as great beauty". Mendl was uncomfortable having any man talking about his wife in this way and shocked himself when he said, "Exactly why I was attracted to my wife, I was attracted to her brain, mein herr, for me her beauty was always the light I have been lucky enough to have shine on me since I met her".

His thoughts turned to her now and he wondered what her day had brought her so far. "She is the brains behind my work, that I know", he said finally, and Bormann fell silent, smarting as his own thoughts turned to Gerda and the relentless growth of their brood of Bormann-Buch kinder. As they passed through Chur, Mendl changed the subject to talk of weapons – after all, he knew little else which might be of interest to the deputy. Bormann remained implacable and silent as the long bonnet of the staff car snaked its way across the still white-dusted passes. They drove past glistening glaciers and sparkling villages on their mercifully short voyage to the stunning mountain village of St Moritz, high up in the Eastern Alps, the "village on the top of the world" as it was called in all of the tourist literature. It had been an unseasonably cool spring and the famous snow topped hotels and shops remained just that, snow-topped. Mendl felt the pain in his lungs in the thinning air as they closed in on the picturesque village and lake, with its handsome hostelries and always-fascinating museums, the Englishman's favourite thing about the busy winter resort. These things and the constantly clanging cow-bells drowned out the people's chatter echoing in the cold air as they milled around the still-iced-over town. There was that constant drip-drip as the watery, slowly-infiltrating sunshine melted the snowflakes on the branches high above. He and Amelia had often talked about it and he knew that this was where they wanted to spend the rest of their life. Little did he know that today his heart's wish was to come true.

Buoyed by the unexpectedly large stash of money he had secured from the Germans – at least twice more than he had imagined - Alan Mendl felt a surge in his confidence and he believed that it was only a matter of days until he would have another large sale. He would also have to exercise his option on those newer DP28s and be ready to supply them at a moment's notice, he believed, but, first things first, he had to get the 26s despatched as his car led the short Horsch convoy to the chalet to which he had planned to retire.

It was as one would imagine a chalet in the Alps to be – built entirely of wood, the gable-roofed, double-fronted, two storey-over basement structure with its balconies and carved cornices was certainly an impressive sight in the bright sunshine and Bormann's eyes adjusted to take in the view before him. Mendl had bought it in the mid '30s as his central European base because he wanted to live close to where most of the instability in the world was still centred, the region offering him the best sales potential. Now Mendl was no daredevil, he had no desire to live life on the edge, but he recognised that to be successful in his chosen profession, he needed to be in a place where he could do business in as short a timespan as possible, and that meant living in the midst of it, albeit that the chalet was in neutral Switzerland. He had weighed up the options carefully when it came to living in the danger zone and decided that St Moritz, with its closeness to the old order in Europe, the Austro-Hungarians, and now, it seemed, the emerging new order of Nazi Germany. With the Soviet Union not far beyond the Carpathians, neutral Switzerland may perhaps begin to play an increasingly larger part in European affairs, and he decided that it was the ideal location. The nearby Italians too had become a force to be reckoned with and Mussolini had been useful to Alan Mendl on two fronts – he had bought arms, firstly, and then given him a reference with Hitler when Hitler was pushing the boundaries on the Treaty. Mendl wanted a base which offered the best combination of convenience, exclusivity and neutrality in these troubled times. He and Amelia enjoyed their skiing and it had occurred to him, on the first of his and Amelia's winter breaks a few years ago to the village, that it was a natural fit for them – cosmopolitan, picturesque, safe. He reasoned - why live like a dog when you could live like an king?

He wondered how his father would have viewed his latest business dealings: Mendl Senior was a died-in-the-wool patriot and his son concluded that his father would not have liked his son's career path in the years following his death in 1930 from an infected gunshot wound. That fatal wound had dated back to the battle at Paardeberg, south-western Africa, Bloody Sunday in February 1900, in the Second Boer War. After he had sustained that wound, it proved to be the last time he would serve in the field of battle - shortly after, he was reassigned to the "bloody desk job" that he remained in until his retirement in 1920. Indeed, his military career had continued during the Great War (as the most recent conflict was now being called) as one of the anonymous strategists in the final months of it. He had been decorated as a hero in South Africa and his Distinguished Service Order medal had eased his passage into the background of that particular theatre and onwards into the background of that subsequent conflagration of 1914 to 1918. These were difficult assignments for Pere Mendl as all he really was trained for was to fight for God and Country – that was all he had wanted to do and he was fortunate that his family's military history carried enough weight for him to be subsumed into the orbit of Entente activity controlled by the War Cabinet of 1914 and beyond.

Miscalculations

These thoughts were swept away with a thud as the impatient Bormann ordered Hoffman to shoot at the front door lock of the chalet, with the three Nazis entering the light-filled open plan living room in pursuit of their prize. "Where are these metal chests with the weapons?", asked Bormann. "The basement", said Mendl, "is usually where I keep deliveries before I transfer them to the outhouse, that mazot out there." He pointed out to the solid brick-built shed which acted as a boundary marker with the neighbouring house. "Then I usually get them to my delivery centres in Poland and Luxembourg but things have been, shall we say, a little bit hot out there", he continued.

It was true that the arms dealer would often take delivery of all of his Soviet-built weaponry in his Polish base near Gdansk as the port was as convenient for his Finnish suppliers as it was for the Russians. It was helpful, too, that there were still many of his business associates who could tolerate his far-from-perfect German conversation, passing through the port. "They arrived just before Amelia and I went out cross-country skiing on the last day of our trip a while back so I never got them out to the mazot", Mendl bluffed. This was an awkward moment for Mendl as he realised that he had simply accepted the delivery without checking the goods against the invoice, something he never did. Bormann was quick to notice the fleeting look of anxiety on the Englishman's face. "I try not to involve Amelia in the business end of my work", he proffered by way of explanation for his oversight in moving the arms to the lock-up behind the chalet. Bormann's eyes narrowed: "Bring us down to them," he quickly ordered.

In the basement, the metal chests lay in the centre of the room, next to Mendl's fine wine collection. The racks of European wines had been accumulated on his travels and his particular favourites were the Scarzello Barolos from a vineyard in the Piedmonte region he had visited many times to build up his impressive collection, en route to his quarterly meetings with the Mussolini government, before he would move on to the Greeks. He had seen himself as some sort of nomadic bon viveur, acquiring fine wines and the occasional work of art with which to decorate his principal residences in Paris and Geneva. He seemed, to his clients, to be a man of culture and it was fair to say that, yes, Alan Mendl aspired to a life far better than the one with which he had grown up. Perhaps that was what had made him irresistible to Amelia - a kindred spirit, he also wanted to rise above the humdrum lives in his small-town neighbourhood and so his accumulation of "luxury" was his way of showing the world that he had arrived. The fact that the peerless Amelia was also his wife could only but confirm to the world that he had indeed become what he had always dreamt of becoming, although the route to that ascension was not always to everyone's liking and he had stood on many toes down the years.

Once again, Hoffman took aim and with one glancing shot, he shattered the padlock on the nearest trunk. The lid swung open to reveal the first cache of arms, with the accompanying ammunition in another metal case at the bottom of the trunk. Hoffman quickly made an inventory of weapons in the chest, counting two hundred guns, which prompted Bormann to order the three SS men to bring the trunks to the cars. As the men laboured in carrying the chests out to the cars, Bormann remarked that the weather still seemed favourable for outdoor pursuits – it was not unusual for winter conditions late in the season, conceded the unsuspecting Alan, as Bormann extended a small gloved hand to the relieved Mendl and said “Mein herr, you have done well and the Fuhrer will be well pleased.” Just then there was the crack of a gunshot outside as Hoffman blasted the lock off the fourth trunk to be carried to the cars. The youngest officer rushed back in, his anguished face masking the exertion he had felt in his short dash: “Reichsminister, Unterscharführer Hoffman and I carried one of the trunks and thought it felt lighter than the ones before – we opened it and there were only one hundred and twenty weapons!”, spluttered the officer.

“Danke schon, Hellman”, said Bormann, turning to face his business associate, cursing him and demanding an apology: “Something told me you knew you did not have twelve thousand and now it turns out I am right. Do you have anything to say, Herr Mendl? Can you give me a reason why I should not demand you to return the money? ALL of it?”, shouted Bormann, knowing that he had his man cornered.

Mendl cursed himself as he knew he had made a grave error and he jumped when Bormann waved his hand, ushering the men back out towards the cars. “Hoffman”, he called, “I was thinking our associate here might enjoy a celebratory trip up to, what is it called, ah yes, the “Cresta Run”” and, turning to Mendl said: “It's where all of you English dogs like to, what do they call it, “toboggan”? “Toboggan”, indeed!”, his voice was filled with menace, dripping with chilling sarcasm. "Skeleton, sir", suggested Hoffman. "Better still, better still!", grinned Bormann, amused at the prospect of this particular Englishman careering down the melting ice chute. Mendl resigned himself to the idea that his misfortune in not diligently doing what he had always done – checking deliveries against invoice – would be his undoing here today, as the cars pulled away to the little enclave of Cresta nearby. They drove up the still-snow speckled hill to the Run and disembarked slowly at the entry point called 'Junction'.

Bormann spoke with mock sincerity: "How unsporting of me, Mein Herr, we omitted to bring the "skeletons"! Never mind, we will improvise. Hoffman!". Hoffman unholstered his Luger from his hip and shot the hinges of one of the crates clean away. He carefully lifted the lid, turned it over, and placed it on the still-compacted ice at the entrance to the run. "I believe you English invented this particular "sport", said Bormann, sounding threatening. "Please, I am looking forward to seeing how it is done", he motioned to the Englishman to embark the makeshift sled. "B-b-but, I have never tried this before! I have no helmet!! I can't demonstrate without a helmet!", protested Alan Mendl, as he remembered two recent accidents involving two very experienced tobogannists whose lives were saved because they wore helmets. Just then, Bormann nodded his head at Hoffman and Mendl's heart jumped when he felt himself being lifted and placed face down, head first, on the makeshift sled. "See you at the Finish, Herr Mendl!", called Bormann as Hoffman pressed his Luger into the arms dealer's back, to stop him from wriggling off the skeleton. Hoffman stood and kicked the lid forward and out into the chute, giving momentum to the Englishman's descent as Bormann and his henchmen waited for Hoffman to drive them down to the Finish.

Of course, Amelia's husband never did make it to the bottom of the Cresta Run: with no helmet and hitting patches of slushy ice in stretches, it was not long before the lid hit a big bank of slush which tossed him high into the air like a rag doll. Except no rag doll had ever conquered the Cresta Run: Alan Mendl's head was cracked open like a walnut on the rocks and banks of earth, which every year supported the man-made sled-run, and the few members of the Toboggan Club in the bar finishing their g and ts and margaritas barely raised an eyebrow to take in the empty sled whizzing past the club verandah. At Finish, Bormann instructed Hoffman to climb up the run to retrieve the wads of cash Mendl had stuffed into his jacket pockets on receiving his payment. "Then let us return to the Fuhrer's side, he needs me", concluded Bormann.

For the most part, however, Amelia's understanding of her husband's disappearance was based on conjecture: there were no eye-witness accounts of his dying moments on their beloved Cresta Run, where every winter they had enjoyed the annual Alpine sports day with their friends, Joel and Ruby Willcox from Southampton. All she had was just a cursory typed note signed by Adolf Hitler, expressing sadness upon hearing from his party colleagues that "Alan Mendl had indeed lost his life in a most unfortunate avalanche near La Diavolezza, caused by a reckless ibex hunter's gunshot. My men were unable to retrieve his body from the banks of snow and they placed a Hakenkreuz on the snow and prayed for his soul at the last place they saw him". That was by way of explanation for his disappearance.

Amelia very much doubted the truth of that excuse, and suspected that the Germans had simply lost patience, raided their chalet for the weapons, and dispensed with him. She doubted too whether the Fuhrer would even trouble his clearly evil self to sign such a work of fiction. However, the letter served to raise suspicions in her that were almost certainly correct and she determined that, one day, she would visit that resting place in the snow and find out the truth for herself. In her head, she promised to retrieve Alan's body for proper burial – she had no doubt that he was indeed dead - and swore that she would remove all trace of his ill-thought dalliance with the Nazi regime, including the cancellation of any and all outstanding orders.

CHAPTER 10

Amelia Lambe Reborn

"What of Amelia Mendl now?", she wondered aloud through misty eyes, clutching the polished steering wheel of the aluminium, leather and walnut cocoon purring it's way towards High Wycombe. The answer came back to her in her head - she had just become Amelia Lambe again and here she was, travelling alone to catch a ferry to the funeral of a man who had touched and loved her briefly. She felt a tinge of self-doubt as she thought of the man she had held and loved so dearly, also gone forever. "Self-doubt? Me?", she thought. For the first time in her thirty-five years, she questioned if perhaps she was cursed never to hold on to happiness. She bit her bottom lip as she blinked back the tears welling in her grey eyes, and wondered what she might do with the rest of her life now that there didn't seem to be a purpose for her anymore.

She smiled as Geoffrey's "High Wycombe" disappeared from her rear view mirrors as she moved along the A4 to meet the junction with the A6, which would swing her north and westwards in the direction of the port of Heysham. She wondered if she might call on her old school pal, Lizzie Dalton, in Thurnham Hall up near Lancaster, on the way but decided, as she turned onto the A6, that that particular pleasure could wait another twenty years or so. Indeed, she mused, remembering Lizzie's nasty lampooning of her in sixth form when she had dropped her hockey stick when all she had to do was round the goalkeeper in that game against the Dolphins, why would she even bother? Then she remembered: had Lizzie not also poached Edward, Eddie, the dreamy-if-dreary head-boy at Eton, from that Irish girl who was Amelia's great pal, the always-funny Siobhán West? This was all the confirmation in her mind that she should give that "pal" a wide berth! She remembered too the time Siobhán had invited her to Ireland and she had the happiest of memories of her time in Enniskerry in the West's estate cottage on the grounds of Powerscourt (Siobhán's father was Head Butler in "the Big House"). She and Siobhán were proud Paulinas and they had always treasured their friendship as much as those school memories, but "yes", she said it out loud, her thoughts turning back to Lizzie, "that meeting can definitely wait at least another twenty years!"

Amelia had not been in the vanguard of her peers, girls who would break the mould – oh, she was definitely bright, but Amelia was never convinced that life in school should mean a life marked by social isolation and reticence. She liked school but she was not inclined to want to work all of her life, if at all, and that, to her mind, was what schooling was about, to turn a girl into either a factory girl, an actress, or a lady consort. It was easy to choose the "lady consort" piece for her, after all, her upbringing had brought her into contact with nefarious duchesses, crown princes, barons and marquises, the various "-esses" and "-inas", of her school days.

Her father had been a career diplomat, having served as a personal aide and second secretary of the British Ambassador to the Ottoman Empire at the time of what had become known as "the Bulgarian Horrors" and, subsequently, through the various brief, but bloody, Russian-Turkish battles. He had performed his duties mostly unaccompanied by her mother as she had remained in England, close to her children and vibrant social life with the other stay-at-home embassy wives. Her father had rather revelled in being the illegitimate progeny of "Serbian royalty" in his youth but when he fell in love with his future wife, he was prompted to salve his itch by completely dropping his birth name shortly after the death of his royal uncle. He adopted the family name of "Lambe"– he thought it sounded softer and he liked the idea that the Christian connotations of "lamb" might be useful in establishing his own dynasty away from the oppressive warring factions of Mittel Europe.

Onwards Amelia travelled north-westwards along the route Geoffrey had planned in the "War Office", as he had (unsmilingly, for once) joked at the dining room table during that "route-planning session". On she drove to Oxford, roaring past Geoffrey's old granite-faced university, opposite the granite-fronted shops on Westgate. It was here that he had formed his idiosyncratic journalistic style as a satirical writer with the ISIS, before an occasional paid stint at the Cherwell gave him to thinking that one could "actually make a career out of this nonsense!". His friendship with "the Waugh chap" had brought him into contact with the owners of the Cherwell as Waugh had been a fan of Geoffrey's writing in the Isis, with her brother conceding in a moment of comical sexual self-doubt that, "Good God, maybe the blighter fancied me!". He was a proud bearer of a rowing team blue – flatfootedness was not an impediment on the Thames - and although a "damn fine rugby player" by his own assessment, his final two years in Oxford were, he would always say, his finest. He had enjoyed the precision of epée as much as the rough and tumble of the inter-varsity rugby matches and he was too much of a perfectionist ever to let the "flatfootedness" thing bring himself down with a less-than-one-hundred-percent effort, even finding himself competing at international level after he discovered a way of compensating for his balance problems.

Amelia had to shake herself out of this cloud of sentimental thought about her brother as she rushed on towards her goal: Oxford gave way to Stratford - she was sorry she would not get to stop in gorgeous Leamington this time, the sun had always seemed to shine that time she stayed in the Angel with the gloriously affectionate Toby Johnson. She was steadily veering left across and up country and soon she was marvelling at the smoking bees nests of the Potteries; then Chester – that name alone rang obvious (wedding) bells in her heart as she zipped around the outskirts northwards towards Merseyside and beyond.

Barely two hours had passed since she had fired up the Atlantic's sleeping horses and she still had less than an hour of travel before the Duke of York set sail. Driving was a passion for Amelia, she had longed for a car worthy of her need for danger and this little lightning rod was her dream car. It seemed no time at all before she was dismissing signs for Liverpool and Manchester off to the right, until grey Preston loomed large in the three-dimensional snapshot of her split windscreen. Unsurprisingly, and as always, the snarl of the car turned heads on the streets, nervous shoppers wondering just who was driving that space age contraption, with its distinctive nose looking like Pluto's comical face: the wide open stare of the divided windscreen, the dip of the bonnet like his floppy nose and the headlamps reminiscent of the cartoon dog's ears. She was well used to the reaction towards her mode of transport for, wherever she went in Paris, that car was the talk of the town. But, you know, she loved it and that was all that mattered.

She stopped at a hotel beside the Ribble – the Trout and Fly, was it? - to get her bearings and she knew it was but a short run to Lancaster and on to the port. Less than an hour later and she had joined the steady stream of lorry drivers with the latest deliveries of Northern Ireland's rations and she wondered how all of these lorries would make the journey. She eased her car along the quayside, its low growl attracting the admiring, envious glances of a large group of teenage Ulster boy scouts, who were heading back across the water after the annual jamboree that was held in the Lake District. Of course, when they saw the red lips and rouged cheeks of the driver, they turned a collective shade of embarassed pink and nudged each other to stop staring. The driver's cheeks too coloured up as she realised they now knew she must also be the owner. There was room only for three or four more trucks on the deck of the ferry and when Amelia tearfully told the stevedore the reason for her need to get to Belfast today, he made quite the fuss, making sure to tell her "Now I'm going against company rules here, Miss", before waving her little car onto the deck.

This was indeed a great fillip for her after the nearly three hour journey – she loved to drive but found that the concentration required, heightened as it was by the occasional air-raid siren blaring in at least two of the cities on her journey, had tired her and she had felt an overwhelming sense of relief when finally the ship and dock had came into view. She was relieved that the trip had been in daylight hours as she found night-time driving added a layer of stress she would not wish on her worst enemy - she had always hated the strain on her eyes of approaching headlights and had, more often than not, found herself pulling into the lay-byes when dazzled by them and that, of course, would only add time to the journey. She felt vaguely ridiculous when she thought about these things, driving her dream car at high speed not just that day but also regularly across the Continent, and here she was, pretty much too nervous to venture out on a long drive after dark.

She was glad that she had resisted the temptation of looking up old school pals on the way to her appointment with the ferry. She had slid out of London, driving past Esther White's cavernous four storey-over-basement house in Holland Park Avenue, remembering how they had entertained their boyfriends, back in the day, with afternoon caffé lattés and luscious chocolate éclairs in Valerie's Patisserie, laughing and joking as teenagers do in the earliest throws of "love". Years would pass, boyfriends would come and go and the women who were girls back then would come to see, independently, that, in fact, what they were experiencing back then was nothing more than adolescent lust and the hope of something more earth-shattering than hot, wet kisses and curious tongues probing mouths for vertical sexual gratification.

Valerie's would also prove to be one of Amelia's earliest experiences of the Parisian lifestyle she would come to embrace with her comfortably wealthy husband a dozen years or so later. She remembered that the waiters would make an embarrassing fuss of them in the Chope des Puces, courtesy of Alan's monthly retainer so that they would always have the best seats for the "Django and Stephane Quintette's" gypsy jazz performances.

Esther, meanwhile, had sadly found herself orphaned, at nineteen, by a horrific automobile accident in northern Italy which had killed her parents instantly. They had decided on a cultural tour of the northern half of Italy and their first port of call had seen them intent on visiting the remarkable Borromeo

Islands in Lake Maggiore. Her father had swerved to avoid a wild boar on the roadway down to Maggiore the day after they had pitched up in picturesque Stresa's Grand Hotel, tucked in on the western shore. Esther it was who had to travel with her uncle, Tony, by car across Europe to the little North-Western Italian tourist haven to tearfully identify her beloved parents. In the face of this most grisly of identity parades, she had remembered all of those holidays in Scotland and the Lake District, the sunburn and her father's waders, and his fishing gear, as she succumbed to tears. There had been a grand turn-out – nay reunion - of their old school year as Esther had been a great friend to all of the girls and nobody had ever had a bad word to say about her, so much so that even the stiff headmistress of the school turned up to pay her respects.

Amelia sat in the car's cockpit for a few minutes as her moist eyes adjusted to the bright sunshine streaming through the driver's half of the windscreen, her body refusing to unfold from its position behind the golden brown steering wheel. "What on earth am I doing?", she thought to herself as, suddenly and quite unexpectedly, a wave of real self-doubt crashed into her: "I barely knew Gordon", she was telling herself, "so how on earth could it be appropriate for me to turn up at his funeral?" She had to concede that it was quite treacherous for his mother to have arranged for her, his brief girlfriend, whom she had met just thrice when Daphne was coincidentally visiting her son in London that week, to attend the funeral, unaccompanied. She felt guilty that she would perhaps be seen as some sort of "special guest" by the other attendees at the ceremony and somehow that would seem unfair. She had met Clarissa just the once and now she would be staying under the same roof as her as her mother-in-law's guest. She was embarrassed. *"How is poor Clarissa going to feel?"*, she thought to herself as she watched the lorry-drivers hop down onto the ship's deck, some with what looked like little food parcels, perhaps rations for their dinner.

She was still contemplating all of this when she noticed a deck-hand walking towards her car. She turned the door handle and pushed the door out towards the oncoming stevedore, the same chap who "had put his job on the line for her" on shore, as she somewhat cheekily reminded him when he drew near. "That's right, ma'am, come on now, you are dead lucky to be on this boat, I really must ask you to go below decks as this crate is embarking on its little journey in five minutes", and he motioned for her to follow the lorry-drivers. She reached her hand out through the open door and the gruff docker, in a moment of unexpected chivalry, took it and helped ease her out of the low-bodied car. "Surely I can have a Bock before I go below decks?", she mischievously asked. The stevedore thought he noticed a glint in her eye as she raised her eyebrows and lifted her fingers to her freshly repainted lips in a mock smoking move. He coughed awkwardly as he imagined she was looking for something far more physical, but that, he admonished himself, was indeed his imagination running wild and she acceded meekly to his request, making her way to the passenger lounge below decks.

Now the word "lounge", it should be noted, is a cover-all name for the less-than-salubrious "passenger rest area", which was littered with today's newspapers and belching, already green-faced scouts and truck drivers. *"Oh dear",* she thought to herself, *"this is not going to be a pleasant crossing".* Sure enough, the next four hours was a comedic series of vignettes of burping, puking, uniformed boys running to the toilets, rushing up to the deck to vomit over the side of the ship, while below decks, the men tried to focus on their card games as the boat heaved and groaned its way through the choppy waters. Amelia sat and drank tea and shared a few naughty jokes with the lascivious truck drivers, as the scout leaders worked hard to keep track of where their charges had disappeared to. They too would discretely "disappear" to the deck to offload the contents of their own stomachs whenever there was a lull in activities. She herself remained unmoved throughout by the undulations of the "crate" and was largely oblivious to the retching schoolboys and queasy rations-bearers strewn around the lounge. She took time to go back up onto the deck to observe the not-too-distant Isle of Man as the ferry followed it's careful sea-route around that strange outpost, as close to Ireland as it was to it's principal benefactor, with it's promenades and stately ballroom and ornate pavilions corralling its community of one-time herring fishermen and curious holidaymakers on some sort of Heaven-made pleasure island. She gazed across the open sea towards the Mann's hazy outline and suddenly felt sad at the overwhelming sense of loneliness in her life. The feeling was symptomatic of the relationship she was now in with Chester: he was a good man, she had decided, but his insistence that they continue to enjoy life as if they were not lovers destined for marriage in the not-too-distant future actually troubled her. She longed for the tie of a relationship with this man, like the one she had enjoyed with Alan, and yet he seemed to prefer to keep her at arm's length and away from his business dealings. She went below decks again and came upon one of the lorry drivers regaling the troop leaders and some of the boys about the many uncomfortable trips he had himself endured before - he was on his three hundredth crossing - and that once he had found his sea-legs, he never seemed to have had the same trouble again.

Amelia was quick to tell him that as far as she was concerned, and she meant "no offence by this", the return trip to Heysham would be the last time she would avail of "this particularly horrific service", over-emphasising the word "horrific" for dramatic effect. There was a ripple of knowing guffaws and one of the scout leaders drew daggers' looks from his fellow volunteers when he called out "Hear, hear!" as if he was in the government chambers in Stormont, not leading a troop of impressionable lads from the Short Strand.

She watched bemused as the scout leaders had ended up arguing amongst themselves as to who was assigned to monitor which boys and so forth, each of them dressed in the leaders' standard issue gabardine uniform of khaki shirt and lanyards. This lurching, stomach-churning journey had seemed interminable and then, not a moment too soon, word came below decks that a horn would sound shortly to let the drivers know it was time to return to their vehicles, a relieved cheer reverberated across the passenger lounge. Finally, this most unpleasant journey on the "Vomit Bucket", as Amelia discovered was the nickname for any ship that plied this short route, would shortly be but an appalling memory and Amelia could make her way to the Anderson funeral.

Soon the ferry was sucked into the Victoria Channel and Albert Dock came into view a short time later. As always, and, as it had seemed to her whenever she had taken the Gdansk to Helsinki ferry with Alan en route to another arms purchase with his shady Nordic contacts, it seemed an age before this ferry glided into its berth on Clarendon Quay. There was a shuddering but reassuring "clunk" as the captain cast anchor in the harbour. Amelia had never been in Belfast before, let alone travelled this hellish route, and she had wisely enquired of the truck drivers the best route to Wilmont House, Gordon Anderson's newest place of work, after he had been selected as First Secretary to the Commander in Chief of the United States Forces in the British Isles, stationed here now in Belfast. The Americans were a-coming alright and their first tentative steps into the theatre of this war were in the unlikely region of N. Ireland, and lowly Belfast had just reared its complex political head above the parapet to put itself on the

Nazi hate-list. That meant, of course, that it now found itself to be a legitimate target.

In her communiqués with Daphne Anderson, Gordon's mother suggested to Amelia that it would be far easier for her to meet her at Wilmont House. It was quite extraordinary that, seeing as she had only ever met Daphne those few times in London, she should now find herself embroiled, for want of a better word, in the machinations of this woman's son's funeral: the last thing Amelia wanted was to appear at the funeral of the man with whom she had had this torrid whirlwind romance, to be the source of whispers as some sort of "scarlet woman", as surely Gordon's widow's friends would likely see her. "*Oh well*", she thought, "*best not get too far ahead of myself on that one. This is for you and you alone, my dear Gordon*".

This first US Army Headquarters in Europe had at one time been the Governor of Northern Ireland's house and it had been decreed by Commander-in-Chief Hartley that Wilmont should be the muster station for the First Secretary's funeral procession to Balmoral cemetery, following what would likely be a rather formal Presbyterian funeral. Amelia's friends numbered Seventh-Day Adventists and Evangelicals, to followers of Eastern Orthodox religions and even Quakers. She had always thought of the Presbyterians as being one of the "purest" strains of the Reformist traditions. Its theology, it had always seemed to her, focused on strict biblical interpretation and the supremacy of God, there was little room for the elaborate vestments and bishoprics of the other, more prominent, denominations. She was quite taken with the idea that Gordon was an Elder in the London City Presbyterian Church on Aldersgate Street, though she could not quite fathom why she felt so moved. Perhaps she was vaguely amused at the notion that, at thirty-two years of age, the fact that anyone could be called an 'elder' at such a young age was something to be simultaneously admired and yet preposterous enough to be appalled by it. It made their brief, highly erotic, dalliance all the more delicious, and she salaciously wondered if dear Gordon had been wracked with guilt or the kind of pleasurable memories she had of their encounter. "Well", she said out loud in conclusion, "we'll never know now". She worried, too, if Gordon had, in fact, taken his own life? She, for one, doubted very much if he had – granted, he was always serious and deep in a book but she just couldn't see him doing something so final. He was well loved and he just seemed so... together, yes, that was it. He was never fazed by new situations or people, he just seemed to get on with everyone he met.

When she had disembarked as part of the small convoy of warehouse-bound rations trucks, she followed the route prescribed for her by Jim, the truck-driver from Wigan, and she pointed her long-nosed chariot into the roadway out from the port. "*Why, oh why*", she had found herself thinking, "*are these entry points to new countries, to new adventures, always so drab and uninspiring?*" She had seen her share of Baltic ports with Alan and she always dreaded the wait for disembarkation. She knew that she should feel, fleetingly at least, like turning around and starting all over again but this trip had been so horrible, that notion was quickly dismissed from her head.

Anyway, she must hasten to Wilmont, it was getting late and Daphne was expecting her to arrive before 10pm. She waited for Bert in his Leyland to pass her and lead her out onto the B23 and she buzzed through the city centre out past Queen's to her left and swiftly on past the Botanical Gardens, before reaching the next stretch of road which she knew would take her all the way out to, or so she had been told, the spectacular grounds surrounding the imposing red-bricked Wilmont. She was surprised to see so many fire-damaged buildings on her journey, many surrounded by scaffolding as homeowners and businesses attempted to salvage their homesteads and livelihoods from the dynamite of demolition. A year on from the Belfast Blitz and the people remained fearful of another devastating Heinkel attack – but still the rebuilding continued, a gesture of defiance in the face of the city's new-found infamy to Nazi Germany as the powerhouse of British shipbuilding and, just now recently, the entry point for US forces into the fray. This had caused the most concern for Belfast's citizens as it only served to confirm that their tiny country was now in the Nazi cross-hairs and, after last year, everyone now knew that it was a reachable target for their bombers. Still smarting that they had received very little warning of that attack, the people were angry that insufficient air cover and limited anti-aircraft installations would still leave the city open to further strife. They feared that, this time, the defence of the city would be short-lived and they questioned if the mainland actually cared?

Onwards to Wilmont and soon Amelia was steadily easing the Atlantic up the long gravel roadway into the estate, past the rose beds and the walled garden, which had escaped damage and remained in perfect decorative order, unlike much of the city a few miles north. She saw the US general's comfortable long nosed and bullet-proofed Buick, its camouflage livery sticking out like a sore thumb. She nervously gasped when she saw Daphne Anderson standing beside the car she had driven in London in 1934. Her two-tone Duesenberg was still in immaculate condition with, much like it's owner, it's style and beauty undimmed by the passing years. The burgundy and black paintwork glistened in the watery sunshine on this eve of the funeral, its hood rolled and pinned firmly down to the rear window ledge in keeping with the pinned-up style of its owner's sand-coloured hair. Daphne Anderson had been in town the same week as that torrid affair between her son and the always elegant, sophisticated flapper girl she had been back then, and Gordon had had no hesitation in introducing the two. They hit it off famously and met for coffees and lunch just three times that week, Daphne had clearly sensed that perhaps, just maybe, this girl could be the one for her son. There was an unpleasant gale just brewing, turning the leaves on the trees upside down as the clouds quickly manoeuvred themselves into the familiar massed ranks of an impending squall as Amelia noticed the first smattering of raindrops on her split windscreen.

Her face broke into a warm smile as she negotiated a parking move between the Buick and the Duesenberg. Daphne was mouthing a cheery hello as she looked into her rear-view mirror, her face beaming that wide, warm smile that had so impressed back in '34. Amelia pushed open her door and unfurled herself from the low driving position into a standing position in front of the older lady. The two widows embraced each other like the old friends they had briefly been in London, and exchanged the ceremonial surprise at how little they had each changed. Daphne was first off the mark to sympathise with her friend on the "tragic loss" of her husband: she had seen the obituary in the Telegraph. Amelia quickly returned the sympathy as Gordon Senior's obituary had taken up some column inches in The Times in '39 and they both quietly contemplated the circumstances of the passing of each of their men. Amelia was unequivocal in her condemnation of Hitler's role in Alan's death, Daphne too was certain that her husband's suicide had been as a direct consequence of the Great Depression's effects on his finances and the Anderson family tea plantation failures following the incessant Kerala monsoons of the mid-30s. The additional financial pressures caused by those extended rainy seasons in those years just served to make things worse.

Of course, they spoke passionately about the deceased. Amelia concluded her eulogy with a wistful "My, how things turned out so differently for us both. Gordon was a good man, Daphne, wasn't he? So caring." "That he was, my dear, he never put himself first, ever", was Daphne's quiet reply, her tear-filled eyes glistening in the gaslight on the porch.

"Come on inside, my dear", said Daphne, "the new general has settled in quickly, and well, here, and he has been such a support in all of these horrendous days. I don't know where we would all be without his generosity of spirit! He has even made his chef draw up a modest menu for a grand dinner for all of those old friends of Gordon who are just coming for the funeral – the Americans have also made up bedrooms for guests to stay over. As I suggested to you, I would expect that you will want to stay with me for the night?", she enquired. "That would be lovely, Daphne, as long as it's not too awkward?", replied Amelia. She wondered how her widowed friend could actually bear to trouble herself with such a palaver, but it was Daphne's way of masking the devastation she felt now that the two most important men in her life had left her bereft.

"Gordon had such a network of friends and ex-colleagues, it was really such a task pulling a list together. I should think half the diplomatic service will be there tomorrow and the other half will be vexed that they never got their chance to bid him au revoir. He was so well liked, you know, dear, I have had telegrams from as far away as Japan and New Zealand – he knew them all, it seems, and they all wanted to pay their respects. And then, of course, he had such a group of close friends and confidantes", she was starting to fill up with the emotion of it all now, "that it would be unimaginable not to have them here. It may seem terribly selfish of me, my dear, but I just had to ask you as I knew you would come too. It's a great comfort to me that after all of this time, you still cared enough to bother. Funny, I have often thought about you, Gordon was so smitten by you and I think you and I will always be friends. What a lovely week that was", she continued. "That it was, Daphne, that it was", Amelia absent-mindedly agreed.

She was remembering that first meeting, the first dance, his dashing attire and his gentle caresses; the gentle first kisses followed by the steamy embraces, his arms surrounding her and pressing her body to his body, the tremors in her loins as his groin touched hers. "What happened to him, Daphne?", she suddenly heard herself asking, it was a question she had not at all planned to ask but, there it was, and she berated herself for asking it. Daphne looked a little brittle again and her face began to colour red a little as she said: "Contrary to what may be doing the rounds, my darling, I'm quite sure he didn't commit suicide. Why would he do something like that? He had it all, m'dear, he really did. Terrific career, respect of his peers, simply adoring wife" - her eyes dipped from Amelia's gaze momentarily at that – "and two marvellous kids". She realised that she had turned a pinkish hue and, embarrassed by her own assuredness on this point, said by way of explanation;

"Anyway, I believe the authorities are looking into some possible bacterial agent which may have caused his death". "My goodness", gasped Amelia, "the Germans have gotten this far??". "Oh, no, my dear", muttered Daphne Anderson, "they're not involved, no. The authorities are investigating the cause of some water-borne thing, it looks like he may have picked up some nasty bacteria. There is no truth in that silly rumour about suicide, for goodness sake, I really don't know why anyone would suggest such a dastardly thing! Suicide . . .! How cruel . . .". She was sobbing now as she dabbed her eyes with her scented kerchief, Amelia wrapping a caring arm around Gordon's mother's narrow shoulders. "There, there, Daphne, it's all been too much for you. How is Clarissa, this must be weighing heavily on her too?", asked Amelia, suddenly aware that she was not to be seen. "Oh yes, the poor lamb has been terribly hurt by those scurrilous rumours – there were no financial worries, none. You know, he would spend a couple of months a year in Kerala working on the finances and planning the harvest - the plantation had turned the corner on all fronts and he was so proud of his father's achievements!" "Truly awful, Daphne, awful", agreed Amelia, though she was inclined to think that perhaps the lady doth protest too much.

"Let's go inside, you can change for dinner in one of the guest rooms, I've organised it with the staff. I will introduce you to the American Commander, Major General Hartle, he is a splendidly mannered chap, quite the gentleman. His wife Lucille is here too, such a caring lady, she has been a rock to me this last week. I dare say that between yourself, Lucille and Clarissa, I will be able to cope with the sadness of it all tomorrow". As she retrieved a royal blue shift dress from her expertly-packed suitcase, with some fresh lingerie and cosmetics, Amelia thought the-woman-who-could-have-been-her mother-in-law was remarkably stoical and strong in the face of the latest tragedy to befall her, but also strangely detached: then she remembered how the desolation had hit her in the wake of her acceptance of Alan's death and surmised that the enormity of the loss would hit Daphne like a sledgehammer in the coming days and weeks, as it had her. "There are some other guests staying overnight here,

I'll introduce them too, a little later", said Daphne. With that, she linked arms with Amelia and led her back towards the front door of the imposing double bay-windowed residence. They turned right and she led her upstairs to one of the guest bedrooms and opened the door into its large dressing room. Minutes later, accompanied by the drone of the conversation in the rooms below, Amelia emerged from a speedy hot bubble bath, drying herself quickly before carefully rolling her red ruche-topped stockings up her legs, locking them in place with the suspender clasps of the burgundy corset she had hurriedly pulled from her case. She wore her favourite purple velvet pumps – it was her secret tribute to Gordon - and matched her smoky eyeshadow to the mauve lipstick she always preferred to wear. Daphne had stayed in the bedroom, sitting on the chaise longue. When Amelia appeared, she too touched up her own make-up and adjusted her charcoal Dior suit of jacket and fitted skirt before they both stepped out onto the landing and strode purposefully down the solid Axminster-carpeted mahogany staircase, lined with portraits of the previous owners and builders of the house, the Stewarts and the Bristows. Daphne explained that the house had been rebuilt in the last century and that "some chap, a descendant of the original owners", had bought it. "That's his portrait there, my dear. The place was then sold on to one of Ulster's greatest gentlemen, dear old Sir Thomas! That's him, a good likeness. He was such a charming man, so devoted to Edith", she recounted, as she pointed to another portrait of a well-upholstered man. "You knew him then, Daphne?", Amelia asked, knowing that the answer would be in the affirmative. "Of course, dear. It's hard not to know the movers and shakers in such a small community and he was certainly that!".

When they reached the bottom of the stairs, their eyes had to adjust to the sudden change in light, first in the hall and then as they entered the main reception room. Amelia could make out a number of uniformed men grouped around the drinks bar while still others were huddled around a coffee table, laden with steaming pots of tea and coffee and Wedgewood blue jasperware crockery. There were overflowing Royal Doulton and locally-made Belleek cake-stands standing sentry over the silver platters of beef sandwiches, others with cucumber-and-salmon and egg-and-chive canapés. There was a low murmur in the group as they spoke quietly and intensely about the day's war news and the uniformed group spoke with twangy American voices that seemed at odds with the quiet solemnity of the seated group of – here Daphne whispered across discretely to Amelia – "Gordon's fellow diplomats and their wives". Gordon's personal friends, his old schoolmates from his Royal Belfast Academicals days, were lining the entrance hall, like some sort of impromptu guard of honour. Numbered amongst them was his lifelong friend, and now "visiting lecturer and Professor of Neurosurgery" at Queen's, Alasdair McGarry, a handsome, fresh-faced chap with unruly curly hair, whom Gordon had mentioned to Amelia as being a bit of a maverick, espousing as he had, eight years ago, the long-term benefits of electric-shock therapy on homosexuals. Daphne seemed a trifle irritated to have to explain this to Amelia, as she introduced them, and that he believed - "it was not an uncommon belief amongst sane people", she suggested - that "homosexuality is a mental illness that can be cured", and his thesis would confirm to the world that *the* most effective cure was electric shock treatment. "Imagine! Barbaric!", exclaimed Daphe, incredulously

"Ah, pleasure to meet you, Miss Lambe!", was the neurosurgeon's affable greeting, "Gordon told me a lot about you, he had enjoyed your company some time ago, when was that? Goodness, must be a good few years now?". Amelia's face flushed a little as she imagined Gordon may have told his friend just a little too much about their intimacy back then. "I think it was around '34, Alasdair - am I right, Amelia?", said Daphne. Amelia nodded her agreement and felt a shock of static electricity in the palm of her hand when she shook his, as he leaned down to kiss her on both cheeks. For him, the electricity he felt was as if he had been hit with a lightning bolt as his eyes drank in that studiously ruffled brunette bob, complementing her startling grey eyes and dark complexion, which seemed pretty much unblemished in the harsh light of the entrance hall. His eyes drifted down the length of her dress and she felt simultaneously repulsed yet inexplicably excited by this odd man's attention, and she realised her cheeks' colour was starting to reveal her innermost thoughts.

Next to him in the hallway stood an impeccably uniformed fortyish man whom Daphne introduced as Douglas, and he did not hesitate to utter the line in an impeccable Scottish brogue: "Duke of Hamilton at your service, m'lady!". He duly jumped himself to attention in his blue RAF officer's uniform, flashed a dazzling smile and seemed, to all intents and purposes, to be a most debonair fellow. "The Duke is here to discuss air operations with the Americans, he is Air Commodore for Scotland, you know?", said Daphne, helpfully. Amelia, naturally, did not know and said as much. Daphne continued: "The Duke is a most experienced pilot, do tell Amelia all about your time over the Himalayas, most fascinating it is, my dear", she said as she slid away to talk to another one of the uniformed attendees near the bar.

Amelia noticed that the Duke appeared to be unaccompanied this evening and had been deep in conversation with Alasdair. She had also noticed that they had both looked a shade irritated by Daphne's intrusion into their conversation. *"Perhaps Alasdair had been recounting his memories of Gordon",* she thought, *as it seemed highly unlikely that* "Douglas" *was of the same age as the deceased.* "I do apologise for that little intrusion into your chat just then, your grace, poor Daphne is trying her best to hold it all together and she was just a little forthright in her introduction, perhaps", she addressed her apology to the Duke. "Not at all, m'lady, and please, *please*, no "Your Grace"", he opined, "I was baptised Douglas, Douglas I remain. Of course Mrs Anderson is reeling from all of this tragedy, of course she is over-compensating and trying to be everything to all men in this situation. How awful for her, awful". "Yes, indeed, she is remarkably strong, you know, it simply can't be natural for a parent to be burying a child. Her only child at that," said Amelia, simply. "Really? Gordon was an only child?", echoed the Duke, seemingly moved by this revelation. "Oh yes, Douglas, yes, Gordon was the sole heir to the family pile and the family's tea business in India", she said sensing the Duke's real motivation for his faux-concern. "Ah yes, of course!", exclaimed Alisdair, "he often talked about India at school, in the summer he would go on business trips with his father and come back with incredible ivory carvings for us in school, we thought he was a great guy!", he remarked as he put some flesh on the bones of Gordon's early life story for the Duke and Amelia. "You know", he continued, "he was the first of us to apply to the civil service but then he was born into that way of life so it was only a matter of time. Often talked about going to London for a spell – he did of course, that must have been when he met you, Amelia. Spellbound by you, I'm sure, if you don't mind me being so forward," Alasdair smiled politely as he spoke, brazenly and knowingly betraying his own suppressed feelings around her. His steel-blue eyes locked with hers and the space between them fizzed fleetingly with an electric intensity Amelia had not experienced since her very first date with her late husband. She was shocked to find herself so taken aback by this, this, well, *stranger*, and she wondered if perhaps she should make her excuses and avoid this discomfort. And then she thought, "No, what will be, will be, I am here for Daphne and to celebrate Gordon's memory, or rather MY memories of him." All of a sudden, she found herself turning to the Duke, saying: "Tell me about the adventures in the Himalayas, Daphne said you spent some time there?" "Ah yes, dear lady, well not so much spent time there, not mountaineering or the likes, but I *was* part of the first airplane crew to fly over those astonishing mountains. By God, they are but towering tributes to the power of Our Lord God Almighty, each peak seems higher than the next, never-ending. No air up there either, and freezing! By God, treacherous! Yes, treacherous – if the cold didn't make your fingers drop off, the lack of air might kill you!", grinned the Duke, pleased at finding a new angle to convey the harshness of the weather he had endured in his open cockpit biplane.

"What on earth were you doing up there, so far away from here?!", asked Amelia. "Oh you know, photographing the land below for the map-makers, really just testing the endurance of these old airplanes, and seeing if there are any improvements to be made to them. Can't say any more than that, my dear, trade secrets and all that!", he laughed cagily, cackling and waving a hand in a dismissive way at his own stuffiness.

"And then, of course, there was the matter of keeping tabs on these infernal Nazis, seems the Nazis are looking for something under the desert, somewhere near Tibet", chipped in Alisdair earnestly, adding a disturbing frisson to what had been a light enough conversation. "Sounds like a load of bunkum, of course", he finished. "How strange", Amelia responded, surprised with the Professor's knowledge of Hitler's beliefs. She had, she recalled now, read a piece in the Telegraph about the Nazis strange fascination with Eastern religions. "Yes", he mused. "Apparently, they have been sending an expedition up into the Himalayas every year since they came to power searching for this "land of milk and honey", or somesuch". "Nonesuch", I call it!", continued Alisdair, name-checking Henry the Eighth's mythical palace. At that, the Duke shot him a withering look. "By Jove, though, it really is quite the most extraordinary story, one wonders if perhaps we British have a greater mission in this world?", Alisdair ventured on, not allowing himself to be muzzled by his companion. Amelia felt herself seething with anger: "Are you implying that the German people are better than us?", she snapped.

The Duke and Alisdair were somewhat taken aback by this beautiful lady's riposte to, first, the Duke's quite innocent meanderings about his dangerous time in the biplane over Everest, and then to what Alisdair considered to be his rather more accurate explanation of how the Duke came to be there. "Hitler is quite mad, you know, quite mad", Alisdair muttered, hoping to appease Daphne's friend. Amelia, on the other hand, was not one bit impressed by his non-reply to what she felt had been such an easy question to answer – a simple yes or no would suffice, she believed. As if to extricate both himself and Alisdair from this very long moment of awkwardness, the Duke sought to conclude matters with: "Quite amazing up there, makes a man realise how insignificant all of this really is, y'know? All of that natural grandeur, one can't help feeling close to God as one looks down at the snowy mountain peaks and shiny glaciers, and then you come to realise "Good God, what an incredible thing to be able to fly, I mean who would have imagined, *fly*, above all of this and come back to tell the tale! It really is a superhuman feat, flying, is it not?".

Amelia was smarting at what seemed like Alisdair's fawningly respectful recant of the Nazi belief in their country's position as some sort of "chosen people", their ultimate destiny to rule the world. "How dare he!", she thought. She was well aware of the German's mistaken belief that they were "God's Chosen People", and she did not like it one little bit. She was also thinking of Alan and she vowed at that moment that she would find his final resting place and replace that swastika, the "hakenkreusz" of Hitler's letter, with a true Christian cross, not some cultish misrepresentation of her God's munificence.

Thankfully, and not a moment too soon, Daphne rejoined Amelia. She had overheard a few titbits, first of the Duke's tale and then noticed Amelia's look of ill-concealed horror as Alisdair had rowed on with his monologue. "Come with me, dear, I want to introduce you to the Americans and a couple of Gordon's old friends from London". Under, her breath, she sighed: "Oh Lord, frightfully sorry you had to listen to that Poppycock, electric shock therapy indeed". "Well he never actually mentioned that but he got my goat up about how wonderful are the German people! I mean, for goodness sake, Daphne, they put up with Hitler! Doesn't say much really!", replied Amelia.

The American Major General was indeed a most splendid fellow and had an encouragingly firm handshake as he greeted Amelia into his little grouping next to the mahogany bar counter. He introduced Lucille, his wife, and the younger officers who had only arrived in this corner of Ireland days previously. There was genuine warmth here for Daphne and her guest, with compliments reverberating amongst the group about how well Daphne looked, ("all things considered" seemed to be the unspoken qualifier), and Amelia felt reassured that here she had met a like-minded group of new acquaintances, at least in their praise of Daphne.

She was introduced to a Mr Du Pont who was a personal friend of the Major General and he was destined for Europe to meet up with his industrialist equals in Farben's. He was a chemist and he held the room in thrall with his obvious love of his deeply technical career. She shook hands with Captain Kirkland and his pretty blond wife, Tanya, and met Lieutenant Colonel Bridges and his equally pretty, petite, brunette wife Pauline. She wondered what these women got up to during the days when their husbands were in the barracks or on overseas duty and considered herself fortunate that, although she may have lost Alan because of his involvement with the fascists, she was not facing into the abyss of possibly losing her loved one because an unknown assassin - a soldier fighting for his country - had taken careful aim and killed him stone dead.

So concerned was she, she couldn't help but ask the question: "What is it you ladies do to while away those tortuous times your husbands are fighting?". It seemed immediately that she had opened a can of worms: the answers came back thick and fast, and perhaps predictably, the answers included reference to "taking care of the children" and "helping out in the set-up" of the various barracks. Some of the wives honestly said they hated the fact that they were "army wives", with "army families", moving from one theatre of battle to another. Some recounted how they had been uprooted from Guam in the Pacific and transferred here to the opposite side of the world at such short notice, some still were excited by the idea that they had a role to play in sharing knowledge on how to make their families feel like they were at home. Amelia deduced that that seemed to mean décor and down-home American homeliness – the aim, it seemed, was to turn these tin barracks into little pieces of America, so as to normalise their husband's lives when they were not engaged in efforts to defeat the enemy.

Daphne gently ushered Amelia across the room towards a mainly uniformed group, which parted like the Red Sea to reveal, at the centre, a grey-haired, Prince of Wales check-suited man in a wheelchair. "Ah, Daphne, my poor lady", intoned the husky home-counties accent of the incumbent. "How are you doing in all of this strife, my dear? Poor Gordon, who was to know this damned thing would hit him? Total shock, total shock", he shook his head as his eyes focused on the floor, suddenly aware that his pronouncement had attracted the eyes of the room on his voice and his "contraption", as he referred to his wheelchair. "As well as can be expected, Charles, as well as can be expected", came the reply and, satisfied, the turned heads all returned to their original conversations. "Charles, I'd like you to meet an old friend of mine and Gordon's, Miss Amelia Lambe. Amelia was a trusted friend during Gordon's posting to London back in '34 and we have continued to be good friends since." Now Amelia knew that was not strictly true but decided to go along with it, in the interests of not wishing to upset her friend. "Charles is involved with the War Department, dear, don't ask me what it is he does – I often wonder does he know himself!", she laughed and he rolled his eyes and laughed along. "All seems so", and here she spoke from behind her right hand, "secretive!". Her eyes darted an exaggerated glance around the room, as if trying to spot a likely traitor in their midst and the little group laughed a nervous laugh. "Enchanté!", came the gallant response from the wheelchair. "Sir Charles Nimmo at your service, my dear!", he said in an unexpectedly bright and matter-of-fact style, as he took her hand and kissed it gently in greeting. The only thing that was missing was the sharp click of his heels. Any notion that this man was a prisoner of his "contraption" quickly faded as he cheerily explained away the affliction that had disabled him so: "Multiple Sclerosis, my dear", he answered her quizzical look and further explained "damn slow developer, my type. Been in this for three years now, and no, not likely to ever get out of it", answered Nimmo in anticipation of the usual questions. "Still, better than being dead, what?!", he laughed. "Decidedly!", replied Amelia, smiling cheerfully as she felt herself uplifted by this charming man's positivity in the face of a slow, cruel, but certain demise. "I must say", she continued, weighing carefully her next few words so as not to sound trite, "you wear it well, sir! In fact, I can honestly say that you are the first person I have ever known to be afflicted with this disease", she continued, "and I, for one, am confident that you will indeed beat it!".

He smiled a smile he had smiled many times before on hearing that particular line: "You are so kind, Miss Lambe, but you know there are some things in this life that one can say with certainty and this is one of them – there is little hope for me, my dear. But, as you say, I damn well do "wear it well"! What's the point in letting it get you down, just dust down and get on with it, it's the only way! Anyway, the King's work must be done and his is my only mission in life now." Amelia smiled knowingly at his rugged face and said no more about it.

Daphne steered Amelia towards the only other gathering in the room and finally she came face to face with Gordon's widow, the rather odious-sounding Clarissa Dwight-Shelby. Or rather the woman known formerly as. She was exactly as Amelia had remembered her to be: stylish in her royal blue jersey bodice and pleated hounds-tooth Norman Hartnell skirt, she looked the epitome of the wife of a diplomat of His Majesty's government. The Dwight-Shelby name had been a force to be reckoned with at the turn of the century in Northern Ireland and the family fortune had been built in locomotive steam engine design and manufacture ("exhaust steam injectors" especially) until the company's demise during the deep economic troubles of the early 1930s. Indeed, much of the family's fortune had been expended on trying to keep this worthwhile enterprise afloat but it was not to be and it was Clarissa's father, Theodore, who was obliged to bring the company's woes to an end in '33. However, it had not lessened the dowry which had accompanied her hand in marriage to the already comfortably-off Anderson chap and her father had embraced his new son-in-law as if he were one of his own.

The two women brushed kisses on each other's cheeks, two widows fleetingly joined together in their own private grief, but for two very different men. Amelia uttered the expected condolences in hushed tones: "so terrible", "such a lovely, lovely man, a real gent", "how utterly horrible for you and the children", these are the words she remembered as her spoken epithet about Gordon to her very distinguished and lady-like successor. One might be forgiven for thinking that Amelia's presence at such a personal, private grieving for her husband would gall the ever-dignified Clarissa, but she was made of the same stuff as her mother-in-law: she was a lady and she would have considered anything less than a dignified acceptance of her forerunner's mourning for her most splendid husband as churlish and ungrateful. After all, he had chosen and married her, had he not? The two women sat uneasily on the cushioned ledge of the bay window to the right of the cocktail bar in the room, more out of a distinct lack of room on the quite narrow ledge. They quietly recounted to each other how each had met Gordon, Amelia editing her particular version of events so as not to offend or upset her co-host and she took the easier option of going second. Clarissa recounted how they had met outside the gates of Drumglass House as a group of Royal Belfast boarders had decided to check out this new part of nearby Victoria College, as it was rumoured to be the girl school's boarders' new home. It was no mere rumour, as it happened - Drumglass was to be Clarissa's home for the next six happy years and she wasted no time in telling Amelia how she had been "bowled over" by the handsome, athletic, if flatfooted Gordon, who had introduced himself to her in second year. It was easy for them both to agree that he had a gift for bringing out the best in all who knew him - he was charming and caring and altogether wise beyond his years, a careful listener with an easy gift for finding the most effective solution to any problem. At the end of their respective homages, they were dabbing handkerchiefs firmly to their watery eyes and Amelia was left in no doubt that Clarissa had indeed gone on to enjoy the most perfect of relationships with dashing Gordon Anderson. She could not help but think that perhaps she would have too.

Their friendship seemingly secured by the very different memories each had of the deceased, they were pleased to find themselves sitting at the dinner table opposite each other, within easy listening and whispering distance. Next to Amelia sat the General's wife, Lucille, and before long she also shared with them her memories of Gordon, albeit her "memories" were from a very short-lived window of engagement with him in his professional role in Wilmont House. One thing they could all agree on was his ability to make everyone seem at ease with each other and it took an ear-wigging Major General just a moment to advise them all that this ought to have marked him out as a potential leader but "some guys just never get the nod from on high". Clarissa thanked him eagerly for his bon-mots and she wondered aloud if perhaps Gordon would have been better off staying in the Navy, where he had a enjoyed a meteoric rise to captain. Daphne, as any mother would, had to agree just a little with her daughter-in-law, which confirmed to Amelia that Clarissa's feet were most definitely under the Anderson table.

By the time dinner had been consumed, the arrow of time was racing towards 11.30pm with tired mourners' yawns adding to the background sound in the dining room filled, as it was, with the buzzing hornet's nest of low murmurs and shrill laughs, interspersed with the musical chorus of American twangs. The Americans had pretty much stayed chatting amongst themselves all evening, Daphne having practically corralled them like a herd of buffalo, first into the dining room then into the drawing room.

Acutely aware that they were an unintentionally awkward presence in Wilmont, Daphne had maintained their formation by seating them more or less together in the central region of the landing strip that was the French oak dining table, it's pie-crust top and brass beading concealed under the crisp white linen table-cloth. Sir Charles sat in his chariot beside the Major General three places down from Amelia and to his left and opposite were his personal private secretary and the two naval officers who always accompanied him, one of whom had previously been Captain Gordon Anderson. The Duke and Alisdair sat at the far end to Amelia and Clarissa and initially were reluctant, and then participated in a surprisingly muted fashion, when conversation turned to the ongoing war in Europe.

There was little in the way of condemnation of the Nazi leadership for dragging the world into conflict again and neither was there much criticism of Hitler's oft-repeated claim that the German people needed "lebensraum" – translated on the BBC newsreels as "living space" so that must be right – and this was why they had expanded their reach into Poland and Austria and as many weakly-led nations as they could crush. Hitler had been aggressively proclaiming his country's right to help countries with an anti-German attitude, no matter how real or imagined. Cinema newsreels were showing his rallies in cities like Nuremburg and Berlin, and all present roundly condemned his pronouncements as just a convenient excuse for invading neighbouring countries.

"I think, gentlemen, you may retire to the main reception again now, I believe brandies and coffees will be served momentarily to all. Of course, the cigars have been laid out for you too and Cranfield will take care of you all", she dismissed them and waved the lone footman to follow the slow trickle towards the main reception.

"Ladies, the conservatory will be nice and warm after the day's sun and I think we shall move in there", prompted Daphne gently, ever in control of the choreography around Gordon's funeral, and always in her own life too. Amelia caught Clarissa's eye as they listened to the wife of the Lieutenant Colonel, also in attendance, telling all about her husband's commission to establish what sounded like a new elite troop of US soldiers, very much in the image of the Royal Marines, whilst here in Northern Ireland. "Thank you, dear", said Major-General Danby, in a none-too-subtle attempt to deflect attention away from his reddening face, "I really think our friends here would find that story just far too boring!". He was also very aware that such plans were strictly confidential and he could not be sure that that would be the case in present company. Feeling chastened by her shy husband's gentle rebuke, Margaret lowered her eyes and whispered quiet agreement across the coffee table to her handsomely decorated husband. All the while, Amelia and Clarissa were watching Daphne, as she worked the room. She was busily pouring teas with the maid-on-duty and carrying a tray of full cups for distribution to the ladies in the heat of the conservatory: "And of course, for our American friends, the coffee is just on the way now", she informed the room. With that, a kitchen hand arrived with a steaming hot pewter pot of freshly brewed coffee and he began surreptitiously pouring it for the gathering's American group. The two new friends nodded agreement that Gordon's mother was indeed made of sterling stuff and agreed at how much they were in awe of her unbelievable stoicism.

The dull sound of jasperware cups being replaced on their matching saucers hung in the air and acted as a sound dampener to the general babble amongst the ladies in the empty chamber of the conservatory. Conversation drifted from the current situation in the war to keeping children safe if there should be more attacks on Belfast.

Clarissa proffered: "Oh my goodness!" - she was wont not to use blasphemy, as would befit the wife of a church elder. "Yes, last year was such a shock, no-one and I mean no-one" – here her eyes were fixed firmly on Amelia "expected that attack. Gerry certainly caught us unawares, hope to goodness that doesn't happen again anytime soon!"

Amelia noticed how little time these women spent on feeling sorry for themselves – the American wives were very much focused on planning "receptions" for their men and making life tolerable in the barracks for them with the local women just talking about protecting their families. They all discussed their children and their education, while the Belfast women, the wives of Gordon's oldest pals, were more concerned with how to overcome the aftermath of the next air strike on the city.

There was concern too amongst the American women for the friends who had been billeted to other provincial towns and villages. This Wilmont-based group of officer's wives seemed to see themselves in the front line as the organisers and inspiration for those very same welcoming receptions and children's parties and they wondered how they might make contact with their counterparts to help out. They decided that yes, this was to be their role, to train and inspire fellow army wives billeted to Ireland and show them how to make life tolerable for all: they determined that Wilmont might become some sort of "training ground" for other overseas wives.

In the main reception room, the men stood with their cigars, billowing their pungent vapours into the centre of the room, the fuzzy clouds of smog floating gently towards the ceiling. They chattered eagerly and robustly, mostly playing out the next moves in the latest war of attrition with the enemy, some recounting the various tales of atrocities which were coming out of Germany and Poland and Croatia. There was dismay and disgust at reports of prisoner-of-war camps where Jews and Serbs and Roma were being imprisoned, some American officers even alluding to the possibility of mass murder actually taking place in these human pens: "Yes, Andrew", said Sir Charles to Captain McNamara of 8th Bomber Command, "I have heard that particular story and I must say, I am not convinced yet – we have men on it and as soon as we prove it, all hell will break loose!". "I should damn-well think so!", agreed the Major General, loosening his collar and swallowing a swig of brandy in one smooth, almost imperceptible, move. Sir Charles was not impressed with that implied criticism from the American but thought better of arguing the toss with him almost as soon as his lips started to form the words, and he grunted a tacit agreement in spite of himself.

Meanwhile, Daphne had interrupted the flow of conversation in the conservatory when she had abruptly announced: "Well now, ladies, I really don't think you should be cordoned off from the men – after all, they will be heading into battle soon enough and it is just not fair that you all should be separated from them at the moment. Bad enough that the children are over in the church hall being entertained by Miss Disoway and her girls! In a little while, I'm going to suggest to the gents that we all should circulate in the drawing room again and quit this silly nonsense. I mean, I know they may like to have their brandy and cigars in a woman-free environment but it's more than a bit unreasonable!". Amelia was chatting with Margaret, the pristine wife of the Major General's aide de camp, the lieutenant colonel, unsure if she should be telling her about her husband's recent mysterious disappearance in Switzerland (and then deciding that no harm could come of it), while Margaret continued to want to talk only about her own husband's mission to train some new elite squad of soldiers. Amelia felt a tinge of sadness for the battle-weary Margaret, who had come from the "Pacific theatre" with her family and, she wondered, who knows what tragedy this war in Europe would bring to all of these American families? She had endured her share herself and it was a lonely place for any woman, whatever her circumstances. At that, she thanked the gods that she had only herself to worry about now.

Daphne became rather maudlin as she listened to the talk of children and husbands and, as a result, found it difficult to stay in concert with any of those conversations. She was agitated enough to remove herself to the large kitchen, where she chatted freely with the house cook, Mrs Armitage, and she talked freely about her son's upbringing and his youth. She spoke too of the many proud moments she and Gordon Senior had enjoyed as Gordon had represented his school at all levels in rugby and had captained first, the junior, and later, the senior, sports teams to the schools athletics Gold Cup each year he was in secondary school. The ladies in the conservatory had, of course, noted her discrete disappearance and nodded sagely when Clarissa saw fit to cover Daphne's tracks by suggesting that she was just too distraught to deal with "all of these family things" just now. This had been a terrible blow to her, she insisted, and she suggested that perhaps this grand sending off for Gordon had not been the best idea, that perhaps they had all needed time to grieve. Still, she acknowledged, that was just not Daphne's way and perhaps that she really should have looked for that space for herself.

Feeling ever more fragile now, Daphne knew that she must return to the men and get them back to mingling with their womenfolk. She pushed open the door to their retreat and was quickly enveloped in the sickly-sweet, smoke-filled atmosphere. Clearing her throat with a dainty cough, more to expel the sickly miasma she was inhaling than out of a polite intrusiveness, she simply announced: "Well now, gents, I have no doubt that you are all suitably sated by your discussions and have come up with a plan to stop this madness? Well, if not, doubtless you will want us all to meet in the drawing room – yes, it's time to reunite with the ladies, you'll forgive me if I say I think you should be with them now, you ought to take every chance to be with them. Every minute is precious, believe me, think of poor Clarissa's situation now". At that, Daphne sniffled a quiet "Yes indeed, poor Clarissa and the children are all I'm left with now". It was a powerfully moving statement as much as it was a plea for time for herself and she caught all by surprise when she blurted out through a shower of tears, "Damnation on this terrible war!". Now, it would be fair to say that this particular reunion had not occurred in the men's minds and there was a muted, mumbled acceptance that yes, it seemed to be the reasonable thing to do. They were, of course, acutely conscious that anything less than a willing compliance with any suggestion from their deceased friend and colleague's mother would look quite futile and so, lead by Sir Charles, they grunted a pleasant acceptance of the notion. There was a perceptibly hurried draining of jasper ware as the coffees were slugged down until the snifters of Remy Martin appeared to be all that stood between the men and their wives and partners.

Sir Charles was first to make the gallant gesture of breaking forward from the massed ranks of male mourners to pull up close to Daphne, placing a comforting hand on her right elbow. "There there, dear Daphne. We are all here out of sympathy and respect for your family's loss, you must know that. You were kind enough to let us know this terrible news and we want to show our solidarity with you all here. Gordon was one in a million, a loyal servant to the nation and me, and one of the very finest friends any man or woman could wish for. I will never forget his tireless work with me in Denmark or the day he saved my life" Sir Charles had been tasked by the naval intelligence unit to forge links with the Scandinavian Resistance and had organised the men in sabotage and other covert missions. Gordon Anderson had saved his life by shooting into the air upon spotting a German sailor drawing his Mauser under cover of the sailors' disembarkation at the arrival of the Kriegsmarine in Copenhagen port: Sir Charles had made the short journey across from Stockholm, with Gordon by his side, as he was leading the "welcoming committee" of undercover allied officers that day, a covert intelligence mission which was to prove invaluable in the planning of Danish resistance to the invaders. Daphne had been completely unaware of this particular story of Gordon's loyalty and bravery and her eyes filled up as Sir Charles recounted the story to the assembly. It was clear that her son had been held in high esteem and this was a comfort to her the night before his funeral. "My word, Sir Charles, how marvellous. He really had nothing but praise for you and for his time with the Section. "The best time of my life", he told me again, only recently."

Daphne's arms seemed to form a cordoning rope around the group as she eased the men towards the open door and across the hallway towards the drawing room. She pushed the door open easily to a cacophony of female voices as the women continued to chat freely together, and then, self-consciously, they moderated the volume of their discussion. Initially, the men were a little intimidated and not a little annoyed to find themselves thrust back into, what they believed could be, potentially, a waste of time.

It was rare that these informal meetings of senior officers took place and, although they were gathered for the funeral of their friend Gordon, they were military men so they saw no reason why they could not take every opportunity to plan on how best to outwit the enemy, be they German or the more immediate enemy in their midst.

As the men dovetailed back into the group of women, it was not long before husbands matched up with their respective wives – as had been Daphne's intention – and those unattached, including Amelia, formed a small grouping near the fireplace. Amelia found herself chatting with an American woman – she had introduced herself as Virginia – and she was a journalist working for The New Yorker in Paris, sending back daily reports. She had a disturbing limp and it was not long before she was recounting to Amelia how she had "stupidly shot myself in the foot whilst out hunting some years back". As a result, "Cuthbert" had been her permanent, silent, partner ever since" – she motioned to her false leg and Amelia realised that was the name she had christened the prosthesis. She recounted a couple of amazing stories about her work to her new friend and Amelia was astounded to hear how she had used her guile to defy German attempts to capture her and stop her reports to New York: her story of her escape from occupied France as the government started to make her existence unbearable was quite extraordinary, almost to the point where Amelia wondered if this could all be true. Even more unbelievable was the story of how she had managed to escape - she and "Cuthbert" had hiked down through France, finally walking across the Pyrenees into Spain where she made telephone contact with her employers who immediately arranged for her to be flown straight back to New York. Now here she was, on the verge of a new era of reportage as part of the US mission to the war in Europe.

Suddenly, the women became aware that they were not alone in their conversation as the Duke and his acolyte, the professor, had sidled up to listen in and perhaps throw in their tuppence-worth: the professor was desperate to ingratiate himself with Amelia after the earlier bad start and his friend, the Duke, had encouraged him to make amends. Surprisingly, and unknown to Amelia, the not-so-gallant Gordon had bragged about his conquest of her back at the time in '34. In challenging Alisdair to seduce his on-off girlfriend, Clarissa, a challenge his friend had refused to entertain, countering with a blunt description of her as "a stuck-up cow with a face like a horse and the body of a Turkish wrestler", Gordon had indiscreetly revealed his brief fling with Amelia. Alisdair's comment resulted in a cooling-off period in their friendship which was to last five years, until, at Clarissa's suggestion, Gordon asked his friend to stand as godfather to their newly-born daughter, Laura. You see, Gordon had been so taken with his new liaison, the fragrant Miss Lambe, that he was prepared to ease himself away from the Dwight-Shelby embrace and had decided that Alisdair would be the chisel to prise Clarissa away from his scheming self. Now, all of these years later, Alisdair saw the opportunity to take up his friend's challenge but this time with the girl Gordon had licentiously described as the sexiest woman he had ever known, the woman standing here before him, the one who got away from Gordon in 1934.

Quite unexpectedly, Alisdair and his new acquaintance found themselves alone and quite apart from the hubbub around the bar. He was quite smitten with his new friend and, truth be known, she with him, excited as she was by his awkward, ogling attention and his absurd teenage sense of humour, with which he had been entertaining the Americans, the ladies especially laughing and twinkling at his every clever witticism and ill-concealed double-entendre. At the same time, he was cultured and exuded a sense of humour as sharp as his dress sense, rarely failing to raise a laugh even in this most sombre of environments. Tonight, however, and out of deference to his great friend's family, he had consciously chosen to curtail his usual quick, acerbic, and incisive witticisms – he wanted especially to appeal to his new friend and he knew he must adopt a certain gravitas to connect with this particular lady. He was, Amelia conceded to herself, quite the dapper and handsome chap and she liked how he looked that night, smart and stylish in his classic charcoal Moss Bros suit, crisp white Lewin shirt and wine and ivory Huntsman twill tie. She wasn't sure about the brown Church's but he was tall and elegant, and she was struck by his confident poise and he carried the look off with aplomb. If ever there was a classic "Professor-style", he had it in spades, she decided. They were wary around each other at first, she sensing his embarrassment at his earlier gaffe and his obvious desire to make amends. She actually broke the shy silence between them when she said “So tell me about yourself, Professor?”.

The Duke had very quickly disappeared into the group of American officers and their wives, leaving the two standing close to the mock Louis XVIth bureau cylindre, positioned along the wall next to the connecting door to the dining room. It was another incongruous piece of furniture which appeared somewhat out of place with its white marble top and mahogany and brass features. It was matched with a Louis XVIth-style deep button leather swivel chair which was tucked neatly into the kneehole to keep it out of the way of passing visitors. She was curious to establish how exactly the professor and lecturer of neurology in nearby Queen’s came to be at Gordon’s funeral. She asked him “So Professor, how did you know Gordon?”. “School”, came the prompt reply, “we both boarded at the Royal. Played our rugby on the school teams – Junior and Senior - and used to spend the off-season playing tennis down at Windsor. Ah yes, we got into some mischief back then too! I remember the time we got chased by park rangers in the Botanic Gardens because we had fished out half a dozen ornamental fish from the water-lily pond – our parents had to pay for new ones and” - here he lowered his voice and laughed at the same time – “we were never really welcome back there again! Quelle surprise, eh?! They never spotted the chunks we took out of the trees, carving our names!”, he grinned as he relayed that gem from his past. “I’m from over west, Florencecourt, near Enniskillen”, he continued, “though we went to London so the old man could be near the War Office. Another army man, you know, he’s the Aide de Camp to the top man of the Imperial General Staff these days, highly thought of”, explained the professor. “Very impressive”, demured Amelia, tempted to ask why he had not shown a similar talent for combat. “I did a year in Portora – Oscar Wilde's old school - before I went as a boarder to the Royal. Great times, we had great times. Gordon could have been a painter or something artistic, he really was more into that, couldn't believe when he said he was sitting the civil service tests", he rolled his eyes and shook his head in mock sadness. "Even worse, he got the damned job!", he laughed as he concluded his brief resumé of Gordon's early career. Amelia smiled - Alisdair had just corroborated what she already knew. She had seen two of his paintings hanging in his apartment in 1934 and had asked him where they came from: she remembered her surprise when he told her that he himself had actually painted them, it was "kind of a hobby". She remembered thinking he was very talented and had told him so – he wistfully replied that it was certainly the career path he had really wanted to take for himself but had almost felt "bound by duty, nay *birthright*", to become "this colourless civil servant, much like the old man." What she was not to know was that Gordon, emotions in turmoil the day after his secret dalliance with her at that hugely enjoyable Mayfair party, had been led to throw down his cheeky challenge to Alisdair to seduce Clarissa. Actually, Alisdair had had to admit to himself, and subsequently to his lifelong friend, Gordon, that his words were ill-chosen and that he, in fact, thought Clarissa was quite the find for his somewhat straight-laced, albeit well-liked, buddy.

Gordon and Alisdair's friendship had continued when they met up around the time Alisdair's father, Alisdair Senior had been assigned to lecture military strategy at the Imperial Defence College. One year later, his father had been appointed to another, similar role, albeit a more prestigious posting, to his alma mater, the Military College in Woolwich, which would prove to be the last of his teaching roles before his return to the forefront of military action in the War Office strategy room. Now, all of these years later, Alisdair saw the opportunity to take up his friend's challenge but this time with the girl Gordon had described as the sexiest woman he had ever known, one Amelia Lambe. Now *that* was some turn-around, he thought, and he winced as he realised he was being just a little too smug. Still, here he was now, contemplating how he might inveigle his way back into Amelia's good books this evening, having made a fairly disastrous start to their acquaintance.

As it happened, the mutual attraction between them made short shrift of any kind of prolonged mating ritual. They found they shared similar tastes in books, good journalism - Amelia found herself telling the McGarry chap all about her brother in London, about his literary column with the Telegraph and how they would spend Christmas together, visiting their last connection with their father, their aunt in Hurstpierpoint. They found that they were both drawn to the finer things in life, with Alisdair clearly trying to portray himself as something of a bon viveur and general renaissance man. On recognising the name "Geoffrey Lambe", he was quick to compliment his writings and align his own particular tastes with this lady's brother. He was quick too, to point out his particular devotion to Ambrose Heath's column which was now a mainstay of the Telegraph following it's purchase of the much-lamented Morning Post and declared that "one day, I will do a tour of the bookshops and purchase as many of those damn fine cookbooks of his as I can find!" For now, he contented himself in the knowledge that he must surely be the only one in the room devoted to the golden nectar of "Old Bushmill's Special", though that did not seem to prevent him from indulging his other expensive taste in Brandy Alexander cocktails. These were being made for him by the Wilmont footman, Revington, with the finest of Martell Cordon Bleu, which was secreted on the top shelf of the bookcase behind the bar counter, and the lightest dash of cream. Alisdair had immediately passed each accompanying Belgian chocolate to Amelia and he watched her delicately bite into them, her finger exaggeratedly catching the liquid cream bursting from each one as it spilled out from her moist red cupid's bow lips.

Of course, he was not to know that none of his foibles really interested this lady who had been in love with, and married to, Alan Mendl, the embodiment of the "bon viveur", a man whose sheer style and self-assuredness meant that his memory towered over most men she came into contact with, including, if she was honest, her new fiancé, the career-minded Chester. Alisdair was left in no doubt that her deceased husband had been a giant among men as she recounted the telling little details of their busy life together traversing the continent, mixing with the powerful and famous as Mendl conducted what, for many, would have been unsavoury business. Sometimes there would be contract negotiations in the military headquarters, oftimes in royal palaces, or sometimes it could be in the back of a bullet-proofed staff car, whichever was most expedient at the time. It was clear that her gilded life with him was all part of the role he had enjoyed playing, parts that included "International Man of the World", and "Friend of Generals, Presidents and Royalty alike". He had enjoyed out-drinking them all and had often found himself discussing military strategy with opposing generals, regularly in the room directly attached to the map-room in which plans were being laid to annihilate the enemy. Amelia had concluded her portrait of Alan Mendl by telling Alisdair that, in her view, he had not realised in his dealings with the Germans that they had declared him an enemy and it had been decided to eliminate him as per the usual means. Why he was an enemy, she could not imagine as "all he had ever done" was sell his weapons to all-comers, including the Italians and the French (she kept to herself the fact that he had effectively defied the law and had also sold the Germans the weapons they all knew they could not have). To Alisdair, these were strange words indeed and he wondered to himself if she did not somehow feel that her husband had been a traitor, a collaborator even, and could perhaps then be identified as a facilitator of the deaths of thousands and an apprentice to the slaughter of tens of thousands?

He was in no doubt too that she was righty rather proud of her brother and her tales of his cultured, literary nous put more than a little pressure on him to impress her to an even larger degree. Geoffrey she had painted as a great raconteur, a literary "man-about-town", a sort of latter-day Charles Lamb-with-an-e but with a type-writer for a quill, and she laughed as she recounted some of Geoffrey's theories on life, living and love. Truth to tell, and this was becoming the theme as he got older, she told her new friend, he was actually a very insecure and shy individual (so much so that he had never even told her about his workplace crush, the love of his iconoclastic life – his fear was that she would just turn up in Fleet Street some day and blow his cover forever). In fact, his views on love had never merited much analysis anyway as, in her view, he was not the marrying kind simply because he was married to his work: she believed that, yes, there was someone out there for her brother but she hoped that he would surface from his solitary life in time to notice "the one" whenever she came calling. He very likely would have been paralysed with mortification had he known of his sister's championing of his increasingly nervous self this night, though he welcomed her undying sisterly love into his life whenever they were together.

Consequently, when the conversation lulled, Alisdair fretted that his conversation might waver and that she might find him to be a terrific bore. He was, after all, a deeply academic man and the notion that he might slip into some recitation on "the development of the human brain" or the "Role of Dendrites in Forming Neural Branches", the subject of his undergraduate thesis, was never far from his mind as he lapped up Amelia's tales of Paris life and holidays in Switzerland. He simultaneously laughed and marvelled at her ability to recount so much detail about life in Paris before 1939 and showed genuine anguish at the notion that the fabled café society of the boulevards had been consigned to the history books for now as the city's citizens laboured under the tyranny of the invading neighbours' jackboots. Alisdair, you see, had hankered after a life beyond the cerebrally confined world he moved in, certainly in this last five or six years, and Amelia was a window onto that parallel universe he had but read and dreamt about since his earliest days under the reading lamps of the library at Florencecourt through to his final studies in Christchurch, Cambridge. He had, he reflected, spent his early life genuflecting to, and learning about, his supposedly noble ancestors and he had determined years ago that he would do all he could to sidestep his accession to the title his father's passing would bestow on him, for that would require him to return to a world so far away from his real life, that he really had no idea how he could ever slow himself down to that pastoral pace of life again. The problem for Alisdair was growing all the while and he had no idea how he was going to tell his family that, actually, his brother Trevor should take the title in his stead. At least *he* was married, to the resourceful Abigail, tray baker and party organiser par excellence, and they had a couple of almost-men sons who enjoyed nothing more than working on the farm, fishing the Erne lakes and waterways and shooting pheasant and quail in the east of the estate. Trevor had not taken the route of académe like his brother, preferring a healthy combination of the outdoor life with his deep interest in all things mechanical, inventing, as he had, numerous devices and associated procedures for suturing work-related injuries and battle scars. Accordingly, his seeming lack of interest in academic pursuit had filtered through to his children, both of whom worked the land around the grand house at Florencecourt which, thus far, had enabled their father to afford to maintain the family seat with some hint of its past glories retained. Alisdair had taken the pre-emptive strike of discussing his thoughts with his brother on at least two occasions but had been disappointed by his younger brother's less-than-enthusiastic reaction to his intentions. For the moment at least, he had decided to drop the subject as he generally liked his brother and had no wish to cause any further unease in their easy friendship.

"So how much did Gordon tell you about me?", he finally heard his companion utter the words that he had been expecting all evening. Though not unexpected, Alisdair was reluctant to divulge much detail about Gordon's infatuation with her in part because he did not want to upset anyone in the room, and he certainly could not let his widow hear of Gordon's true feelings for her. He turned to her and lowered his voice: "He was very taken with you really, and I have to say his descriptions of you paint a very smart, very pretty, ingenue!" They both thought about that word for a moment and the longer it hung in the air, the higher went Alisdair's temperature and colour. He actually had no idea where that one-word description had come from and he realised that he had, once again, made himself look quite childish. The word he had meant to use had come to him in that pause but he bit his tongue: she was never to learn that the professor had thought of her as an *enchantress.*

It was plainly obvious that Amelia was no ingénue for she just did not fit the role of the innocent, inexperienced young lady which that word implied. The academic began to wish for a hole to open in the ground below him and, for Amelia, she took it all in the spirit in which she believed it was meant, quickly interceding to rescue him from his embarrassment. "Oh, that's such a flattering thing for you to say, how sweet!", she replied, and she touched his arm so tenderly they both coloured up instantaneously. Their eyes met and held each other for an awkward extended moment and Amelia surprised herself by coyly smacking the back of his hand, much as a girlfriend might playfully admonish a boyfriend for a thoughtless word or deed.

It was around midnight when Daphne sidled up to Amelia and gently interrupted the flow of conversation with Alisdair: "Well now, Amelia, Holmes is warming up the engine in the Duesey, are you ready to retire yet? Not rushing you, my dear, but I do so need to get home now. Holmes will return anyway as he will be needed to clear up when all of the guests have taken up their accommodation for the night. I can see you are getting along famously with Gordon's lovely friends, I'm sure you all have a lot more to share about him. Me, I'm afraid my night owl activities don't stretch much beyond the midnight hour these days and tomorrow will be such a long day. I think I shall take my leave now, my dear, I hope you don't mind. Holmes has laid out your bedroom back at the house, and, as I say, he will return here once he has left me off – I will ask him to make cocoa for you and show you to your room on your arrival. I do hope you can excuse me, my dear, I really must sleep"

Amelia felt an urge to leave with the exhausted Daphne and, as it happened, Clarissa was also taking her leave with her mother-in-law. The urge to leave, however, was somewhat dampened by the prospect of sharing the back seat with her newly-widowed and wary acquaintance, for there was no doubt that Clarissa remained uncomfortable in Amelia's shadow. Amelia had a long tiring day, she had already had had a long, tiring day, having wound her way that morning out of central London up England's western border and she had endured that frightful boat trip with its collection of rations-carrying Octopuses and Comets. Her eyes turned to Alisdair and she admitted "Oh dear, Alisdair, I do apologise but I think I *will* go now with Daphne, it really has been a very long day, please forgive me", she pleaded. "Goodness, not at all my dear, yes, it sounds like you have had the day of it getting here", he gently replied, adding, with a roll of his thickly-eyebrowed eyes as he animatedly glanced around the uniforms in the room, "I shouldn't think I will get to bed anytime soon here, I can see the gents are piling their loose change on the coffee table which can only mean a deck of cards is not far away!". He brushed her proffered cheeks with his Bushmills-coated lips and winked at her as she hurried towards the open door into the hallway behind the ladies. She felt another flash of excitement as she quickly waved a hand and disappeared. "Damn!", Alisdair whispered under his breath, as he suddenly felt cheated by her swift exit, almost as cheated as his new friend had felt when she flicked her hand in a wave of farewell. She sighed to herself as she exited through the stately hall-door, a sigh of regret as she wondered had she not just left him feeling a little let down as she made what was, for her, an impromptu exit.

Perhaps because the intuitive Anderson mère had sensed the unease between them, Clarissa it was who was directed to the front passenger seat of the seven litre straight eight on its short journey to the Anderson family home up through the Malone Road and on to Balmoral Avenue. Amelia left the

Atlantic in the driveway and sat with Daphne in the sumptuous leather of the back seat and joined in when Daphne engaged Clarissa in some idle chat about the "wonderful turn-out for Gordon", as she put it. Amelia felt strangely detached as the two recounted his many achievements in the diplomatic corps and the mysterious "Special Operations" services he had served in. They expressed delight at the presence of Sir Charles as it had been "a few years" since Gordon had moved on from Sir Charles' London office in Baker Street. Daphne had felt obliged to relate this to Amelia in a low voice, as if the Dusenburg's's body-work had been infiltrated by some enemy spying device, speaking as she did from behind the shield of her right hand. "Perhaps Holmes is a foreign spy", Amelia mischievously surmised to herself, especially now the Americans had arrived in Northern Ireland. It was all the talk now, the mighty USA had gotten behind the Allies once again. It had come as no surprise to her as she had watched the story unfold in her brother's London apartment through his daily consumption of the various London broadsheets' anxious headlines, strewn across his coffee and dining tables, in fact, on every available flat surface, it seemed. The "will they, won't they" anxieties had been placated finally with the news that platoons of soldiers were packed into ships crossing the Atlantic en route to the fray in Europe, via, of all places, the North of Ireland. Of course, the touchpaper had finally been lit in the Pacific and the Americans had been left smarting and wanting for revenge, with Eisenhower perhaps sensing that small victories could simultaneously raise and distract the nation's spirits. Britain had breathed a sigh of relief at the news, as had, indeed, the occupied nations, as the Nazi war machine relentlessly blitzed a path ever westwards towards Britain, crushing every borough in Western Europe in its path.

The drive to Balmoral took no more then fifteen minutes, barely enough time for the emotionally drained women to formulate coherent thoughts about the day ahead. To be fair, it was late - it had been a long day and at least one of them had travelled by car and a most unpleasant boat journey to be there, some 300 hundred-odd miles. The conversation was, at times, uncomfortable and they strove to recount the highpoints of the evening amongst themselves: Clarissa had met a few of Gordon's old school friends over the years, most of whom were paying their respects at the wake in Wilmont House, and she recounted the heart-warming story of Stephen Bainbridge and Fiona Butler and how it had come as a bit of a shock to discover the two had in fact married some six years ago shortly after Stephen's hospitalisation in the Royal Victoria with a bout of Pontiac fever. This he was thought to have developed after a visit to what should have been the restorative waters in the spa town of Bath, that particularly balmy summer to help ease his usual summer asthma. It was the wealthy farmer's daughter from County Kilkenny, Fiona, who had nursed him back to health when he had fallen ill and was rushed for treatment to the Royal United. She was a final year student nurse and she had been somewhat lovestruck on meeting the ten-years-older Oxford graduate, with his silky Dunmurray accent and fashionable suits and cravats. Clarissa enjoyed telling her companions how the happy couple had retold the story of their meeting and courtship and laughed about the obstructionist ways of the Bainbridge parents in trying to delay and prevent the inevitable marriage of the two. His parents just could not imagine any son of theirs marrying a "Free stater, Protestant or not!". Conversely, her parents feared should it become known that if any daughter of theirs "consorted with a Northern prod, let alone marry one", it would have repercussions in the tighty-knit Craig community and so they watched helplessly as the two fell in love before their eyes. Fiona had been embarrassed at telling that part of the story to Clarissa and Daphne expressed her shame that parents of her generation held such narrow views on life.

Amelia appeared to be nodding her head in sympathetic agreement when, in fact, her head was lurching forward and back as she began to feel waves of tiredness seep up through her body. Daphne, meanwhile, in exclaiming her great delight at hosting Sir Charles, recalled her first ever meeting in London with him, remembering his charm and easy gentlemanly streak. "Oh yes", she was reminded as she thought back, "he was not wheelchair-bound in those days, he was a six foot two Adonis, dapper in his usual houndstooth three-piece wielding his silver topped cane", which she now realised he was using to maintain his balance as the early stages of his condition had begun to affect his toned body. "Yes, Gordon introduced us in the London offices when they were in the Ritz. Odd really, a government department based in a hotel – I suppose it gives good cover". The younger ladies listened and mumbled how they had missed out seeing him at his best, while Amelia began to imagine that perhaps her night should indeed end at Daphne's five bedroomed villa-style house after all. Perhaps sense should prevail, she thought, but she had a niggling feeling that she had unfinished business to tend to with the professor and she noticed the thought rather excited her in a quite unexpected way.

After a quick introduction to her night's sleeping quarters in Daphne's company, she discretely established when the return journey would be made by Hughes and she determined that she would quietly slip away in the back of the Duesenberg in the prescribed twenty minutes. What she subconsciously avoided taking account of was how on earth she would get back to this Balmoral respite: truth be known, she had given it no thought at all, so consumed she was by the notion that she must complete some sort of liaison dangereuse with Alisdair. "Bugger the consequences!", had become her over-riding belief (the consequences apparently excluded all thoughts of loyalty to the hapless, if always absent and busy, Chester).

And so, once she had acquainted herself with the mirror in her en suite, and had subtly reapplied a dab of rouge and co-ordinating lilac eye shadow, she lightly stepped back down the double-width thirteen steps to alight in the hallway of Daphne's home. She looked around the hat and coat stand but remembered that Holmes was household staff so would not have left his outer garments on it. Surely Holmes had not left? She heard muffled laughter and followed the sound to the scullery door around to her left and back by several yards. He was behind it, standing talking to Daphne's housekeeper, Mrs. Davis. On seeing the refreshed and resplendent Ms. Lambe, Holmes snapped his brown shoe heels to attention and moved self-consciously and silently towards the hallway. Amelia followed him without word and very quickly she was luxuriating in the nubuck scent of the tan leather seats of the Duesenberg left-hand drive monster. He held the gate-side maroon door open and flicked a bluebottle off the satin and walnut internal panel. Amelia could no longer contain her curiosity about this incongruous beast: as she settled into the sumptuous back seat, she said "You know, Mr Holmes, I remember seeing Daphne with this car in London in 1934, how on earth did this palace on wheels end up in the Anderson family? And in Belfast?! I was too shy to ask my old friend earlier". Holmes suppressed a grin and said: "Actually, Mr Anderson Senior acquired it some years back from an American film-maker and learned to drive left-sided when he was stationed in Hungary."

And so this elegant paeon to the glamourous years of Amelia's twenties glided out of the Balmoral mansion's driveway, its white-wall tyres and fiercely polished lights and kickboards silently carrying Holmes and his secret passenger, like some Hollywood movie star, south towards Wilmont and its impressive grounds. Amelia wondered if perhaps, on her return, she would find that the drawing room and lounge had respectfully been hushed as the guests had one by one, or two by two perhaps, retired for the night and for the emotional day ahead. And for the first time, she wondered about Alisdair: could she have been wrong about that frisson of animal attraction she believed they had for each other? It was too late now to doubt that and, damn it, she was going to see if she had been right! He was unattached, at least for tonight, and she too felt, with Chester in some faraway place as always, very much unattached and very much needing the company of a man. And, she had decided, this man in particular.

Sure enough, on entering the old house, only an hour after she had made the short journey to Daphne's house with her overnight case, she could see that a number of Gordon's local friends had retired to their comfortable nearby homes for the night. There was a murmur of American accents in the drawing room still, the one with the drinks bar, and she made her way towards it at the prompting of Holmes. He disappeared as he helped Revington to usher the last of Gordons' friends towards their cars and then to tidy up the reception rooms. Amelia started when she spotted Alisdair and their eyes met as everyone turned to see who had entered the room. "Amelia, my dear", she recognised Sir Charles' cultured tones and he came into view through the group surrounding Alisdair and the Duke, "we thought we had lost you for the night! We were just talking about poor Gordon, shocking business, this fever, what?", he enquired with a quizzical look. "I'm sure it is, but I missed that conversation", she replied honestly. "Yes, I think Daphne mentioned it earlier.

Silly me, of course", here she punctuated her sentence with an embarrassed roll of her eyes, "I imagined that Gerry had used some diabolical chemicals or somesuch and had started to target our American friends here before they have even started to help us. But yes, poor Gordon, its horrendous!"

The Duke it was who pointedly suggested the remaining few ought now retire to be ready for that emotional and draining day ahead. First to take the cue was Sir Charles himself: in his front-line career in the 1914-18 conflagration, he had been known as "Rip Van Nimmo" for his unshakeable ability to sleep through the thunderous Howitzer firepower of the German artillery regiments in the oppressive grime of the Ypres salient. He was a much admired officer, the "toff who never forgot his mates", as he was also known. He had refused to be desk-bound in London, preferring instead to stand with his men, much as Wellington had done over a hundred years before. At first, he had commanded a battalion of Royal Dublin Fusiliers, known as the "Old Toughs". Even though he was the quintessential Sassenach in charge of those mostly Irish troops, he was held in great esteem and he had felt a surprising affinity to that most loyal bunch of lads, for "lads" was all they were. Even his stiff upper lip had twitched when news came through that his young gofer, Tommy from James's Street in Dublin, sixteen if even that, had been mown down in a hail of bullets fired by a Maxim barely one hundred yards in front of his marauding battalion at Ypres. Sir Charles, plain Charlie back then to the lads, knew poor Tommy was one of the many teenage lads from Dublin looking for a better life away from their doting mother's apron strings. It was a tragedy he came to see over and over and it had saddened him profoundly to find his worst fears coming to fruition time and again.

At last, the remaining guests followed the example of Sir Charles, including his aides de camp and the Duke, and retired to bed. Amelia found herself alone in the drawing room with Alisdair McGarry.

She glanced at him, she thought discretely, but his eyes met hers as he said "So what *really* has you here? I mean, Clarissa is a darling, what on earth could she be thinking seeing some distant girlfriend at my old pal's funeral, what?!?" "I think you ought to ask his mother, I can't possibly know what was going on in her head. Believe me, I have asked the same question myself. It's not like his funeral should be some sort of spectator sport. I'm here for Daphne and indeed Clarissa, now that I've finally met her. Gordon was a terrific fellow, Clarissa did well there, absolute gentleman and a real tower!", was Amelia's thoughtful reply. "Are you in love with the Duke?", Amelia surprised herself by absent-mindedly asking. "You and he seem so very much to sing from the same hymn sheet and there never seems to be much distance between you two either in distance or agreement": she knew she was taking a big chance saying this but, much to her surprise, the Professor just grinned and said, with an amused chuckle, "Sharp! Very sharp, my dear! Of course I have great admiration for m'laird. You know, if he had been given the chance, he would have ended this little argument with the Germans last year. But no, oh no, Montgomery knows best and the Prime Minister backs his man all the way! You know, the Deputy Fuhrer was all set to come here to do a deal but our little "government" up here" – he was making his disdain clear for Craigavon's administration – "said "No way! How dare he invite Hess to our shores!" Now look at the mess we are still in".

The professor had become surprisingly animated, thought Amelia, and she could have been forgiven for thinking that perhaps he seemed just a little too enamoured with the Nazi leadership. Then he embarrassed her as he whispered "Gordon told me about you alright, said you were the best lover he had ever had! Not that he had many, of course". He continued on, and she raised an intrigued eyebrow, "Oh yes, Gordon was quite the ladies man, my dear Amelia. Quite the most popular chap with the ladies, never seemed to be without a beauty on his arm, took Clarissa a lot of perseverance and persistence to finally land her catch. I have a lot of respect for that gal! By Jove, he could be a terrible cad," he concluded, with a mischievous grin as his eyes seemed to search for some distant landmark.

She was quite taken with his tone of voice now and she felt herself beginning to feel quite relaxed in his company. She wiped an involuntary tear from her left eye. "There now, my dear", he empathised, reaching out to her and gently pulling her towards him. She noticed how soft his hands were as he ran his fingers across her face. They smelled vaguely of the Pears soap on the ledge of the bathroom wash-hand basin, while his 4711 cologne reminded her of Alan. She was strangely impressed with the girth of his biceps as his arms enfolded her proud shoulders and, as sudden as it was unexpected, their lips met. After the first kiss, there was a pause.

Amelia it was who momentarily felt desperately embarassed as he, unabashed, pondered his next move. He had to admit to himself that his plan to seduce his friend's old girlfriend was gathering encouraging pace. Amelia quickly decided that she rather liked the warmth of his breath on her nose and the tremulous heat of his lips on hers. She had not felt so aroused since the last time she and Alan had made love, two nights before his final trip. She put a hand behind his head and pulled his face to hers again - this time she locked her lips on his, hungrily opening her mouth enough to allow her saliva to burst into his mouth. He responded in kind by parting his lips and driving his cigar-flavoured tongue into her willing mouth, his invading organ taking her breath away as it collided with her own excited tongue as she roughly ground her lips onto his. His head pulled back slightly and he murmured "Wow, I think I just found heaven". In the throes of this surprise interlude, he actually thought he had. She grinned a slight grin as they continued to lock lips, their tongues eagerly exploring each other's dentistry. She found her body quite overwhelmed with an intense feeling of pleasure and, in another first-since-Alan, she experienced a spontaneous orgasm there and then. She was as wet as she had felt when Gordon first trailed his tremulous fingers across her body before he had pulled her on to that bed in the house in Mayfair in 1934.

With Alisdair pressing his stiffening and tightening groin into her tingling pelvis, she began to feel overwhelmed with a sense of ecstasy she had not felt since that last night with Alan. She could remember that night so well and, knowing that she would always have to compare any man with Alan, she had to admit Alisdair was an adroit kisser. His lips were alternately urgent in their strong pressure and then, coyly retreating, holding her lips, her breath, in a gentle tantalising thrill, forcing her to lunge back needily towards his departing lips, starving as she was for physical love and affection. They gasped as their mouths crashed, lips sticking together in a hot frenzy of saliva and tongues as their trembling hands began to explore each other's firm bodies – she had been impressed with his body, developed and maintained by his daily exercise regime of forty press-ups, followed by the forty sit-ups to maintain his tight abdomen. He was excited by her curves now at his fingertips: he ran his hands expertly up her back, starting at the top-most curves of her firm behind, massaging each contour of her tightly sculpted back with his gentle strokes, easing each fold back into its natural position before gliding onto the next undulation.

He whispered in her ear, "Hhhmmm, my dear, you keep yourself in exceptional condition, quite exceptional!" She was not sure how she was expected to respond to this remark and said curtly "Is that a compliment? Do I say 'thank you'? Or do I smack you?" She watched his face for a response as she could see she had given him a fright. She was determined that he should understand that she was 1) engaged and 2), quite recently widowed of the "exceptional" Alan. Alisdair was more than a little confused now – here was this wonderful woman responding to his touch on the one hand, and then...

He was rescued from his embarassment once again when Amelia squeezed his hand and her hands moved up to cup his face as her mouth closed in on his. They kissed long and hard standing near to the drinks bar and jumped nervously together when Holmes gently opened the door and called out into the room, "Miss Lambe, I am leaving in five minutes. If you are ready, I will see you out at the car then..." He left the sentence open as if knowing that, in all likelihood, he would be leaving alone. "Thank you, Mr Holmes", she called out in reply, giving him his title out of her usual common courtesy, "Five minutes, I'm sure I will see you then". This reply sparked a look of some surprise on Alisdair's face and his kisses became suddenly more passionate, more insistent, as he realised his chance may be snuffed out in under three hundred seconds. Amelia pressed her body tightly against him as she sensed his increasing anxiety that she might leave and she wanted him to feel that she had no intention of letting him down in such a cruel way.

Three hundred seconds later, Holmes repaired to the Duesenberg. He looked at his watch and saw it was coming up to 2am: he watched as the light in the drawing room window went out and waited in the car for another ten minutes before deciding that he would be travelling alone that night. The sleek American car eased its way back out onto the Avenue and diligently wound its way out of Wilmont, to return to Daphne's Balmoral home.

The love-making over, they lay on top of his bed and reflected on the passion they had just shared – it had been explosive. Amelia was mid-stream in her thoughts when she felt Alisdair's wet lips nuzzling into her belly button, his busy tongue at first flicking, then oozing saliva, into that strangely erotic opening in the human body. "Ooohh," she gently moaned, still thinking of that last night of passion with Alan. "That's so good, Alisdair, it's all so good. Alan would do that to me too, he would slip his hands under my behind and lift my groin up towards his face so he could bury his face down into me." Alisdair, sensing that he was being prompted, duly obliged and massaged her buttocks with an emphasis on upward movement, so that within seconds her neatly cropped bush was lightly tickling his lips, inviting his tongue to invade her, to bathe her sex in the distinct sweetness of his oscuro-wrapped Havana breath. Sensing an opportunity to further ensnare her in his passionate grip, he found himself drawn to that pulsating opening, his tongue thrusting up into the delicious darkness, his teeth colliding tenderly with her engorged sex as she ground herself against his wet face. She was falling under his spell and he was intoxicated with her passion, drowning in her wettest orifice, she writhing in ecstasy under his touch.

He found himself so aroused that he was compelled to lift her gently and mount her onto his glistening member, as if she was an apple waiting to be covered in Hallowe'en toffee. She worked his tireless sword between her legs as he pawed at her perfect breasts, his long sinewy fingers eking, in turn, each swollen nipple towards his ever-eager tongue and willing mouth. He had never enjoyed such pleasure before, and she was relieved to have, at last, found a lover who she could compare favourably to Alan. She had to admit, not even Chester measured up to this experience. They both reached a swift, tumultuous climax together and minutes later, she fell off his retreating tool onto the bed beside him. They lay in silence looking up at the ceiling, occasionally glancing at each other just to make sure that the other did exist. He had very little to say about the Americans and their commanding officer, other than a cheap aside about their "recall from Guam or wherever" for this "man's war in Europe".

Chapter 11

Alisdair and Old Lace

He had said little too about his friend the Duke, prompting Amelia to question, in her mind, if there was actually a friendship there at all, and that her latest suitor was little more than an admiring fan of the noble earl. She wondered this aloud and Alisdair seemed affronted by the suggestion. "Are you implying I am some sort of sycophant?", his eyes softening as he asked again, "Are you? I really hope not. It's been an education to meet the Americans, though I doubt they are going to add much to the Allied cause at this point. My eminent friend thinks it won't be long until they get run back home by Gerry. Must say, I'm not convinced that their Commander is the right man for the job, seems quite unsure of himself and not at all mindful of the might of the enemy. I do hope he wakes up to reality soon!", was Alisdair's cryptic view. "I'm sure you are wrong, can't imagine the Americans sending an inexperienced troop over as the kingpin! This is no easy run for whoever has the lead in Europe, I'm sure", was Amelia's measured response.

She had felt uncomfortable at the dinner table when talk had turned to the latest crisis in Europe and her senses told her to say little and so she had found herself silently observing the Professor and his friend. She had been to a number of sales meetings with Alan and had observed first hand just how devious and malevolent a certain kind of man could be. She sensed that ugly feeling from the man who had just seduced her, and it quite made her skin crawl.

She shifted on the bed and rested her elbows on his outrageously hairy chest and, as she looked down at his glowing face, said

"So tell me about the Duke and his friend, the Nazi's deputy leader. You mentioned it earlier . . .".

"I did?" replied her conquest.

"Yes," she quickly said, determined not to let him off the hook. She could detect some unease in him as he attempted to deny he had ever said a word about it.

"Are you telling me that was a bit of a lie then, Alisdair?", she pushed him.

"Good Lord, not at all!", he countered. "Actually, when Daphne told me about my old pal dying like that, I was on my way to Dunglaven with my father to see Douglas", he said.

"Douglas? Dunglaven?", enquired Amelia.

"The Duke and his Scottish home, my dear", continued Alisdair. "As I say, the old man's a military man and he had some war business with the Duke to thrash out. All gone by the wayside now, of course, had to cut short that visit... We flew over here when I told him about the funeral. Daphne wanted him to know anyway. Must say, Gordon does appear to have been a "national treasure" to some people in Belfast, seems to have been everyone's friend", he concluded and his voice tailed off.

"Did you two keep in touch after school, then?", Amelia enquired.

"Not hugely, no, careers went off in different directions really, but we would meet up a couple of times a year just to mark time and chew over the old times. Just catch up really", he said.

Their conversation circled on in this manner for another ten minutes or so and they eventually came round again to the events of the day, the preceeding day as it was now. Then Alisdair said something Amelia registered as more than a little odd: in analysing the Americans in attendance, he was even more scathing about the US Commanding Officer than previously. She was puzzled by this, as she saw it, unnecessary hostility towards a representative of a friendly nation and she said as much to him.

"Really?", he said with an eyebrow raised. "I think our "friends" sometimes need a reminder that we Anglo-Saxons are simply friends because of a shared history, that they can't always change our direction to suit their world view". He said all of this with alarming venom and she did not like that he was behaving in this most disagreeable way.

Exhaustion took them over and they both fell asleep until, just over an hour later, Amelia sensed her sleeping partner slipping from the bed covers. She watched him through her eyelashes, careful to keep her eyelids motionless. He retrieved a vial from the top pocket of his jacket which was draped on the back of the chair in the room, and he moved stealthily towards the bedroom door. He eased the door open just enough so that he could slip out onto the landing in one swift move.

She decided to follow him, intrigued by his cat-like movement and his shifty behaviour with that vial from his jacket. "What could he be up to?", she thought, as she tiptoed to the door. She opened it noiselessly until a crack of light shone through into her eyes. She took a moment to focus on the two figures on the landing as she realised that she was looking at both Alisdair and the Duke, with the latter holding the vial up to the light and pointing down the landing at the last door on the left. "What on earth could all of this mean?", she thought. Slowly, the realisation began to dawn that dirty work might be in train and the vial seemed likely to be the conductor of this nastiness. Alisdair was carrying the vial now and he appeared to hesitate in moving down the landing towards the door indicated. Who was in that room, what was in the vial, what was going on? She was still watching the goings-on through the crack between the door and the door-frame, when she noticed the contents of the vial being poured into a glass of what she assumed was water, carried by the duke and which he handed to Alisdair. She silently watched as Alisdair crept up to the door at the end of the landing, noted his shifty glance over his shoulder and, suddenly, he had disappeared beyond the door. Moments later, he re-emerged empty-handed and made his way back down the landing towards his bedroom door, the door concealing Amelia. She had already hopped back into the bed and was feigning sleep as he crept back into the room. He undressed and lay down quickly and Amelia shifted her position so that an arm fell across his chest, her fingers gently grooming the thatch under them. He couldn't tell that she was, in fact, awake but he liked her strokes and he kissed her arm in appreciation.

It was no time at all before she realised that he had fallen asleep. She thought about what had gone on on the landing and was anxious enough to feel that she ought to at least retrieve the glass. But who was in that room, she wondered, and could she take the chance of also sneaking into it unnoticed?

When she had stroked Alisdair to sleep, she repeated his stealthy moves along the landing and found herself, moments later, removing the glass from the bedside locker of the Major General: she recognised his army uniform hanging on the front of the wardrobe door and she paused to watch his chest rising as he slept noisily beside his wife. She could see, even in that light, that the water had an oily scum floating on top and she became convinced that it had been contaminated by the contents of that vial: could it be that Alisdair was attempting to poison the Major General? She crept downstairs to the scullery and poured a sample-sized amount into a tiny empty spice jar and screwed the lid tightly on it. She thought it smelled quite sour as she poured the remains of the liquid down the sink - she was shocked when the liquid sizzled as it glugged its way down the plughole, much as caustic soda reacts with water. She resolved to save this sample of the liquid because she was convinced Alisdair was up to no good. Having secreted the little bottle down the front of her brassiere, she returned silently to Alisdair's room and, concerned that it might be found, she tucked the spice bottle into the ripped lining of her handbag.

She lay down next to Alisdair and, this time, it was she who fell asleep within minutes, lulled as she was by the sound of his rhythmic breathing in the gloam of the room. They were rudely awakened a few short hours later by a brain-numbing breakfast gong, which reverberated around the walls of Wilmont like the explosions which had so damaged the city the preceeding year. Both awake now, Amelia immediately expressed her concern at not having a change of clothes because, in fact, she had not returned to Daphne's house after all. Her concern was compounded by the fact, she slowly realised, that she would have to come up with an excuse for the other guests as to why she had not returned to Daphne's Balmoral home: this she told her suitor but his sympathies did not extend much beyond a shrug of his shoulders and his declaration that he would soon be visiting "the real Balmoral" to rejoin his father for their "annual fishing expedition". Luckily, she had a good representative collection of her cosmetics in her handbag so that she was able to reapply and refresh her look, even if her clothes were quite another matter. Happily, she remembered that the clothes she had travelled in during the day just finished were, in fact, still hanging in the dressing room in which she had changed last night and she resolved to have them pressed and starched later on by Wilmont household staff, if there was anyone available. There was a certain strange tension now between herself and the Professor as she wondered about just what had gone on on the landing earlier. He was acting a little oddly and she found she was watching for signs from him that he might tell her about what had unfolded during that time he had seen fit to slip out of their lovenest, without a bye or leave.

The funeral morning unfolded with breakfast commencing just after that gong had been sounded at 8am. Predictably, the military men and their wives were first to surface in the dining room, which had been set by Holmes and Mrs Armitage two hours earlier. There was a strong smell of freshly brewed coffee and Mrs Armitage's butter pancakes, with traditional American maple syrup, were piled high on two three layer cake stands (Wilmont's cook had learned how to cook and serve pancakes American-style with the Major General's wife, suppressing alarm at the whole notion of *pancakes* for breakfast! Whither the rashers and sausages and eggs and soda farls, the traditional Northern Irish breakfast? And *tea?*).

By the time Daphne and Clarissa arrived down at 8.45, a second round of coffeepots had replaced the first. Outside, the wheels of the Duisenberg crunched on the gravel driveway surrounding the front of the house. "Oh no", thought Amelia, as panic began to set in: "what is my excuse going to be?", and she really wanted the earth to swallow her. As they entered the solemn dining room, she could see that Daphne and Clarissa had both been crying fresh tears, at the realisation that this was Gordon's last day among them was hitting home. "What must they be thinking of me for not returning to Balmoral?", she was thinking, overlooking the fact that they actually had an entirely different thought on their minds, that would be laid to rest in his casket sometime between now and lunchtime. It took Daphne to remind her of that as Amelia self-consciously began to apologise for her absence on this, "of all mornings"; for to have been "so overwhelmed with exhaustion, so much so that she had fallen asleep in the drawing room and never made it back at all!" Holmes, hovering in the background, read the script and concurred with that version of events: Amelia's apology was complete.

Much to her relief, neither Clarissa nor her mother-in-law paid much attention to her excuses, Daphne indeed apologising for "inflicting such a harsh trip on" Amelia: "Don't be ridiculous dear", said Daphne, "of course you were, *are,* exhausted! My word, what a couple of days you have had!" With that, the three women sat down at an untouched corner of the dining table and after a short wait, ate softly poached eggs and some smoked bacon, accompanied by triangles of white soda farls and Northern Ireland butter and preserves. "Gordon Senior's favourite breakfast!", exclaimed Daphne, Clarissa smiling and nodding in agreement with her mother-in-law. They ate quietly and reflectively to the dull background musicality of American voices and the occasional awkward, stifled giggle. The mood was suitably dark in the room generally, and Amelia amused herself by talking to Sir Charles across the table. They reminisced about London in the 1930s and found they had an interest in Hollywood movies, and, much to her delight, she discovered Sir Charles was an aficionado of both Harold Lloyd and Buster Keaton and that he had never really been convinced by 'talkies'. He was a fan of Korda's movies and was at odds with the critics' view that his work was not "art" – he considered "Rembrandt" to be one of the best films ever made. Amelia, taken aback by his knowledge of the subject, could not agree about "Rembrandt" as it was the only one she had not actually seen. They concluded that London of the thirties had been a grey, uneven period in history, hamstrung, as its people had been, by the Great Depression, its confidence shattered by memories of the Great War just over a decade earlier.

Time was racing on and ten o'clock came and went. At eleven, Daphne finally entreated mourners to move towards St John's on the Malone Road. She had, surprisingly, allowed her daughter-in-law to pick her own Anglican parish church as the location for her son's funeral and so she had had to embarrass herself with excuses to the council of Gordon's own Presbyterian church. A sturdy body of men quickly volunteered to meet Daphne's request for the short final parade of honour to the church.

Amelia was impressed to see her conquest, Alisdair, be the first to propel himself forward for duty, quickly followed by the Major General, his aides de camps, and his honourable friend, the Duke. They assumed a formation of four men to each side of the casket and the undertakers hoisted the load with ease onto the pallbearers' shoulders. The average heights of the men was such that Gordon's coffin was propped firmly between them, fully five feet five inches above the ground, at least for these first few yards as they all moved to the fleet of long black cars and American staff cars waiting for their human cargo on the driveway. Moments later, the convoy snaked out of the gateway of Wilmont onto the Upper Malone. Curious residents filed down their gardens, heads lowered and turned respectfully in the direction of the slowly moving vehicles. They reached the junction with Balmoral Avenue. It was as sobering a sight as it was unexpected - US military uniforms, a cape-wearing academic and a tartan-kilted, black-blazer wearing duke amongst the pallbearers, closely pursued by more American uniforms and a wheelchair carrying a three-piece houndstooth-suited knight of the realm. They followed in silent solidarity with the unfamiliar figure of the black fitted coat-clad Clarissa, replete with fashionable black velour slouch hat, embellished with a ring of faux pearls and black looping. Moving slowly forward, her children five paces behind her and with their solemn-faced grandmother beside her, Gordon's widow paused to wipe a tear from her right cheek. Amelia was a further ten paces behind the children, walking quietly with the senior American officer's wives. There was an eerie silence echoing an accompaniment along the road to St. John's. The cortège drew to a slow halt at the entrance to the church and the coffin bearers found it hard not to heave a sigh of relief as the undertakers took over the mahogany casket and slid it onto the low-slung trolley for the first leg of Gordon's penultimate journey. They sailed silently through the red-brick arch of the doorway and up the nave of the church, leaving the casket a respectable ten feet shy of the altar.

Amelia sat alone in a pew mid-way down the packed church. Not only were Gordon's friends of last night here, but there was also a considerable turn-out from Gordon's own Presbyterian parish. Amelia supposed that the devout Gordon of 1934 had changed little in that regard and that would be no surprise to anyone here today. She blushed when

Alisdair motioned that he wanted to sit beside her, a blush that could mean only one thing to him - that he thought she was embarrassed by the previous night's furtiveness. In her mind, she had decided that, somehow, she would have to find a way to close this fling down but that would have to wait until after the day's order of ceremonies.

Neighbours, too, some of whom had watched thoughtfully from inside their garden walls, lined the wall at the back of the packed church and sang for their lives: "Onward Christian Soldiers" was a bravado performance from the massed ranks of the US Army, aided and ably abetted by the massed ranks of Presbyterian male voices, corralled together mid-way down the left transept. His old schoolmates in the congregation, childhood friends all, joined in a rousing rendition of the Boys Brigade anthem "We Have An Anchor", a hymn which he had always said he wanted to have sung at his funeral, in honour of his Uncles Jimmy and Willie who were two of the hundreds of HMS Indefatigable dead in the Battle of Jutland.

Finally, "The Lord's My Shepherd", with its perfectly timed changes in cadence and power, crashed into Daphne and Clarissa, with the effect that their sobbing could even be heard above the organ's deep timbre. It made for an eerie finale and Amelia felt simultaneously bereft and helpless as she reflected on her own situation and the life ahead for these two women and Gordon's handsome children. She glanced at Alisdair as they were both coming to terms with the sadness of the morning's events. She whispered: "Oh Lord, Alisdair, what ever will they do? He was their rock, no doubt about that". "I'll say", he replied, looking at the floor, remembering just how his old school friend had been an inspirational leader in everything he did.

"Will I see you after this?", said Alisdair, catching Amelia by surprise. "I mean, can we have a bit longer together? I'm afraid I've rather grown an attachment to you, my darling. Sorry, forgive me for being quite so forward, you see I find I am quite helpless in your company", he whispered, eyes lowered, pink cheeks glowing. She was, she told him, terribly flattered by his attentions and that their meeting and intimacy had been truly breathtaking for her, all quite unexpected. "I am, of course, engaged so I can't see how much more I can give", she said. That line hit him hard and neither said anything more about it. The vicar blessed the congregation and the ceremony finished with the always heart-wrenching "Abide With Me", the singing of which ensured that both Daphne and Clarissa would leave the church heartbroken today.

The final verse was accompanied by the opening of the great doors, and the congregation was dazzled by the bright sunshine of the glorious day streaming through the tall archway. Amelia watched as Alisdair rejoined the pallbearers in what would be little more than half a mile of shouldering the remains of Gordon Anderson to Balmoral Cemetery. This would be a long walk with a heavy burden but one the US Army was ready for, whatever about poor Alisdair and the Duke. She came to wondering again about what had gone on on the landing during the night and she knew that she must somehow find out what had caused that sickly-looking slick in the water in the Major General's glass. What if it was poison? And what if the Commanding US officer had imbibed it? Alisdair was certainly most charming, she thought, but something was not quite right.

She disappeared into the comet-trail of mourners walking behind the procession and marvelled at how something as mundane as a funeral procession could still bring spectators forth in such numbers. She walked beside Sir Charles and he regaled her with tales of his time working in the chemical weapons division of the War Office when he had come back off active service. He had been disappointed to find that his worsening symptoms had made infantry work impossible for him. He told her how he had come to now work in the "Intelligence Services" and she was minded to tell him about the sample she had taken of this unknown substance last night. She described the slick it created in the glass of water and he slipped the sample into the top pocket of his jacket, with a promise to "get it analysed". "From what you describe, it could be cyanide or zyklon B", he said. The procession turned onto Balmoral Avenue and all along the avenue, curtains twitched upstairs and downstairs, the more adventurous daring to inch into their gardens, nodding to neighbours over the garden wall that yes, this one is for "someone important". Although a few recognised Daphne, they chose not to engage her with meaningless platitudes: now, seemed to be the unspoken view, was not the time.

After what seemed an age walking with a small portion of weight on his right shoulder, arm linking under the coffin with the Duke, Alisdair heaved a sigh of relief when the graveyard gates came into view across the railway track and the road junction. The funeral proceeded on through the gates of the cemetery, winding its way down the leafy tranquillity of the South Walk, until, eventually, the family plot was reached. Amelia had been intrigued, bemused almost, at the near-New Orleans-pageant that today's event was in danger of becoming. She berated herself for thinking these thoughts and her face flushed with personal embarrassment when she concluded with the notion that "Good Lord, this could do with a few jazz players to keep the watchers happy".

The Anderson family plot was an impressive sight indeed, comprising as it did a granite vault lying at the base of a five foot high Portland stone obelisk, with a white marble inset inscribed with the names of Gordon's father, his paternal grandparents, and his great-grandparents. It was not what Amelia had expected: ostentatious, she thought, the mini obelisk with its discrete Masonic skull inside a Star of David inscribed at the centre-top of its white marble panel, two carved serpents framing the marble panel being the only hint as to the family's leading role in freemasonry in Belfast. Few knew that Gordon had followed his father's footsteps and, in the last year, had already worked his way to Grand Master grade. He fervently believed, with near-missionary zeal, that the secret society could eradicate poverty in his hometown, no matter what political or religious allegiances might ordinarily dictate.

The human train having shuddered to a halt, Amelia soon found herself in the company of the Professor again as he bypassed Hamilton, Sir Charles and the senior officers, the men he had mingled with the previous evening, to appear at her side. He was like a puppy, except Amelia neither called him to her nor had she used any kind of inaudible dog whistle to bring him to heel. He was enthusiastic, she had to give him that, but she was troubled by his strange activity just a few short hours earlier. "Oh, hello," she said, turning sideways to take in his patrician side profile. He was handsome, she decided, despite the hawkish nose and unkempt eyebrows, and, she could now confirm, he was quite an athlete "in the sack", as she knew he would have put it. Maybe that was what appealed to her, this clever man with his academic's cape was quite earthy in his conversation with her and he had made love to her like it could be his last time ever. "Where will you be heading after this?", he anxiously enquired, suddenly realising that he likely would never see her again. "Well, as the vicar said, Daphne wants for everyone to go back to Wilmont. She said there will be a cup of tea. I don't know when I am leaving yet, no . . .", she replied. "Of course, the Americans are staying there, aren't they? And Gordon's closest friends are local. Like yourself, indeed", Amelia was quick to point out, acting as though she suddenly was not that interested in his attentions. "Yes, yes, the Americans...", he mumbled and seemed agitated at the idea that they would also be in attendance. "No, I shan't be leaving straight away", she conceded. She knew that she would most likely have to stay another night as she actually had not booked a return ferry to England. She felt no great urgency to embark on a return journey on that awful "floating death-ship", as she had described it to her paramour. She sensed too that there may be unfinished business between them as his eyes darted across her body again, drinking in every taut curve.

The casket lowered to its final resting place, Clarissa and Daphne stood staring into the inky blackness of the six foot hole under the uppermost vault stone. Clarissa pressed a dainty handkerchief to her eyes and heaved a mourn-filled sigh. Daphne hugged her daughter-in-law to her and sobbed uncontrollably, her shoulders rising and falling with each breathy sob. Some of the American wives reached out to her and touched her arm tenderly as they turned to join the massed ranks of uniforms and fashionably broad-shouldered, besuited wives on their retreat down the tree-lined walk and out through the gates. Two Rolls Royce funeral cars and the three army staff cars were parked up outside the railway station across the road. The Duisenberg was there too – Holmes had been detailed to collect as many of Gordon's friends as he could manage, even if that took more than one trip. With Daphne and Clarissa seated into the lead funeral car, Amelia took her place in the stately Duisenberg's front seats, for this car accommodated a driver and two passengers up front.

It goes without saying that that spare front seat was ably filled by, of course, one Professor Alisdair McGarry. Amelia saw a chance to perhaps delve into the reason for Alisdair's earlier carry-on, while he saw an opportunity to perhaps quiz her a little on her husband's dealings with the Nazis as he mistakenly thought that perhaps he had found someone who may share his grudging admiration of Germany.

"You said earlier that you had met Hitler and the inner sanctum of the German government in Hitler's mountain hideaway? How exciting!", he gushed and turned crimson when he realised that was a completely inappropriate thing to say, particularly in view of the company in the back of the car. Sir Charles was singularly unimpressed with Alisdair's remark and it simply served to confirm to him his deeply held suspicion that the "academic class are sympathetic to the Nazi cause". He said nothing though, just registered the awkward moment in his forensic mind. Amelia, meanwhile, saw Alisdair's embarrassment at his gaffe and made no further comment, deciding that she would wait for a better opportunity to probe him about his post-coital activities.

The convoy had taken to the open road and it was no time at all until they reached Wilmont again. Inside the grand house, Amelia partook of tea, salmon and cucumber sandwiches, even potted shrimp on soda farls, as the staff flitted around the assembled throng once more like black and white dragonflies, serving tea from china teapots, freshly brewed coffee from those pewter coffee pots and carrying trays of dainty sandwiches on doilied silver trays. The dull clunk of the jasperware once again absorbed the murmur of American voices and the shrill, stifled laughter of Gordon's old schoolmates as they recounted yet more tales of school life, sounding as they did like the happy bunch of teenage boys they had once been. Alisdair stayed close to Amelia, even as she chatted animatedly with Daphne and Clarissa, she trying to remain oblivious to his claustrophobic attentions.

"So, my dear, when do you think you might leave us?", enquired Daphne. It has been so good to see you again! As I said to Clarissa, it is such a long time since those games in London, I really had no idea if you would even remember our teas in the Savoy and Café Royale. Very many thanks for coming, Amelia, of course you are welcome to stay with Clarissa and I for as long as you need", she concluded. Turning to the professor, she said "I see you have acquainted yourself with my old friend here, Professor, I imagine you might have met your match! Brains to burn, has Amelia!", she laughed. "Yes indeed, Mrs Anderson, not much she did not know on the Dendrite front!", he lied, with a twinkle and a nod to Amelia.

Just then, the Duke appeared and addressed Alisdair: "What-ho, Alisdair, what are your plans for the rest of the day?", he asked just a bit too loudly. "All depends on how things pan out here, but Scotland beckons", he replied with a glance across the room towards the Major General. "Ah yes indeed, Scotland – I see", said the Duke, barely concealing a glance across at the American commander. It seemed as though they perceived something was not quite right and their body language seemed strange to Amelia, as if they wanted to move on but were waiting for some signal, something to happen to propel them on their way. Amelia was intrigued and she realised they were indeed waiting for a sign – could it have anything to do with the Major General? Had that been poison in the glass? She sipped her coffee and watched the two men closely for any indication that they were expecting something to happen but, eventually, the men parted company as the Duke was engaged by two of the captains in recounting his flight over the Himalayas.

Quietly, Amelia took Alisdair by the elbow into an empty corner of the room and thanked him for his pleasant company. She saw her chance to query his strange activities: "Well, I must say, Alisdair, I rather enjoyed our time last night", she whispered from behind her hand, "but was most distressed when I realised that you had slipped out of the room! Talk about "here's your hat, what's your hurry!". She went for the kill: "What on earth were you up to out on the landing anyway?" Alisdair's forehead crinkled as he thought up a makeshift excuse – he knew he was close to being exposed here. "Stupid me, I had forgotten to drop some Milk of Magnesia in to the Duke, he mentioned that he suffers from terrible acid, I always bring it with me!", he stuttered brusquely, hoping against hope that his answer would be good enough so that he would not be questioned about it again.

But she continued from behind her hand: "I had been hoping for some more "activity"!", she whispered with an open-eyed smile. He smiled: "I was thinking the same thing! You think we might before leaving?", he asked quizzically, she smiled as she realised he had misinterpreted her comment on last night.

His comment though was more a statement of intent. “What is that building out there? I’m going to pack up my car in a little while, why don’t you meet me in there? Looks deserted . . .”, she remarked. Alisdair was unexpectedly energised and relieved that he may get an opportunity to delay her departure and he replied: “Absolutely – I think it may be an ice-house, not sure it will be ideal, but if it has to be . . .”, he tailed off, brimming with ill-concealed excitement.

Chapter 12

The Icehouse Cometh

It occurred to him that not only was he delaying Amelia, he was also delaying himself from the next stage of his "mission", a mission with which he was beginning to feel a little uncomfortable. In fact, he thought, the first stage seemed to have failed – the Major General should be dead, did not drink the water, it was clear – he should be dead. Whatever, the next phase would have more finality about it, there would be no relying on chemistry, just a well-aimed gun-shot should do it. Within the hour, Amelia was making a move and, having retrieved her case from the Duisenberg, she checked to make sure everything was present in it. Alisdair took in her every move and readied himself to co-ordinate his exit with hers. He said to the Duke, as Amelia appeared to be readying herself to go to her car: "That reminds me, sir, I think she", Alisdair raised an eyebrow in Amelia's direction, "may be on to us, something she said about last night . . .". "Well then, you know what to do!", was the Duke's curt reply. "Yes", said Alisdair and that gave him the excuse he needed to leave the room. He exited the house the way he had come in and swung around to the ice-house, out of view of the majority of the mourners.

Amelia had just gone out to the gleaming black Atlantic and had deposited her bag in its trunk when she noticed Alisdair disappearing though the door into the small outhouse. She glanced around the garden – she had no idea why – and swiftly darted to the ice-house door. It was slightly ajar and she pushed through it easily. Her final rendezvous with the professor began moments later as he turned around and with open arms, embraced her to him tightly. "My love, my love", his lips were close to her face, "whatever shall I do with you? My heart will break when you are gone!". The melodrama in his voice sounded alarm bells in her ears as he clutched her tighter to his body. It was too tight and she found that she had to break free from his embrace. His change in mood scared her so that, from having been ready for a steamy interlude, she now found herself being reticent: "What's the matter with you, Alisdair? I thought this opportunity was what we both wanted?", she enquired of him. "Tell me what you saw last night, Amelia?", he responded, then, softening his tone, "What has troubled you so, hmmph?". She steeled herself before saying "I saw you with the Duke, you poured something into a glass of water. But he never drank it, you brought it down to another room. What was going on, Alisdair?".

She knew that what she had said was very direct and his face turned white, then red, as shock, then anger, seemed to convulse him. "What's wrong? Are you angry with me? I thought you were falling in love with me, I had wanted you to stay last night. I want you to make love to me here, now". She hadn't wanted to sound pleading, but she knew that was how it seemed and how he would want it to be. He looked away from her, as if searching for something. He turned around swiftly and held Amelia's face roughly, squeezing her cheeks so that she found it a strain to whip her face out of his grip. "What

ARE you doing?", she said, when he finally released her, she feeling very threatened by him now.

Suddenly, he was filled with remorse, emotions confused by a sense of duty to his "mission" and his new-found passion for the woman in front of him, hoping for her to love him right here, right now. He knew that she could unravel his mission, and he wondered if he could convince her to come on his adventure. No, too risky, he decided: "Don't be a fool", he thought, "she is onto me, us, Hamilton's right, damn it, I have to eliminate her!". The thought repulsed him and at that moment she knew she had to protect herself, for she had seen that thunderous look in the eyes of the Nazis in the Eagle's Nest, the madness. He sobbed, taking her by surprise: "Oh Amelia, I have been a fool, a fool! Too many innocents could die because of me", was his barely discernible cry, as he flapped around wildly like a child trying to banish a toothache. Amelia was worried for her own safety now and she looked around the narrow passageway, weighing up how she might get out. Meanwhile, Alisdair had recovered his composure and had turned his face back to her. This time he gently pulled her to him and kissed her tenderly on the lips, tasting her as if for the first time. She wondered what he had meant when he said too many innocents could die because of him.

Suddenly, they fell back onto the cold stone staircase and they fumbled at clothing. Deep kissing was followed by deep penetration as Alisdair's tears trickled onto Amelia's flushed face. His hands, a source of immense pleasure minutes ago, now gripped her neck, her throat, and she gasped for the sharp, cold air in the narrow stairwell. Her head was beginning to spin as her airway was closing, her hands flailing against the gritty wall in the semi-darkness. She felt cold steel - her fingers tightened around a sharp pointed object as his fingers tightened on her throat again. She vomited into his face as her fingers found the ice-pick handle and she jabbed it hard into his back. It punctured the skin between his shoulder-blades, penetrating his left lung. He gasped and exhaled a stream of blood and when she pushed him off her, his limp body bounced down the stairwell into the freshly broken ice below.

She remained seated on the step she had made love on, nearly died on and, now, the step on which she had saved her own life. She watched as the ice coloured red ten metres below her. "How will I get away from this mess?", she thought, her clothes a mess of vomit and Alisdair's blood, how was she going to escape this gruesome scene? She told herself to stay calm and she inched her way back out into the sunlight. She looked around the clearing at the entrance: she knew she had seen an urn near the opening and she poured rainwater from it onto one of the kerchiefs tucked up the sleeve of her messy blouse. The water could have been fresher, certainly, but it did a job and, with the help of a handful of ivy leaves, soon she had mopped the human mess from her face and decotellage.

Her mind racing and filled with anxiety, she retrieved her case again and decided to slip back into the house. Somehow, she managed to vanish upstairs to the bathroom unnoticed and continued her clean-up, regaining both her composure and devising a reason for her dishevelled state: she would tell Daphne that she had stupidly dropped her handbag into the old blackberry bush near her car and had fallen into it trying to retrieve it. Sure enough, when she reappeared downstairs, that was the story she told – Daphne was horrified, not because of what had befallen her friend, but was aghast that no-one, including herself, had seen what had happened or had offered to help.

Re-groomed and refreshed, Amelia returned to the drawing room where most of the mourners were now gathered. Gordon's old friends were readying themselves for home, but not before they took the opportunity to talk about old times for the umpteenth time. The army personnel had mingled with the locals so that the room was a giant hive of musical voices and the occasional muffled laugh. Talk returned to the attack on Belfast last year and the Americans admitted they felt that the Germans would soon turn their attention towards Belfast again. The Duke made his excuses and was the first to leave, claiming "pressing engagements in London" meant he had "to shoot back to the House". Sir Charles, always wary around the Duke, wheeled across the room towards Amelia and was quick to comment: "Splendid! I do believe this is my first chance to talk to you without the close attentions of that Professor-chap!", he had lowered his voice after his initial loudness. He had alarmed Amelia and her face coloured as she thought of the ice-house. "Was it that obvious?", she whispered back to him. He lowered his voice also: "That little bottle you gave me? I had some chemical friends here take a look – you know something, just by looking at the chemical reaction, they say it *is* cyanide, absolutely lethal!", confirmed Sir Charles. "Well done for retrieving it, I must say I'm not comfortable around those two oddballs – that Hamilton chap has just departed, wonder where the other fellah got to? Probably left too, I shouldn't wonder . . ." Amelia stifled a blush but her discomfort was obvious to the wily man in the wheelchair, as he continued "Don't worry, m'girl, whatever happened between you two is your business. What's the matter, Miss Lambe, you look like you have seen a ghost!".

"I... I really don't want to talk about it, Sir Charles", she stuttered, as the shock of what had happened minutes earlier struck home. "What on earth happened to you? My poor girl, you are most distressed!", he said, his kind eyes transfixing her in his gaze. She choked a sob as she told him about her "fall into the fruit bushes minutes earlier" and how she "had injured" herself. But to a battle-hardened infantryman, he could tell she was covering her tracks and, therefore, the truth.

She could feel her emotions bubbling over, tears beginning to form and it was all she could do to persuade Sir Charles to take a walk around the grounds. She knew she couldn't contain this tale much longer and the intelligence man in the wheelchair might be her safety valve. Thus far, he had confirmed her suspicions about the Duke and Alisdair, they had been trying to poison the US Commander. The ice-house incident confirmed for her that the two men were highly dangerous and that they had questionable loyalties to the Allied cause, even if one of them was a member of His Majesty's government.

Sir Charles listened intently as Amelia unburdened the story, barely thirty minutes old, of how Alisdair had met his demise. He made no comment as he listened to how her fingers had found the ice-pick as she scrambled around in the semi-light for air and for her life. "Good God! Jolly good riddance to "him, my dear!", he finally exclaimed as she recounted how Alisdair's blood was now staining the ice. From his seated position, he could see the finger marks on Amelia's neck and he was in no doubt that the incident had taken place as she described. She had been frightened by her own ability, she said, to so coldly stick the ice-pick into such a large man's back and to make sure that it was so embedded that it killed him. Sir Charles was impressed by her cool bravery and had nothing but praise for her resolve, even if, as he was quick to point out, Alisdair's demise could present new problems for the still-new American contingent. He knew that many of the women who worked for the Executive were trained to be absolutely ruthless but many managed to hide their darker side from view by being, at first glance, the "perfect wife", or the perfect "lady-about-town" and they often out-killed their male colleagues in the field. "Was he working alone or was the Duke in on it, do you think? Did he give any indication at all?", suddenly the questions were flowing from Sir Charles as he became more like his usual commander-class. "Well, if the Duke was in on it, I don't really know. But it certainly looked rather odd. The Duke gave him the glass of water, yes. He made no reference to anyone else though", she answered, then: "No, wait, Alisdair said he was going to the "real" Balmoral after here, something about meeting his "father" for their annual fishing trip", she recalled. "A-ha!", said Sir Charles, "Amelia, my dear, I think we need to head to Scotland, posthaste!".

Chapter 13

A Lambe pursues A McGarry

The look of surprise on her face made him realise that this job was something he could not reasonably be expected to be a part of. The plan crystalising in his mind involved Amelia as a new recruit, a recruit he could mould into a female version of the operative he had always wanted to be: she had "brains to burn", he was sure of that now, and her detached manner around her elimination of Alisdair was exactly what was required – no emotional attachment to him had been forged and she had been ruthless in her precise slaying.

"Oh, my word, Sir Charles, whatever purpose do you think I might serve?", she said, incredulous at the idea of travelling with a wheelchair and the, frankly, invalided former soldier. He stroked his chin thoughtfully and seeing the look on her face, said: "Dead right, Amelia, I would be an awful hindrance to you, you must make your way by yourself." Make my "way"? To where, exactly?, she said, her incredulity growing by the minute. Sir Charles excused himself and clarified: "Why, dear lady, from what you say, the bounder clearly had it in mind to pay our Royal Family a visit, and I shouldn't think he had an invitation for tea, would you? I'm afraid I have no idea what you had planned to do after today's events but I'm asking you, in the name of King and Country, to make that visit to Scotland in the Professor's stead!"

Amelia was overwhelmed by the importance of Sir Charles' proposition: "But what do you think I will be going there to do?", she said anxiously. "Listen, my dear", he began, "we have known for some time that the Germans see the King as the primary standard-bearer for the nation, the key to a peace deal, the only man who might dissuade Churchill from continuing with this battle of wills. Hess blew it last year when he crashed his 'plane on the way to see our "friend" the Duke, he thought he could do a deal to save the Germans' faces! They look less and less likely to get the upper hand now that the Americans have arrived. And they know that!", he smiled as he continued: "The news we have now is that some of Hitler's pals in high places *here* want to see the King dead, or at least off the pitch, seem to think it would destabilise the whole country's resolve for victory and a Britain with a German Chancellor will be better than a defeated people with Churchill!"

"Good Lord!", exclaimed Amelia, "What appalling stuff, I can hardly believe that there are people in this country who want to see the King dead!". "Believe me, dear lady, Hitler has a surprising amount of support in this country! Now, you are a lady who has experienced this enemy first hand and has lived to tell the tale. If you are willing, I need you to work with my agency to find out what you can about what was going on with the Duke and this McGarry chap – obviously dirty work afoot, as you rightly suspected. What do you think they were up to? I mean, Balmoral . . .",

Sir Charles was stroking his chin as he reflected, his mind filling with the audacious possibility that the academic may indeed have had plans to wreak havoc on that other Balmoral residence too. Amelia was alarmed to see his brow creasing, then his eyes widening, as he announced: “My dear, you know, this fellow may well have been public enemy number one! Did he say who his father is? “A McGarry, doubtless”, he murmured quietly. “No, don’t worry”, he quickly said as he could read her blank face, “I can easily find that out. Now, my work gives me the authority to give you special privileges when you are there, if you agree to go on behalf of the Executive. Not that you will be working “for us”, of course”, he corrected himself and looked away from her, the crimson flush of his face giving her a start.

Chapter 14

The Enemy Within

"You can update me with telegrams from post offices, probably best not to use a telephone for the moment as the Germans have sophisticated listening devices. We need to be very discrete, if you do decide to take up the opportunity to join with us in defeating the enemy within. Here, take this", he said handing her a small envelope. She opened it immediately and saw what looked like code words, with lines like "the weather is very inclement for the time of year". The contact replies "Yes, but the sunshine can't be too far away" which indicates that it is "not a good time to be seen together talking". She thought it seemed terribly stilted but Sir Charles continued: "You will meet a man at Glasgow University who will give you further instructions, he works in the library there. Just follow those instructions – are you with us?", urged Sir Charles, the head of this "Executive", as she would later discover. "I was not sure I had the choice, Sir Charles", she smiled, "but yes, of course, I want to find my husband, even if it is only his corpse", answered Amelia. "I will say my goodbyes here now and head for Scotland?", she continued, energised by the thought that she might actually be starting the journey that would bring closure to the most important time of her life, and not having the slightest notion as to how she might get across to Scotland.

It was Sir Charles who came up with the solution to her travel problem:

"The Strathairn is carrying troops to Scotland first thing in the morning from the docks, Amelia, to Gourock, just a few miles from Glasgow centre. I imagine that might be a good point of arrival. The university library is in the west end of town so not too far, less than an hour's drive. Oh yes, your car – there will be army vehicles on deck, I will make sure there is room for yours", he finished. She shuddered at the memory of her recent previous crossing, barely forty-eight hours before – the puking scouts, the *squalor,* yes that was the word, squalor, of the "lounge". Of course, it did mean another night in Belfast and she determined to stay in a hotel near to the docks. So after saying her goodbyes to Daphne, Clarissa and the Americans, she loaded up her trusty Atlantic once more and made her way into town. Daphne had recommended The Merchant after a sulky argument with Amelia as she felt affronted that her guest should seek to leave so soon – she could not accept that her one-time prospective daughter-in-law wanted to be as close to the docks as possible so that she could exit Northern Ireland discretely, avoiding a repeat of that most unsavoury of trips across the Irish Sea back to her original point of departure.

Following her 7am breakfast, a full Northern Irish special replete with warmed soda farls, baked beans and two soft-fried eggs, she joined the couple of thousand combat-ready American servicemen dockside. She sat in her car waiting to be waved up onto the ship's deck, positively revelling in the feeling of cleanliness and freshness that a freshly pressed and well-tailored Chanel suit always brought her. Alan had introduced her to Coco in 1936 and she remained in the famous designer's contact book, which secured her a place on Coco's shortlist of her most eminent clients. She reflected too on the last forty-eight hours: the journey from London to Belfast and the corpse she had left at the ice-house, her confession to Sir Charles, and his careful suggestion of this latest trip. Her thoughts were interrupted as she was requested to follow five Rolls Royce armoured cars up the metal ramp onto the Strathairn's open deck. She did as she was asked and parked beside the car immediately in front of her, the bonnet shaded by a lifeboat's shadow. This time, she was relieved that the journey seemed to pass quickly, water mercifully calm, with not a single sign of a seasick scout or a be-toggled over-grown scout master. Of course, she had had to endure the lecherous attentions of a battalion of American GIs for the duration of the journey but it was good-humoured banter and she felt comfortable knowing that they could take her equally sarcastic and raucous wit as just that. She felt that she had become a different woman in this last couple of days and that she now understood the kind of detachment these men were trained to feel in combat situations.

It seemed no time at all before she found herself back on dry land, and with her Ordnance Survey Scotland map unfolded on the seat beside her – what would Geoffrey have to say about *this* trip? - she was soon powering her way steadily towards Glasgow and the university. Passing signage for the scenic lands of Argyll and Bute to the north and west, she remembered Marjory Fletcher from Dunans in Argyll.

A very matter-of-fact gal, her father, Dougie, was the head of Clan Fletcher and judging by her various stories about him, he loved nothing more than whiling his weekends away shooting his estate's abundant pheasant, snipe, and wood pigeon which would be disturbed by the household staff and the family's three lively cocker spaniels. The Fletcher's were the major land owner in the region and the family wealth had grown exponentially, and quite unexpectedly, with the continued success of the family's artisan distillery malt, "Fletcher's Own". Unknown to her parents, Marjory had hated growing up in Dunans and never liked how remote it was from the kind of bustling city life she so thoroughly enjoyed in London. Yes, there were lots of hidey-holes and secret passages to please children of all ages – she had even seen one of the three ghosts not once but three times in one year. Well, maybe, she had seen all three and she had always felt embarrassed whenever talk turned to "staff", even amongst her well-heeled schoolmates. She had foolishly admitted one day to a household retinue of twenty-two staff, including her own personal maid, a "lady-in-waiting" if you will, when she was growing up. That on top of the personal tutor her parents had thought was something "every wee girl should have". Despite that cloistered start, she had grown up to be a very independent woman, very much unsullied by the life of luxury foisted upon her by anxious parents who had, after all, only wanted for the best for their only daughter.

She confounded them because as a teenager, and seeing their cloying need to please her at her every turn, she cruelly ignored and sidestepped them as if to prove the point to her peers and her two brothers that she neither wanted or needed their attentions. The last Amelia heard from her friend was of her fulfilling her ambition, working as a doctor in the field in Gallipoli. She recalled too that her father had died in a fierce aerial battle, during the Battle of Britain in 1940, for she had sent her regrets at not attending that funeral. He had been a veteran flier from the earlier battle and had become a much decorated Spitfire pilot, flying daring missions over France and the Lowlands: he had been caught unawares when a lone Messerschmitt surprised him from below, on his flight back from a mission over Guernsey, and had shot him down fatally.

The smoke-stacks and bustle of Glasgow were within touching distance inside the hour as the black bullet ate up the few road-miles to her destination. Lunchtime in the working city was approaching as she followed signs to the University, passing Govan and Ibrox on her way to the Kingston Bridge to bring her over the Clyde. She drove the full length of Sauchiehall Street before making the final turn which would bring her up to the University. Her contact, according to Sir Charles, works in the library and, as she parked her car under the grand entrance tower to the university, she thought about what Sir Charles had told her about how she should make contact with the next stage in her journey to Balmoral as she swept through the grand mahogany doorway into the reception hall and headed for the Library.

Heads turned as she appeared in the library reception – dressed in her emerald green boucle Chanel suit with matching laurel-style brooches, she cut quite the most distracting picture for the exam-weary student and fusty academic alike. Staff had nameplates on their individual desks so it was not long before she found herself standing in front of Alexander Brigham, her contact in Glasgow. He was a well-groomed man with blond hair and blond eyelashes, bearing a passing resemblance to the movie star, Peter Lorré, although he spoke with a much less menacing East Fife brogue. After the charade of the exchange of codewords about the weather, he led her to a small office beyond the ranks of history books on sentry duty on the far left wall of the library. There was something too about the scent of old books which beguiled her – just the smell got her to thinking about Dickens, well-lived lives and far-away places - and the powerful funk of the many antique tomes on display was working like a drug on her receptors. She had succeeded, by her own merit, in securing a Saturday job in Foyles in London, which developed into a summer holiday job for three summers, earnings from which she spent on the latest fashion trends and make-up. She had a habit of saving her monthly allowance towards the little train journeys to the seaside she liked to take with the other Paulinas who had no home to go to during the summer breaks. Brighton had been a favourite haunt, it had always reminded her of the time her father had brought the family to Constantinople, the minarets of the Pavilion acting as the backdrop to the whispering palm trees dipping and bowing in the gentle south-easterlies. Once, during their dalliance with all things gothic during their "vampire" phase, the girls ventured well beyond their comfort zone to York city and took the train out to Whitby to have tea in the hotel in which Stoker had invented Dracula little more than a half a century before. She often thought that, someday, she too would take a quill in her hand and write her own tales of wonder and delight, but perhaps knew deep down that it was a preposterous notion as patience was not in her gift.

Here she was now, a woman a million miles away from those halcyon days of her youth, standing in these wood-panelled offices as Brigham revealed his knowledge of the reason for her seeking him out at the university. He unfolded a map of Scotland on a Victorian green faux-leather topped mahogany desk as he said "Well, Miss Lambe, CD has told me that you are going to attempt a rendezvous with this

McGarry-fellow's father, that is of course if he even exists. He wants me to show you your route to Balmoral. T'is a wee bit tricky y'see, very hilly up in the Cairngorms. Don't suppose ye have much experience of hilly terrain, do ye?". "Actually, I have a chalet in St Moritz and I have driven through the Alps numerous times", she said, deftly deflating his bubble and wiping the grin off his oily face, feeling just a little bit thrilled to have done so and with such panache. "I see", came the thoughtful, slow response as he suddenly found himself face to face with, as he saw it, a very unusual woman. A bit too assured for his liking but, definitely, a woman of some substance. "CD?", she said, an inquisitive eyebrow raised. "Oh yes, that's how he's known to us. Real name . . .", he paused, dredging for it in his memory, "Nimmo? Poor blighter has that multiple sclerosis-thing, wheelchair now . . .", came the spot-on reply. "Okay then, not easy tay git to", he said in his thick Scots burr, switching back to the job in hand. "Must be why they like it", he continued. "Follow this route tay Aberdeen. Ye'll be watchin' oot for signs for Ballater, a wee bit afore it. The castle is just before it agin. I believe the owners have taken up residence early this year, must be something to do with the air-raids on London. CD says you will have full back-up from the camp at Oldmeldrum – must be expecting some trouble so the plan is, if ye git yerself into a pickle, telegram me here and I will mobilise the boys in the camp there, ye need have no worries in Scotland!". "Excellent, Mr Brigham, truly excellent", she replied, "though I must admit, I have little intention of making that alarm call!", she replied. Easily said, she thought, just beginning to feel that she had volunteered herself to do what should in all probability be someone else's work. She paused momentarily and thought: "No matter, I am here now, best get on with it", whatever "it" might be.

She climbed back into the Atlantic and resolved to call it "a journey", not allowing it to become a mission, and she saw the journey as an attempt to ensure that Alisdair and the Duke's skulduggery would not cross the sea from Ireland. How many others, she wondered, were involved or were sympathetic to the Nazi cause? What of Alisdair's father? Would she meet him, she wondered, now that that seed of doubt had been sewn by Brigham? The windscreen of the Bugatti framed the three dimensional world outside, the reality of a Glasgow very much at war, a world filled, seemingly, with more smokestacks than Stoke-On-Trent, coughing out the thick smog of industry, camouflaging an industrial powerhouse, driving the Allies to victory. There were the ship-builders' imposing gantries on the horizon, looking like futuristic steel spiders, standing on stilts and painted in camouflage shades of grey and bottle green. Below these were docked the fruits of the shipbuilder's hard labours – frigates and patrol ships, ready to be launched onto the Clyde. Some were moored quayside, already in active service, carrying troops or rations or army vehicles on their regular travels to and from Liverpool or London or Belfast.

She had followed the road north east out of Glasgow and it was not long before the old royal seat of Stirling Castle came into cinematic view in her roadster. She marvelled at how the daylight here in Scotland seemed so much brighter than in the rest of the country. Oh yes, the air was fresh and clean but how she longed for the rapturous, dizzying brightness of the Alps, the sun of Monte Carlo, the tranquillity of the azure seas off Valetta. "How selfish of me", she thought, as her thoughts turned to how easily she had forgotten about the darkness enveloping Europe again. She remembered her nervous drive up through England to catch the ferry to Belfast – had the country she passed through not also seemed dark, the kind of gloominess that is normally only banished when someone turns on the electric light? There was a doom-laden eeriness to the greyness wherever she went and she hated it: you could taste the fear, the sense of foreboding with every siren wail, with every night-time volley from the ack-ack guns. She thought of her lot, of Alan, of that encounter with Hitler, and she cursed the enemy.

Soon Perth was disappearing in her rearview mirror and she sped her way out of the old Pictish capital, as if being pursued by McAlpine's ghost. She was cruising north-north east towards the Cairngorms and her map showed that Balmoral was little more than an hour away. Sir Charles had told her that the elder McGarry was "probably holed up", as he had rather coarsely put it, in nearby Ballater village, just a stone's throw from the castle, but that he was unable to give her his exact whereabouts there. "Oh Lord", she thought, as she read his message again, "how on earth am I supposed to know what he looks like or where the devil he is staying? I mean, I can hardly approach every man in his sixties and ask him 'Is your name McGarry? Are you waiting for your son, Alisdair?'. She balked too at the notion that she may be the one to share the bad news about his son's demise but she put that thought out of her mind by deciding she would share that information only in the most extreme of situations. Her thoughts instead turned to what other benefit it could be to track down and befriend that brief, pleasurable, acquaintance's father – what might he tell her about his son's friendship with the Duke, did he know there might be a possible attempt on the Major General's life, and if there were other plans in train to cause strife. There were many questions she *could* ask, yes, and she shivered when she started to question if, perhaps, McGarry the elder was party to his son's disloyal leanings.

Chapter 15

A McGarry, Like Father, Like Son

Amelia filled her journey with these thoughts as her elegant car buzzed a lonely swathe through the undulating grey valleys, the light from her headlamps shining a path through the light misty rain. She pulled in to the side of the road and rolled down the front passenger window to get a better sense of what was going on out in the wood: she was sure she had seen men on horseback in the trees to her left.

A scene unfolded and she realised she could hear the sounds of a stag hunt: bugles and hooves and shouts echoed in the shallow valley and the distant holler of men was offset by the sorrowful howl of their quarry echoing across the glen. It was a terrifying scenario and it all came into view at the top of the climb that would naturally set her on the downward swoop towards its origin. The stag, his majestic antlered head silhouetted against the watery sunshine, was out-jumping and outwitting his frail adversaries, determinedly evading and repulsing tracker dog and voracious hunter-on-horseback alike. He had defied these usually in-season hunters for eight, maybe ten years, but now he had been surprised by this much earlier Royal party as London had become just too precarious for Royal living. The shouts and barks came and went as the hunt rampaged across the mossy forest floor, water splashing as the hunting party followed its prey through the little Dee tributary on his suicide route back towards the castle.

Then, two triumphant rifle blasts shattered the sunshine-dappled spectacle as the hunting party of King and acolytes cut short this, unfortunately-monikored, "Royal Stag"'s vain show of strength. Amelia pulled in to the narrow hard shoulder and watched open-mouthed as the silhouette sank into the ground slowly, each bone in its agile limbs seemingly folding and sinking into the mossy, peaty soil of the forest floor, pride and strength annihilated and wasted. Oddly, she felt a good deal more sadness for the innocent stag than she did for the man whose blood now tainted the ice in Wilmont House and that wave of empathy was helping her to ready herself for whatever lay ahead. Fleetingly, she worried that maybe, just maybe, the second blast had not been aimed at the beast - what if the King was no more? No, no, surely the voices would be at a crescendo of panic as the enormity of that treason would quickly become clear?

Shortly after, Balmoral's fairytale turrets came into focus but quickly became a distant blur as she pushed on past to nearby Ballater. She enquired at the first public house as to the likely resting place for the King's "outer circle" of friends in the Royal hunting party. She was directed onwards to Profeits Hotel in the next village, Dinnet, - some of the King's party would be staying there, she was assured, and she may also find a room suited to her needs.

She drove on to Dinnet and quickly found the hotel. She decided that, at this stage, McGarry Senior would almost certainly have been appraised of the Wilmont situation and she had no desire to come face to face with him at this early stage in his grief. The hotel appealed to her as a base, at least for the night, it had the look of a small estate house, with a welcoming façade and a turf fire in the lobby. Her immediate concern now, of course, was trying to identify Alisdair's father: Sir Charles had given no indication as to what to watch out for, there were no distinguishing features, no indication as to any distinctive mode of dress, no physical markers that might make her task that much easier. As it happened, Amelia did not have to do any detective work as the men not staying in the Castle entered the village astride their handsome and sweating, mostly chestnut, horses. The small clutch of triumphant riders trotted their horses up to the yard beside the hotel where they dismounted, and removed their rain-stained, velvet-covered riding helmets. Steam rose from the hunter's waxed jackets as their horses' well-tackled backs dribbled steaming sweat from under the saddles and the hunters dodged the splashes as the sweat hit the cool paving below.

Alisdair McGarry Senior was immediately recognisable: McGarry Junior had been an exact replica, albeit Senior bore a neatly manicured pencil moustache on his top lip. When he had quite carefully removed his helmet, she stifled a grin as she noticed that he sported a, frankly, feral hairpiece. It was a decidedly incongruous, out of place toupee, and Amelia's eyes, on spotting the wig, swiftly averted focus down to his face just as his steel-blue eyes met hers. She felt confusion as a sense of déjà-vu became muddied with the fairytale notion that her unfinished romantic interlude could yet continue, albeit perhaps with this older reincarnation of her

Belfast seducer. He was unexpectedly attractive in her eyes, certainly in his mid-sixties, and clearly The Elder's style had been a significant influence on the Younger. He wore a moss green Donegal tweed jacket over his blue Prince of Wales check poplin chemise and a close-fitting cherry-red waistcoat, his fawn riding breeches splattered liberally with shards of Cairngorm moss and splashes of peaty soil.

She was standing in the hotel's entrance lobby with her one piece of luggage – she and Alan had made it a rule to always travel light – and her vanity case, as the gaggle of steamy hunter-gatherers moved en masse towards the cramped reception desk. The two ladies stationed behind it slid sideways out from behind the desk and pressed their delicate piano-fingered hands into the damp and sinewy hands of this bunch of modern-day conquistadors. They exchanged pleasantries with their charges for the night: yes, we are here doing some "out-of-season hunting at His Majesty's invitation" and, to the taller of the two ladies, "How splendid, you are a direct descendant of Dr Profeit himself!", a line which unfailingly ensured that she would recount her long deceased great-uncle's duty to the Castle's first owner, Queen Victoria herself, when her ladies-in-waiting were searching for a place for the household staff to stay, whilst their quarters in the Castle were being made ready. McGarry Senior made a bee-line for Amelia and in gentlemanly fashion wrested the larger piece of luggage from her right hand, brusquely introducing himself without handshake, for he carried his helmet and riding crop in his left hand. His right hand was now tightly clutching the handle of Amelia's brown leather portmanteau. "Good day, to you, ma'am, Alisdair McGarry at your service!", he barked, and she had to contain herself from letting him know that she was all too aware of just who he was. "Allow me, Miss . . .?", his voice tailed of with a deliberate question mark. "Call me Amelia, Amelia Lambe", came her quick response, surprising herself with the authority in her voice as she realised that, actually, that was perhaps the first time outside her circle of friends that she had not called herself Amelia *Mendl* in rather a long time.

"Enchanté", he replied to the tune of a theatrical click of his heels. She steadied herself as suddenly she was in a déjà vu situation: it was most odd. Her face coloured up as she remembered Belfast and she wondered if her dashing aid actually knew that his son was dead, his lifeless body lying in the broken ice in the icehouse? "My word, young lady, where have you come from you look, if I may say, heaven sent, completely out of kilter with this ugly bunch of bruisers here today!", said McGarry, his cheeky grin catching her unawares, nodding across at the small group of fellow riders mulling over the evening menu. "I came over from Belfast, stayed with the US commander and some of his troops there the night before", she replied, "had a funeral to attend there, terribly sad, even if I had not seen poor Gordon in such a long time. Quite a sudden thing, I'm afraid."

McGarry caught her a little off guard when he said "Good Lord, I wonder is that the one my son went off to at a moment's notice? We usually do this annual fishing trip up here and suddenly he was meeting up a bit early with Hamilton and off they went!". Her heart was beating fast as she said: "Perhaps it was, perhaps it was, but I should think it was but one of quite a number in Belfast in the last couple of days". She was distracted now by the nerves tightening in her stomach and she knew she was a terrible liar. "Yes, yes, indeed so," he found himself giggling as he agreed with her, upon realising that what she had said made perfect sense and that he had made very little. She felt a wave of relief as he seemed to enjoy the tangent he had embarked on and she realised she had avoided more serious discussion on the matter. There was no way she could reveal that, yes, she was at *that* funeral. For now, she sighed a little sigh of relief and asked "Do you fish in the River Dee?", as she sought to bury any reference to Belfast. "Used to always, my dear, we would come up on the Messenger and stay in Dinnet with the Dumfries. Stayed here in Profeit's a few times, when my son was growing up, though. Loves his fishing, it would be the Dee or the Don, the other big river up here", he nodded in the general direction. He spoke of his son as if he were still that young lad "growing up", his eyes giving away his delight at the memory of those days. "Oh, I see, TWO good rivers", she said, perspiring uncomfortably and desperate to change the subject as quickly as possible. "Yes, plenty of salmon and sea-trout, we would often bring some to Balmoral's residents, great way to get invitations to the goings-on around here and find out what really goes on in London, what!", he said cheerfully. "Why, yes, I should imagine so!", she quietly replied, and they continued chatting, really about nothing much in particular. She liked his easy manner and engaging laughter, very much reminiscent of his son. He, equally, was impressed with her knowledge on a wide range of subjects – they talked about the ongoing war, the arrival of the American military, the Nazis, the Alps and other parts of Europe, there seemed to be a lot of common ground. He made allusions to business he "had to conclude in Aberdeen" as he lied that he "worked for the War Office as an Ordnance Specialist". His training had pointed him towards 'officer-class' and he had served as an artillery engineer first with the army then as an officer-teaching in "the Big Two military colleges", as he called them. He had returned to the frontline briefly before his assignment to Woolwich. McGarry appeared to take everything in his stride and he revelled in telling Amelia that his frontline attitude was "Always, if they kill me, they kill me, no point crying over my spilled blood!". "If it ever gets to that stage . . .", he concluded, clearly supremely confident that it never actually would. The talk turned to the day's hunt and, at the end of it, Amelia had learned that, in fact, that second thunderous shot on the glen had not been a carefully aimed shot at the King from McGarry's Webley, but that it was actually the fatal shot, fired by one of the Scottish dukes (Buccleuch, she thought he had said), in the party. She metaphorically wiped her brow as she had worried in vain that McGarry might have been teeing up a pot at His Majesty and he seemed quite frustrated now that the King's rifle had been credited with the kill this afternoon, a frustration he made little effort to conceal.

Soon, 2am came and went and they found themselves sitting on the sofa in front of the crackling embers of the tartan-wallpapered lobby's open fire. McGarry stoked the glowing remains of the pine logs with the brass pentagram-tipped poker he had retrieved from the coal-bucket on the black-and-white mosaic tiling of the hearth. His stirring in the remnants caused a spark to crack another piece of the original kindling into life and it fizzled with a bright orange burst of flame before settling into a smouldering red flare atop the white-hot coals. He looked into Amelia's cool grey eyes and jumped as he thought he saw his son reflecting back at him: he gasped and shuddered simultaneously, so that his late-night companion gently pressed her right forefinger on his lips to gently comfort him. Immediately, she began to apologise for seeming so forward and she asked him what was it that had caused him to shake so suddenly: "I . . . I thought I saw my son in your eyes, my dear", his eyes were stretched wide open, as if in surprise. "Gave me a fright, I do so apologise", he said. Amelia was taken aback – what ever would she do? Should she not tell this handsome gentleman that his son is almost certainly dead? No, no, that would incriminate her, give the game (it had been no "game") away.

"Silly! You probably just saw a reflection of your own face", she replied cheerily. Then, fearing that he might think she had actually met the younger McGarry, chimed in with: "I'm quite sure that your features have been inherited, I mean 'good-looking father begets . . .'", she laughed as she worked hard to retrieve this awkward moment. McGarry blushed pink and thanked her for her kind words, not even questioning her convincing quoting of a self-invented turn of phrase. The mahogany grandfather clock propped against the wall to the right of the black alabaster fire surround chimed three in the morning as the hour hand pointed at the twin pillars representing the number three and the minute hand stood erect pointing at the compass and set square, representing the number twelve.

The hoteliers had long since gone to bed, having served round after round of Dalrimples and Chivas to the three other Balmoral hunters, leaving the two unaccompanied in the hotel's lobby for the last two hours. Without warning, the elder Alisdair, who had slipped his right arm around her shoulders, pulled Amelia closer towards him and kissed her firmly, his left hand cupping her face delicately. She was taken off guard but responded in timely fashion by cupping his face in her own hands and opening his lips with the force of her own pliant mouth. They kissed like this for fully ten minutes it seemed, before his hands moved up under her bodice and his fingers skilfully undid the stays of her nude-and-black coloured stockings, rolling first one, then the other, down her legs. He kneeled on the floor in front of her as he massaged her rose-scented feet, unabashedly kissing each one as he had done her mouth, letting his tongue linger on each toe as he licked and excited her. He lifted her gently upwards so he could tug her skirt down to expose the black cotton knickers with lacy black panels to the front and his tongue took an evermore northward direction, trailing wetness up the inside of her warm legs. He buried his face in the black underwear and she shifted herself on the sofa so that her sex could be bathed in the warm dampness of his breath. She was exhausted but could feel the sexual beast in her body reacting to his seductive cajoling as saliva exploded from his mouth and into her most intimate crevices. He used his fingers to caress the mixture together as she stifled her moans while her head lolled back on the couch. He felt invincible, insatiable, as he thrilled her with these most gentle and subtle of probings until her body shuddered with that final crescendo of pleasure. He spent an age with his face just pressed against her damp underwear, kissing her inner thighs and inhaling the sweet smell. When he resurfaced, his wide shoulders moved his face up towards hers. As she kissed his face and licked his lips clean of her juices, he assured her that he was simply too exhausted for her to, as she put it, "return the favour" and so they simply clung to each other in the low lamp-light.

They slept on the sofa, arms entwined, only to be wakened at five o'clock as the first of the hotel food deliveries, courtesy of the baker's boy, arrived. They woke abruptly and McGarry wasted no time in telling Amelia that he must catch the train up to Aberdeen, that he had pressing "matters of State" to follow up on. He clearly had no inclination to explain what those matters entailed but Amelia was well aware that the senior McGarry was a military man and she assumed it must be war-related duty. They both needed to freshen up, it had been a long day of hunting wild animals for McGarry and an equally tiring day for his yawning conquest. Each went to their own room to reunite with their luggage and it occurred to her that she should, in fact, offer to bring Alisdair to Aberdeen. She reckoned that would enable her to keep tabs on him without seeming too "clingy" and she imagined that Sir Charles would applaud her ingenuity: if McGarry was trouble, he needed to be monitored closely, what better way to do that than to offer to be his driver? She took the bull by the horns and stepped across the landing to his room and gently rapped her knuckles on his door. It opened quietly with the light force of her knock and he smiled expectantly, and then nodded agreement, as she suggested she could bring him to Aberdeen this day.

"Need to make sure the defences are well co-ordinated up here", confirmed the academic's father, in his abrupt, truncated-sentence style. She wondered if his thoughts came to him in that measured, matter-of-fact style, and concluded that yes, they most likely did - not for him five hundred words when fifty would suffice.

Quickly bathed and powdered, she dressed in last season's Chanel jacket and a fashionable beige gabardine utility skirt; he in yet another tweed ensemble and check twill chemise, teamed with yesterday's brown brogues, they met at ten in the hotel lobby. They enquired of the elegant Ms Profeit as to the likely journey time to Aberdeen, the University specifically, and nodded relieved agreement that the journey may be not much more than an hour of steady driving. Of course, their innkeeper was not factoring in the mode of transport – the Atlantic would eat up the miles and in no time at all, forty-five minutes later, the pair were facing the granite gateway to King's College. It seemed McGarry had meetings set up with the local artillery school and soon he was in deep discussions with a Colonel Wishaw and a Captain Whitehead about local defences while Amelia busied herself with reading about the college's impressive history and its alumni, in the library. There was one name in particular which McGarry had mentioned numerous times on the journey which stood out from the crowd: Hector MacLeish who, she deduced, was some sort of local "chief of operations" and the man her charge seemed most keen to meet.

She watched from an ante-room next to the library, a dimly-lit reading room, as finally McGarry stood in front of McLeish, a small effete man in his early fifties, sporting a greying beard and dressed in a light-weight suit made of the ancient MacLeish tartan, a subtle check of blue and moss-green squares on a weave of pure new wool. He had bushy sideburns to match his neatly parted, sandy hair and Amelia liked the liveliness in his face. There was a nod across the hallway to her as Alisdair told his new companion that "Miss Lambe very kindly drove me up from Balmoral". They proceeded to move out of view into an unoccupied room down the hall and Amelia was unimpressed to find herself excluded. She had a bad feeling about the elder McGarry built up from their often uneasy conversation in the car about Hitler and she decided that the best way for her to keep tabs on them would be to bring in a tray of refreshments. She enquired of the librarian how she would get to the refectory and, once there, enquired politely if she could bring tea to her travelling companion and his associate. Having pressed a guinea into the hand of a young cook as an encouragement, she was soon knocking politely on the door that the men had disappeared behind.

Once inside, she placed the silver tray of Doulton on a side table and poured two cups of steaming Earl Grey for her charges. She had been amazed to see a slim sheaf of ten pound notes, held together with a thick rubber band, being tucked surreptitiously into an inside jacket pocket of MacLeish's suit jacket as she entered the room. The men acted as if nothing had happened and she caught what was clearly the end of their discussions. Surprisingly, McGarry turned to her to bring her into the conversation and proceeded to tell her that MacLeish was in charge of the anti-aircraft gun battery a few miles east beyond the docks, on the Aberdeen coastline.

"Nice to meet you, Miss Lambe!", burred MacLeish when McGarry introduced the two.

"Delighted, I'm sure", she said as he brushed her hand lightly with a dashing kiss. The men's conversation now seemed to become stilted, "constrained by what?", Amelia wondered.

"I dare say if there was no ack-ack up here", began McGarry, "Jerry would be trying a pot-shot at HRH!" He looked into Amelia's eyes for affirmation that his comment was absolutely correct, but Amelia felt that nowhere would ever be safe from enemy attack and she said as much.

"I don't know, Mr McGarry", she preferred to call him by his formal title, "I think it is very difficult to feel safe anywhere in the country now. I thought I was safe living in Paris and Geneva, but now...?", she trailed off.

"I'm afraid you are so right, m'dear, dinnay know when those blasted sirens will go off! Ach, I suppose we are lucky up here, the extra miles are a wee bit of a drain on the Heinkels so we haven't been bothered too much", replied MacLeish. "Still, must be vigilant, look at that Hess thing, imagine if it had been an entire squadron!"

"Yes, could have been a much bigger incident", agreed Amelia, only dimly aware of that most peculiar occurrence the year before.

It was not long before she began to feel extraneous to requirements in the room as it became quite clear that neither man was keen to enter into in-depth discussion whilst she was in the room. She found this quite frustrating so to relieve the palpable tension in the room, she made her excuses and decided to head back to the library.

McGarry felt a twinge of embarrassment as he quickly said out loud: "I'm going to catch the Pacific, due out at two o'clock, perhaps you will join us for lunch at one? Leaving it a bit tight for the train but I've done it before . . ." She mumbled agreement that yes, she would come back to them at that time, that she would have to return the tea items to the refectory anyway, and she made her way to the library again. *Hhhmm, he must be in quite the hurry, the Pacific is such a fast train,* she thought, as she went back to reading some local history pieces in the reading room.

She leafed through pamphlets on Royal Deeside and its railways; she learned about the ancient Picts and their graveyards in Perthshire and beyond; she read the introduction to a little handbook on whiskys and read a brief history of kilts. If nothing else, she would come away from Aberdeen with a head expanded by little-known Scottish facts and historical trivia. At ten minutes to one, she reapplied perfume and lipstick before returning to the sideroom where she had left McGarry and MacLeish, only to find it empty. She checked her watch to confirm that she had not mistimed her return – she had not – and, quite panicked now, decided to return the tray to the refectory in the hope of making enquiries as to the men's whereabouts and to, perhaps, gather her thoughts in planning her next move. Perhaps she needed advice from Sir Charles but, soon after, she was to get her next cue – on passing the library again, she saw MacLeish and McGarry disappearing behind a white door behind the librarian's desk and she waited at a sidetable beside a white alabaster column in the hallway for the men to reappear. Minutes later, the door opened slowly again and the two edged their way out of the library, heading back towards the room they had left just minutes earlier. She followed them more closely this time and embarrassed them when she reappeared to them in the anteroom. "Ah, Miss Lambe, I do so hope that we have not upset your plans for Scotland? Hector here must make his way to the coast whilst I'm afraid I must head for the station – am I still able to avail of your kind offer of a lift there?", he asked, sheepishly. "Of course, Alisdair, and please, no more formality, my name is Amelia!", she laughed with a pleasing flourish of her hand. "Perhaps I can come back and bring Mr MacLeish to his destination?", she suggested. This seemed to worry the two men and McGarry quickly said "Oh no, he has a motor car with him, as quick as yours I should think, a lovely Austin, nippy blighter!", he said with a glance at his associate, who simply flashed a smile back at him. "Yes. I will be travelling on out to the searchlights in my other guise as Commander of the AckAck unit at the docks (this surprised her as she did not see him as the combative sort).

They all exited the university and Amelia reunited with her dynamic Bugatti whilst MacLeish hopped into the cockpit of his Austin Seven. McGarry travelled light and once he had retrieved and placed his one piece of luggage on her back seat, he settled himself into the front passenger seat. Amelia eased her motor onto the road from its kerbside berth and headed towards the station. She travelled down King Street and cut across to Union Street before pulling up outside the classically styled granite terminus. McGarry pushed his door out and clambered from the low passenger seat, stopping only to retrieve his case and to thank his chaffeuse. The Pacific's steam billowed over the bright building's rooftop and, as he was engulfed by the exhausts, he took in Amelia's exotic Mediterranean profile. He wondered if he would see her again and felt a tinge of self-pity when he concluded that, in all likelihood, their tryst was as good as it got.

She, on the other hand, was anxious to see exactly where MacLeish was headed and rushed back down Union Street towards the docks and out beyond Torry. She had monitored his journey in her rear-view mirror following her down King Street and had noticed his racing green Seven sloping off in the direction of the docks. She felt herself to be driving into a narrower and narrower cul de sac until, eventually, in the distance she could see what she supposed was the searchlight control station. It was a low plain brick building with slits in the walls for windows and, shortly after, she spotted the Austin parked up on a bank of earth some distance behind the low, featureless, concrete structure. She braked firmly as she had no desire to drive her conspicuous roadster much closer and she parked well short of the unit, on the steep incline down to it. The searchlights themselves were not as big as she had imagined – the powerful shafts of light were emitted from electrical rigs not much bigger than a kitchen sink, she thought, and she marvelled that such simple compact machines could prevent such unfathomable death and destruction. Suddenly, she spotted MacLeish skulking around outside the back of the control unit and she quickly ducked back into the shadows to monitor his movements, all the while she was keeping an eye on his actions as he appeared to be unravelling something. He was certainly acting suspiciously and he anxiously looked around to his left and then his right as if expecting to be rumbled. He was definitely up to no good, thought Amelia, and she stayed in the shadows to watch him.

"Hamish, Hamish!!", came a sudden cry from nowhere. MacLeish was startled by the shrill call and he swiftly pocketed whatever it was he had been unwinding and rushed towards the nearest searchlight, about ninety yards further on. It appeared the operator had called him over and they quickly got into a deep discussion, distracting enough for Amelia to take her chance to investigate what MacLeish had been doing. She crouched low as she moved swiftly towards the wall of the base furthest from the men. She found the wire pressed into a small ball of putty, so that it sat about five inches above ground level. She traced it to the left around the bottom of the wall (in order not to encounter the soon-to-be-returning MacLeish) to a point around the gable end where suddenly the wire sank into the freshly-disturbed soil. All seemed most suspicious and, on hearing the men's voices getting closer, she rolled into the building via a wide low window slit and lay completely still and silent. She could see the men's ankles just outside the slit and heard MacLeish tell the operator that "I have it on good intelligence that the enemy has heard the King is in Balmoral, so be very alert to attacks!". Then he revealed that his next destination was St Andrews, en route to Edinburgh – his mission was to ensure the Scottish East Coast could secure the King from attack and that all precautionary measures were being acted on. "It is vital that the Royal Couple are safeguarded, the King is the nation's talisman and, make no mistake, the consequences for failure in this most simple of requests will be monstrous", were the last doom-laden words she heard from MacLeish as the ankles walked away into the distance.

Minutes later, an air-raid siren began to wail and as the two men rushed back towards the control unit, it was all she could do to affect her unseen exit through a side door in the unit. She felt panicked now, the siren doing nothing but adding to the confusion of the searchlight crew and her own fear of being caught. *Wait a minute*, she thought, *caught? Doing what, exactly?*

Suddenly, through the shouts and the distant drone of the enemy bombers' propellers, the ground around her was strafed by machine-gun fire from an advance party of buzzy Messerschmidts. The high intensity light-tubes of the searchlights shone their fierce white light up at the angry metal wasps and the anti-aircraft shells traced their way skyward as if being drawn onto the sky dot-by-dot. MacLeish had assumed his control position and was in radio contact with the searchlight operators as he located the hulking shadows of the Heinkels on the horizon. The fighter 'planes' guided by the bright discs of light on the ground below, dived lower and released volley after volley of machine gun fire at the grouping of men and machines in their cross-hairs. There was a heart-stopping explosion as one of the lines of bullets ripped into the piece of ordnance treasure MacLeish had buried just outside what might just have become his own concrete coffin. Amelia heard screams and saw silhouettes fall in the early evening gloam as the heavy bombers flew high overhead. She scrambled frantically back up the hill to where she had left the Bugatti and was relieved to see it remained undamaged by the destruction that had been visited here this evening, although the bonnet had picked up a small dent caused by a flying piece of masonry from the concrete structures below. Unsure of MacLeish's whereabouts now, she had to conclude that he was trapped, perhaps dead, in the pile of rubble that the base had become. She decided that she would make her way to Edinburgh via St. Andrew's as this had been his last hint at what his itinerary would be.

It was after six in the evening and Amelia unfolded a map to plan the best route to St Andrew's. She knew she had a long drive to Edinburgh ahead of her so she decided to take it step by step: she would drive to Dundee this evening and hope she could pick up a spare room to overnight in. She drove due south towards Dundee, ever watchful just in case the Messerschmidts might reappear, but they did not. She was clear about one thing – she abhorred night-time driving, the strain on her eyes and concentration always tired her. The lights of her car seemed to be making no impression on the darkness surrounding her, and she was driving further into the increasingly wet abyss. When whizzing past the fairytale entrance to Arbroath Abbey, her lights picked out the rain shadow effect on its entrance towers, the light refracting through the raindrops and pulling her ever onwards towards Dundee. She arrived at the northern outskirts some time around eight thirty and skirted the shoreline past Scott's Discovery. The freshly painted Tay Hotel frontage rose like a ship's beacon in the twilight and it was here where she would make her bed for the night.

There was a telegraph machine in the hotel lobby and she immediately made use of it, even though it was late in the day. She doubted if Sir Charles would get her message until the morning. She was excited by the day's events and needed affirmation that her plan to follow MacLeish's route was the correct path to take.

She had only just sat down to dinner in the hotel's softly-lit dining room when the wine waiter came to her table and, blushing, handed her a long white envelope with her name emblazoned across it. "For you, madame", he said. She was taken aback as she had not expected such a prompt reply. The reply read: "Wonderful news you bring! Follow your head for it will surely bring reward. Visit the Uni, that light pattern will doubtless fall again". *Good Lord,* she thought, *whatever is all that gobbledygook supposed to mean?* She didn't expect her every contact with Sir Charles to be so obtuse and, as she pondered the meaning, asked her waitress where the University was located. She was relieved to discover that it was nearby and she decided that she would pay it a visit – perhaps if she mentioned MacLeish there too, she might pick up more information about what was going on. She was not to know that he had been a librarian there in his youth but she had been instructed that the library should be her first port of call: perhaps he was known here, in the same way it seemed he was known in the others, was her reasoning.

The next morning, after a light breakfast of poached eggs on toast and tea, Amelia made her way down Nethergate and took a side street up to the University. She parked on the street and was soon standing at the library's lending desk. She mentioned MacLeish's name and was promptly ushered into the Chief Librarian's office. "Well now, I believe ye're an old friend of Hamish, young lady? My name's Martin Campbell", a voice spoke from somewhere beyond the back of the bottle green leather swivel chair and wide mahogany desk in the middle of the room. The voice was cultured Scottish, more Cambridge than Dundee, and he turned slowly to face her: he was well-upholstered like his swivel chair, with thinning but neatly combed sandy hair and he wore a three piece charcoal worsted wool suit, the waistcoat finished with what she presumed must be the bottle green and dark blue check of the Campbell tartan. She noticed he wore a silver tie-pin which looked like it could be a family coat of arms. She had not said that she was a friend of MacLeish but decided to stretch the truth a little and said "Yes. Well, rather more acquaintance than "old friend". The name's Amelia Lambe". They shook hands stiffly and she was less than impressed with his clammy and, frankly, limp handshake. She suddenly had a change of heart and decided to play it a little closer to the truth – she was nervous and she felt uncomfortable about creating a persona for herself which was far from the reality. He talked about MacLeish as if she really did know him well and she probed him to see how much he knew of his friend's moonlighting as a searchlight commander in Aberdeen. It turned out that he knew very little but surprised her when he told her that, in fact, his friend thought of himself as a crusader for the rights of the German people and that he believed the terms of surrender in 1918 were unduly harsh: "Our friends in Germany were good people and our people inflicted misery and ruination on an entire nation", he stormed, and she could not quite work out if these were his views or McLeish's.

"Ach, he was always trying to get me to do the same job down here but I just don't have the time, library staff in short supply in these parts. So short in fact, I am also the librarian in St Andrew's two days a week. The previous chap signed up to fight, something about it being in the family, his father had been an army captain at Paschendale. Poor bugger never made it back but that didn't stop my old pal", he recounted. "But that's the way. Funny what war will do to good men", he muttered, and his voice trailed off. There was a sharp knock on the librarian's door and a young female pushed it open: "Visitor for you, Martin", and she waved through an anxious interloper, who pushed past her gruffly. Amelia felt the colour drain from her face as, incredibly, she found herself confronted once again by Hamish MacLeish. She looked down quickly to avoid MacLeish's gaze. "He should be dead!", she thought to herself. Granted, his face was covered with cuts and bruises and he had an arm in a sling. "What on earth happened, Hamish!", exclaimed Campbell to his old friend and colleague. MacLeish took him by the elbow and led him out of the room, as if he had not seen Amelia at all. What would she do now? She felt panicked and out of her depth as she waited to see if they would return. But she realised too that she actually had nothing to fear from an encounter with MacLeish as she must surely be above suspicion – she had done nothing wrong to his eyes so there could be no need to be afraid. But she decided to make an exit before their return, try to regain the initiative, and perhaps also find out what MacLeish's immediate next move would be: she dare not let him out of her sights now.

She slipped back out onto the narrow hallway and was just in time to see the two men exit the library onto the neatly manicured lawns of the college courtyard. MacLeish made a bee-line to his Seven and she rushed back to her Atlantic. Following him out of the grounds at a discrete distance, she soon noticed that they were following signs to St Andrew's. After an uneventful journey, they entered St Andrews and he pulled his car up in the main street, got out and entered what looked like an antique shop, although there was no name above the door. The window display contained old ceramics, bric-a-brac and old paintings. She sat in her car and watched him talking to the shopkeeper. She squinted into the shop when he disappeared into the background and breathed a sigh of relief when he re-emerged ten minutes later. The shopkeeper stood at the front door in his white cotton bib apron and passed what appeared to be quite a light package to MacLeish. She could see symbols emblazoned on the apron – around a golden square and compass, she could make out an impression of two golden pillars either side of those symbols and what appeared to be one of those all-seeing eyes perched atop the square and compass. Was this an antique shop at all or was it, as she was beginning to think, something entirely different? What was in the oddly-shaped parcel tucked firmly under MacLeish's right arm?

The shopkeeper spoke to the librarian and motioned in her general direction – he had spotted her and was telling MacLeish, at least that was her reading of it. MacLeish looked in her direction but seemed to be focused on something beyond the car and was gesticulating with broad hand movements as if indicating that there was something of interest in the wider blue yonder. He was talking to the shopkeeper and he held up the parcel as they spoke: Amelia decided that she must find out what was in the package. At least with McGarry safely despatched to London, she had only MacLeish to keep an eye on now.

Her charge put the package in the boot and got back into his car. She watched as many as twelve men file past the shopkeeper out of the building and disperse into the streets of the university town, destined for where? Well, she thought, her first concern must be to keep watch on McGarry's friend so she pulled away from the cathedral precinct wall in unison with the Austin. Keeping a full ten car-lengths behind, she trailed the nimble Seven as it made its way east and she could see the coast in the distance. Out of nowhere, there was the familiar sound of an air-raid siren - it made her want to pull in but she could not as the Austin's response was to move faster and she knew that she must not lose track of MacLeish's whereabouts now.

She was not to know that MacLeish had been watching the low black car in his rear-view mirror for the last ten minutes. He was driving towards Kingsbarne, but suddenly he took a right turn and sped off at breakneck speed up a very uneven and narrow road. The siren's blare seemed to have panicked him and he knew that it was an imperative for him now to get to the searchlight installation on the Isle of May as quickly as possible. His car bounced violently over the road and he found himself hoping that the detonator was secure. This shortcut would take him south-south-east to the ferry at Anstruther, where he stopped his car no more than ten yards from the ferry terminal. Amelia had followed as closely as the uneven road surface would allow her and she stopped her car at the post office down the road. She watched as MacLeish took the package out of the car and carried it into the terminal. She abandoned her plan to find somewhere she could shoot off a telegram to Sir Charles and hurried down the road on foot to the ferry terminal. She made the ferry with moments to spare – it was leaving on the hour, barely five minutes hence. She was fortunate that there was a platoon of Highland soldiers embarking the small vessel and, wrapped up warmly in her grey gabardine overcoat, hair pulled back off her face and hidden under her beret, she crushed in behind the servicemen who had been scrambled to the artillery base. As she paid for her ticket, she saw that it would leave the island on the return leg at ten pm. She remained on deck as the men made their way through the small doorway to the cabin below deck. She would keep her head low and do her best to avoid detection by her prey, Hamish MacLeish.

He was, of course, fully aware of her presence from the start: his sixth sense told him that something was not quite right today and he was quite aware that she had followed him in her little sportster. Now he could instinctively sense her presence on this short journey and there was no doubt in his mind that this lady was trouble: first, he had seen her fleetingly at the anti-aircraft installation in Aberdeen and he had been lucky to escape the ruins that that had become. This time, she was positioned on the deck so that she could see a fair proportion of the platoon through an open porthole and, best of all, she had a clear view of McLeish. She numbered the times that he checked the mysterious package - seven times - and she counted her blessings that, so far, none of the military passengers on the deck beside her had even noticed her, never mind ask her her name. She had not realised that there were gun emplacements on the Isle and barely thirty-five minutes later, they all disembarked at what had been a hastily-assembled wood and stone dock, finished just last year, the stone of which had been there since before the turn of the last century, maybe even a left-over from the one previous to that one.

MacLeish assumed control of the detachment, ordering groups of men to gun batteries to the north and south of the tiny island. Once Amelia had slipped out onto the island, she looked on aghast as she estimated that another two-to-three hundred men had materialised and merged with this new platoon. They all seemed to willingly take instruction from MacLeish and she slunk into an outhouse, grateful to finally don an ill-fitting protective skull-cap. She used the chin strap to anchor the headgear low on her forehead and looked over the top of her printed instruction set: for the first time, she realised that this tiny piece of land was covered in Nissan huts and cowsheds and she noted MacLeish disappearing into one of the larger cowsheds, alone. Others disappeared in groups of three or five into the other metal structures, from which she could see gun turrets protruding from the roofs. She supposed that that line of open-roofed huts housed some sort of aerial defence system and the occupants would follow any incoming aircraft in the white tubes of light criss-crossing the Firth. With the island commander, this supposed august defender of the Eastern seaboard of Scotland, now out of sight, Amelia found herself admiring and watching the diligence of the personnel in assuming their defensive positions on the island. It was well-rehearsed, and the weeks of training for just such an event was paying off. It was obvious that the little island was a very open target for an aerial bombardment, which scared her.

With the calm dispersal of personnel, she made her way up the island with a small detachment moving towards the hut closest to the shed that MacLeish had entered. The three-man crew rushed in and the one closest to her put on headphones and nodded wisely when he heard the instructions being issued from the control station. Moments later, the monotonous buzz of the Messerschmidts was overhead as the enemy was making its way towards the Rosyth shipyards and factories. The firecracker crackles of the anti-aircraft guns all around her made little impression on the fleet of fighterplanes as they carved the way for the Heinkels' attack further up the Firth. Amelia got to the leader's base on time to see MacLeish discard the packaging on his parcel and attach the contents – some sort of mechanical device wired to a clock – to a round grey metallic object. He looked up at her, surprised to find he had been followed and he said, his eyes glowing demonically, "I am going to light this island up like one giant firework!". Amelia looked at him and heard herself say: "Don't be a fool! We will all be killed and you will let the bombers through", but it was too late, he pushed past her through the doorway, still carrying the round object. He threw it away towards a gun emplacement and they watched it roll fifteen, fifty, eighty yards, down the field. Seconds later, it came to a stop in a divet, and, as if he really was possessed, MacLeish ran after it and dislodged it from its resting place. He held the device at arms length but at that precise moment, the large bomb detonated: the Commander of Eastern Scotland defence was blown to smithereens and the blinding flash of the bomb acted like a magnet for the metal dragonflies overhead. Amelia's eardrums were traumatised and, as she dived for cover behind the only stone pillbox on the island, she was hit by some of the debris landing all around her. She lay on the floor of the pillbox, protected by its stone defences, as the enemy aircraft strafed the island with machine gun fire and the island's guns fired ineffective volley after volley into the sky.

The gunfire slowly abated as the drone of the Me9s faded into the distance. She stretched out her fingers and grasped the shiny metallic object that had bounced off her nose: it was MacLeish's clan tie-pin, with some blood-stained tie still attached. Surely this time MacLeish was no more? She struggled to her feet and moved back out into the smoky cordite-laden vapour enveloping the field in front of the control station. What she saw shocked her to the core: practically every Nissan hut had suffered damage from the fighter planes' strafing and men staggered around the field dazed by the ferocity of the last few minutes' hail of bullets. Some were badly injured and had garrotted their own limb wounds with belts and tied handkerchiefs around hand wounds, many were moaning and crying and falling, appearing to hit the ground unconscious, to be surrounded by groups of nurses and medics who were leaking out of hospital huts on the western side of the island, and were tending to the victim's injuries. It was a scene unlike anything she had seen before, and she had to accept that it was a scene she may indeed see many more times before this war was over.

She checked her Patek Philippe, the watch Alan had given her on their very first Christmas together – she had forty minutes until the ferry set sail for the mainland again and she knew now that she had been right to try to keep one step ahead of MacLeish. What would have been his next destination? Was he guilty of setting up the island for enemy attack? She found herself being guided into the well scrubbed, antiseptic-smelling confines of a tiny field hospital hut, a field hospital which was never intended to be so inundated with wounded men.

It was starting to look like a scene from the trenches of the last great battle. Men, barely able to sit up, asked of the whereabouts of "The Boss" and she realised that these men were actually loyal to the gruff, evasive, McLeish. She confessed to them that she had watched him run after a bomb and she quite deliberately and melodramatically held his tie pin aloft – "this, gentlemen, appears to be all that remains of "The Boss". There were gasps of shock (although someone clapped cruelly), at the news. "Och, this is terrible news!", one of the injured said loudly. To her mind, MacLeish had engineered this attack on the island through his quite deliberate detonation of what could only have been a sizeable bomb. He had almost had them all killed but it was, she realised, a measure of the man's standing that they chose to overlook that final treachery of his. She saw too that the work she had taken on at Sir Charles's charm-filled behest was potentially going to kill her but this adventure had become part of her journey to get to the truth behind Alan's death so she swore to herself, there and then, that this was all essential and was part of what she would do to avenge his death.

Her mind was filled with plots and sub-plots - what *really* was going on? MacLeish had been involved directly and indirectly with two deadly enemy attacks on Scottish soil, something that had been not been heard of up until now. Both attacks had been an attempt to illuminate targets for Nazi fighter-planes to attack, and both had had a measure of success. Was this MacLeish's goal, to make it easier for the enemy to eliminate obstacles deemed to be in the way? She asked casually about "The Boss" – what did they think of him, was he not one of the army "elite", thereby to be regarded with suspicion? Or was he "one of the boys", and then she got to wondering what his next destination might have been: she guessed Edinburgh and she knew that this must be her next port of call. She needed to touch base with Sir Charles in order to discuss McLeish's possible route.

She made landfall on the Fife headland before eleven o'clock and on that short journey, sitting under the stars on the deck of the tiny ferry, had smoked two Bocks as she thought about an expedition to Edinburgh. Her telegraph from the transmitter on the island to CD had been unsatisfactory – he was dismissive of her decision to head for the city as he had "been forming the view that these traitors are trying to sabotage, maybe even eliminate, our defence mechanisms", to weaken the ability of the country to withstand enemy invasion. He could see no useful purpose, he said, in following in the likely footsteps of such a dubious character. Unknown to her, Sir Charles had understood from Intelligence reports that searchlights, as part of the defence of the realm, had become viable targets. Here, though, Amelia questioned why MacLeish had sought to light up potential Nazi targets with fireballs. Sir Charles' immediate concern was with the proposition that the enemy's focus was all about knocking out the country's defences, especially the anti-aircraft searchlight bases. With the searchlights eliminated, only then could the Nazis consider a successful land invasion. *Proceed with caution*, she thought to herself, suddenly not feeling so sure of the support of Sir Charles in London. Then she thought: *"Wait a minute, I AM only doing this because of what happened in Belfast and because I want to get to the truth of Alan's disappearance! I am going to get to the bottom of this.*

Chapter 16

McGarry, The Monk and The Mouse

After an uncomfortable two hours sleep in her car at Anstruther, she checked her route again on her map and struck out for Edinburgh. In the absence of guidance from London, her instinct was to head for the University library as, it was clear and it seemed likely, MacLeish was well known to the university libraries the length and breadth of Scotland. Her previous visit to St Andrew's had been quite an inspired move, even if it had produced a hair-raising moment or two: she had taken a gamble dropping his name, it had worked, so why not try it again?

This university was a much different proposition – slap bang in the middle of this most cosmopolitan city, it felt like it belonged to every citizen of Edinburgh. She parked up on South Bridge and walked the short distance to the library building. It proved absurdly difficult to even catch a library assistant's eye and when she did eventually succeed in turning a listener's head to her theatrically-raised eyebrows, she was delighted by the immediate reaction to her query: "Hello, I am here in place of Hector MacLeish, I wonder could I see your Chief Librarian. My name is Amelia, Amelia

Lambe". She had decided that she had better start to use her maiden name to, as she thought, cover her tracks here in Scotland. If she was honest, she had no idea why she had just introduced herself as if she was actually some emissary appointed by MacLeish – emissary for what exactly, she had only scratched the surface of what his role was, of being some sort of co-ordinator of East Scotland defences. Was he really that loyal? She was ushered into a high-ceilinged, all white room, with a calfskin-topped mahogany desk in front of a wall symmetrically covered with framed master degree scrolls of the incumbent of the chair behind the desk. She glanced at the name plate which confirmed that yes, this was Murdo MacLintock, the same name inscribed on the yellowed vellums on the wall. His ego allowed him a little internal smile as he could see the light of confirmation in his visitor's face, watching her gaze shift between the wall ornamentation to his desk. He looked as odd as his alliterative name sounded, wide-shouldered and narrow of body in his MacLintock-tartan tank-top of red squares framed by steel-grey tramlines. The top two buttons of his poplin check shirt were open, and the collar was spread over the v-neck of his sleeveless knitwear in a surprisingly louche manner. As he stood up to shake her hand, she could see that the look was finished off in good taste with a grey tweed kilt and, she presumed, MacLintock tartan knee length woollen socks. "So then, madam", he started, "why no Hector today? Get caught up in Haddington again?". Of course Amelia had no idea what he was alluding to and he could see that in her face straight away. "Ah yes, bit of a "ladies man", dear old Hector. "Or "Lecher-on-the-Leash", as we used to call him!", said MacLintock, grinning broadly and rolling his eyes gratuitously. "I see", said Amelia calmly, grinning, "well I never saw *that* side of him. Rather glad I didn't, actually", she muttered, under her breath.

Her attempt to silence any more indiscretion went unnoticed, it seems, for MacLintock proceeded to tell her about the "time good ol' Letch" had travelled out beyond Garvald and Haddington, to "look in on proceedings at developments in the new base there". Unfortunately for Hector, he had come down from Buchan via Aberdeen and had had to overnight in a hotel in the centre of Haddington before travelling on the windy road out past the mountain hamlet the next morning. MacLintock continued: "Now Hector was a bit of an aficionado of malt whisky, more Cragganmore Single than Dalwhinnie's finest, y'understand?", he said, as if this was of some import to someone who only knew Glenfiddich and the Irish distillations in her brother's apartment. "Oh, right", she smiled back at him politely. "What happened?", she continued, feigning interest in his tale. He took a breath and said "Well, he got into an argument about whisky with a local and the only way to resolve it was the local way: they had the same six fine malts placed in front of them, one from each of the malt regions, and had six minutes to identify where each one came from, and whoever lost had to buy a round: "The Whisky Six", it's called. Letch won of course, and his hapless quarry wasted no time in buying the six bottles to share around the hotel bar. Oh and yes, MacLintock made sure another two or three bottles of Talisker Twenty-five year old was downed that night, though I doubt any of the paying customers saw a dram. Anyway, seems the whole affair turned Letch into quite the hit with the ladies-about-town and he made very firm friends with more than one young lady that night!", said MacLintock, with a lecherous grin. Amelia kept her counsel and instead asked about the base near Garvald – would it be an army base or an air force base, was it far from Garvald, but she fell short of asking if he planned to visit it.

MacLintock was quick to point out that MacLeish had even trained up one of the religious, an enemy sympathiser, in the Abbey out there. This, thought MacLintock, was an ingenious way to ensure all enemy activity could be monitored at the searchlight station when the air-raid siren was activated. After all, it was highly unlikely MacLeish's replacement would be able to scramble from St. Andrew's, and certainly not from Aberdeen. "I mean, if you couldn't trust a man of the cloth, who could you trust?", he asked. *Interesting, yes, it was clear that MacLeish could never be bilocational* she muttered to no-one in particular while she congratulated herself on her decision to absolutely pay Garvald and this monk a discrete visit.

MacLintock too was in no doubt that MacLeish's attractive stand-in would indeed travel out on that road and, as soon as she had left the office suite at the library, he rang Peter at Sancta Maria: "Troubling development today – some nosey parker, stand-in for Hamish, came-a-knocking, nothing to say for herself, be wary, visit imminent. McGarry in Napier to meet Walker about new club, apparently", were the key phrases she would have heard had she stayed on. "Thanks for the heads-up, Murdo, I will put down the usual smoke-screen. Do you need me to delay her a little? Or will McGarry let the mouse run free this time?", replied the voice at the other end. "No, no, let's see how she runs, shall we? I do think it might be wise to get in touch with the island though and let Meixmoron know about this strange occurrence, don't you?", MacLintock replied. "I have a funny feeling about it to be honest, charming though this Lambe woman might be", he concluded on a note of caution. "Yes. Yes, I think you're right. I will take care of it", said Peter, and he immediately sent the same succinct, carefully coded telegram to McGarry and then to Meixmoron:

“Andrew’s man in thrall to Lambe, threat imminent, will have to eliminate asap. Stop.”

Barely an hour later, with the accelerator pressed hard to the floor, the Atlantic was easing Amelia south-eastward through Haddington. She slowed to take in the quaint main street, and she noted the white-washed and turreted Hotel, which she guessed must have been the one MacLeish had stayed in. The town’s buildings had a very European look, she thought, feeling quite at home in these surroundings. She followed the handwritten signs for Gifford that took her further east towards the monastery where she hoped to meet with ‘Brother Peter’. Perhaps he was the key to finding out just what was going on in these parts: she was getting very suspicious indeed.

Chapter 17

Brother Peter

The road to Gifford was a narrow, undulating strip of hard clay, marked out over the centuries by plough-horses, then pilgrims on horseback, then pilgrims shanks mare, and now, latterly, by motorised vehicles. The village itself was nothing to write home about, a collection of small sandstone houses and a half-dozen or so understocked shops – a grocer, a post-office, two taverns, an undertaker. If Gifford was nothing to get excited about, then Garvald excelled – it essentially was made up of the nearby red sandstone monastery, a post office and an underwhelming and understocked provisions store. Still, it's picturesque and rural charm elevated it into lettercard status and Amelia felt a cold chill as she contemplated how she might go about meeting Brother Peter. It was not long before she pulled into the grounds of the red sandstone sanctuary perched on a hillside above Garvald. Built in the Scottish baronial style, its towers appearing at once majestic and yet oppressively dark and menacing - surely not built for a band of Cistercian monks – it harboured someone who was apparently trained to command an anti-aircraft unit at the airforce base on the nearby shoreline of North Berwick.

She drove into the courtyard of the monastery and pulled up beside a grove of mature willow trees, the last of their new leaves unfurling in the dapple of early summer sunshine. She had smiled at the sight of two rabbits disappearing into their burrows as her wheels crunched the pebbled concrete of the driveway and she eased her way down the thoroughfare. Parking under an archway to the west of the old red-bricked building, she got out and entered it through a split door less than ten yards from her car. This was not the main entrance to the monastery and so she was very wary, soon finding herself tiptoeing down the narrow corridor behind the door. With what little light was left streaming through the coloured glass fanlight over the door, her heart jumped as an electric light suddenly illuminated her pathway. Grateful for this timely if anonymous assistance, and not a little startled at its unexpectedness, she soon emerged into a bright lobby-type area and, as she blinked furiously, her eyes were immediately drawn to a black-clad figure silently disappearing through another door just twenty yards away. She thought nothing of following the mysterious figure and she too passed through the same doorway in pursuit of this first sign of life in the remote abbey. Why she was following, she had no idea, but she felt that by following, she might find her way to some answers. She needed to catch up with Brother Peter, or whoever this was, there were questions she wanted answers to: why had the anti-aircraft facilities on May been targeted by enemy fire, why was there no warning from London or the Eastern coastal defences? She wondered to herself if MacLintock was involved in other, more sinister, goings-on? The incident in St Andrew's was a worrying sign that something was not quite right.

She moved swiftly through the claustrophobic and cold souterrain, monitoring the dark silhouette now only fifty paces ahead. The silhouette came to a halt, in front of another silhouette, the original silhouette seeming to have become quite animated, hands gesticulating and fingers pointing back down the drafty passageway towards Amelia. Had she been rumbled, she thought? Suddenly, and she had not been expecting it, she seemed to have caught up with Brother Peter, and almost collided into the silhouette. She was face to face with the shadowy figure and was astonished to see that "Brother Peter" was, in fact, a nun. The other silhouette's head, no more than a few yards away, turned in its cowl and its female voice hissed "Petrina, I think you had better talk to this woman", which also appeared to be an instruction to her companion to say as little as possible.

Petrina!, thought Amelia, so she had misheard the name as "Peter". "Where is MacLintock?", "Sister Petrina" wanted to know, suddenly whirling around, a quite beautiful face framed by the colourless cloth of the wimple draped around neck, chin and cheeks. She had an elegant, easy presence which she quickly relaxed into when confronted by her stalker. "Oh, he has had to travel back to St Andrew's and then he heads back to Dundee", I'm new, Amelia Lambe's the name", she heard herself say. Amelia was fascinated by the idea that "Petrina" had been trained to take charge of the searchlight station in North Berwick in the (all too likely) event that MacLintock was unavailable. What if she herself was unavailable? Was she really up to the task? But much to her surprise, Amelia found that Petrina was willing to be more than a little forthcoming with the kind of detail that she knew could be very useful – perhaps it was the opportunity to talk to another woman, another woman perhaps unburdened by the strictures of her own life of servitude?

Amelia was surprised when Petrina said that there was a cabal of well-to-do Scots who were happy *not* to play their part in the defence of Britain, that they may choose to play into the arms of the Nazi cause through, initially, inaction. She rattled off the names of dukes and lairds and whisky heiresses who perhaps fitted that description. There was even a government minister's name she recognised and Geoffrey Lambe's sister found herself wishing that her brother had been a more inquisitive journalist - this stuff was dynamite, she reckoned, and she found herself concentrating hard on the nun's every word because she knew she would have to get a message back to London as soon as possible.

Then the nun said something quite unexpected: "I agree with MacLintock, we must be vigilant around these parts. After all, the Americans have got a foothold in Britain now, what if they see our country as more than just an aircraft base, what if *they* want to conquer us? What if we are just a stepping stone to Europe for them? Perhaps it is *they* who have become our enemy and we are putting up all of these defences against our German friends when really we are letting a new enemy take our friendship for granted by giving them free reign on our land?" These were very odd words coming from a religious sister and Amelia stood silently amused as she looked into Petrina's face. She could see a disturbing intensity in her eyes as she said those unanticipated words. To be honest, it was the same look she had seen in the younger McGarry's eyes in Belfast, the same look as she had seen in his father's eyes here in Scotland and it made her think that there was something bigger going on that she was just beginning to get a sense of. She decided to change tack: "So what *is* MacLintock's role around here then, Sister?", she asked.

This question seemed strange to Petrina as she thought Amelia had been sent by MacLintock in his stead: "Oh, I thought he had sent you here?", she asked in reply. Amelia's face flushed pink as she was suddenly taken off guard. "Yes, yes he did", she lied, "but you can appreciate, I don't live in Scotland. I've only really just arrived from a funeral in Belfast". "Belfast?", repeated the nun in a soft East Lothian lilt. "You mean, you have not come from London? I thought that if MacLintock was not available, a replacement would have to come from the south. Or at least a local..., oh, that sounds awful Miss Lambe, forgive me, I really don't wish that to sound harsh!", said the nun, her eyes cowed because of her sudden embarrassment, her hands fidgeting with a set of mother-of-pearl rosary beads. "Oh, that's fine, Sister, I understand your frustration, really I do!", Amelia reassured the clearly stressed nun. The other nun was still nearby and Amelia started when she raised her arm suddenly and silenced them with a loud "shush!". They became aware of the distant wail of an air-raid siren and Petrina immediately adopted a commandeering air of authority as she turned to Amelia and said "You have a car, could you run me up to the searchlight station?" Amelia confirmed yes, she could, and minutes later, Petrina changed from the monastic-wear of a Cistercian nun into more appropriate khaki gaberdine slacks and sturdy black infantry boots. She lowered herself into the front seat of the Bugatti and off they headed for the Berwickshire coast. Amelia stifled the questions swirling around her head about Petrina's moonlighting as, as she saw it, a vital cog in the southern Scottish defences.

As the almost prehistoric outline of the Atlantic growled its way out of, and beyond, East Linton parish, "Petrina" revealed that her real name was Anna Ramsay. She described how her German mother, Eva, had met her father, Edinburgh councillor Struan Ramsay, when, as a young lance-corporal, he rescued her from a collapsing building in her hometown of Dusseldorf in 1918. It was love at first sight for her parents and even though her father had returned to his hometown of Arbroath in early 1919, her mother remaining in Germany, they wrote to each other every day and had risked their lives to be together again. By the end of 1922, they had married in Westminster Cathedral, honeymooned in Newmarket, and set up home on the south coast. Incredibly, and after ten happy years in Bournemouth, they relocated to Edinburgh so that her mother could work again as a college librarian: a job had come up in Heriot Watt after the Chief Librarian finally succumbed to the injuries he had sustained in the Battle of the Somme and his passing and subsequent replacement had allowed for a ripple of new positions in Merchiston. Remarkably, her German accent and outlook failed to deter the selectors from making her their choice and she was delighted to finally get the chance to use her German qualifications, ameliorated by her two years study in "Library Science" at Southampton University while they lived in Bournemouth. Her father, retired now from the army, had thrown himself into the textile industry in Edinburgh and had used his inheritance to buy a kilt shop on The Mound in the city centre. The shop came with a loom and, after a crash course in weaving, he propelled himself into making Cowan's Kilt Shop the number one destination for the lairds and ladies of the Scottish east coast. Anna, "Petrina" as she was inexplicably nicknamed, knew that he was looking to their elder daughter to take over the business but she had decided that she wanted to dedicate her life to the Lord above and the Cistercian way of life was the one she wanted above all else. She conceded to Amelia that, yes, she had behaved quite selfishly really but her parents had never been anything but supportive of her solitary life. Then out of nowhere, along came MacLintock last year, searching for help in the development of an initiative of "extreme national importance" and she felt quite compelled, no doubt by God, to put herself forward for it.

The air-raid siren had been growing louder as the little black sportster sped its way down off the hilly roads of East Linton towards North Berwick until, finally, the searchlight installation came into view. Petrina pointed directions for Amelia to follow and minutes later, they were both rushing into the control unit for cover as the first flight of German fighter aircraft's waspish black bodies came into blurred view in the watery light of the evening sun. Amelia had not expected to find herself thus caught out by the need to take shelter with the nun, a woman of the cloth who nevertheless was charged with no less a job than acting as Eastern Scotland's deputy air defence commander. How strange, she thought, as her reflexes forced her to dip her head low as the fighter planes swooped low on the anti-aircraft guns that were firing volley after volley from the natural amphitheatre of the base. As they reached the entrance porch to the control unit, a stream of machine gun fire ripped into the adjacent concrete anti-aircraft gun base and was tracing a line along the soil leading to the command unit. Suddenly, Petrina lost her footing and her trailing right leg was hit by not one but two twenty millimetre bullets and her screams stopped Amelia in her tracks. She turned to see the nun clutching at her right leg, her grey/blue slacks colouring crimson as the blood seeped into the cloth. There was a coil of insulated wire on a chair at the entrance to the command unit and Amelia quickly decided that she would use it as a tourniquet on Petrina's leg. This may stop the bleeding and she would use her kerchief, perhaps even tear a sleeve off her shirt, to stem the flow of blood. She stooped as she ran and she reached out to Petrina, lifting her up into a crouched position so that they could both move swiftly into the building, heads lowered. The nun grimaced and gasped as the pain tore up her leg into her body and they both fell scrambling for sanctuary in the main room of the control unit as the Messerschmidts' machine gun fire ripped into the grass around them. Amelia pulled the nun's slacks down at the waistband but no further, as the right trouser leg clung to the nun's bloodied leg. Amelia had to use her car key to tear a hole in the saturated cloth clinging to the fleshwounds, before applying the tourniquet. Petrina screamed loudly at this move and Amelia took a clean kerchief from her pocket and knotted it tightly around the nun's injured calf. The piece of linen turned red instantly and the blood seemed to be flowing ever more strongly so Amelia hit on the idea of using her own brassiere to stem the flow further. This was a more successful procedure as the brassiere wrapped around the injuries twice and the elastic held the "bandage" in place.

If Amelia surprised herself with her Girl Scout proficiency, Petrina surprised her by telling her that she would be letting down MacLintock because she would not now be able to travel to Durham due to this "set-back". "Durham?", repeated Amelia, suddenly sensing that perhaps Petrina was on the verge of unveiling more details of what was going on. For fear that she wouldn't be able to identify what was materialising, she decided to put herself into the centre of action: "I can bring you to Durham if you like?", she offered, seizing the opportunity to be close to the key player now that MacLintock and the elder McGarry were out of immediate reach. Petrina was startled to find such a willing chauffeuse but was cautious in her reply: "What a kind, kind offer! I really don't believe I will be able to travel but if I do, I think I will stick to my original plan, there may be more danger ahead." "Danger?", repeated Amelia, "what danger lies ahead? And how are you going to get there anyway?". "Did I not say?", said the nun, "I will be travelling in an armoured car to Durham. Hamish" – and here her unadorned face turned from its usual rosy hue to bright red – "insists that I travel safely and incognito, whenever possible. As does Father Benedict". Amelia hid her amusement at Petrina's discomfort - why does she become so embarrassed when she mentions MacLintock? *Incognito? In an armoured car? Hardly undercover, now, is it?* she was thinking, but then the nun came back: "I can see what you're thinking - the drivers always use different routes. It's quite safe, it really is", she said, knowing that she was probably losing this argument. Amelia took her cue to ask what kind of dangers she should expect. The answer was inevitably airborne - fighter planes and their machine guns and bombs coming from above were the number one danger, but "the ack-ack guns will get them first", was Petrina's confident prediction. Amelia was not so confident.

Within the hour, and after a five minute consultation with the military medical team, a hastily reconstructed Sister Petrina was helped into the Daimler for her journey across the border to Durham. Amelia was aghast that the nun, fit lady though she may be, had elected to make the odious journey down the A1 in the pre-arranged Dingo and, although she was feigning that she herself would be returning to Northern Ireland the following day, her real plan was to follow Petrina's heavy chariot at a discrete distance.

CHAPTER 18

A Lambe chases a Dingo to Durham

The Dingo, a camouflaged, stubby, unattractive vehicle, careered south at high speed down the carriageway of the main North-South artery towards Newcastle-Upon-Tyne. It was a shockingly unstable machine, bouncing and swinging wildly across the median into the fortunately-unbusy, northbound lane. The hundred or so miles should take under two hours to cover and Amelia found she had to keep the accelerator pressed to the floor to keep the Daimler in her sights. She, too, was driving at breakneck speed to make sure her own car stayed true to the increasingly wet conditions as, very quickly, she had been forced to switch on the windshield wipers and headlights to keep her view clear in the pelting rain.

The day had turned quite grey, a turn up for the books, the day having begun with the promising sunshine of the early morning. She detested driving at speed in this kind of weather, and she was straining her eyes to keep the khaki colours of the Dingo in some sort of view. This squall was making for very uncomfortable driving: the brewing storm was doing everything it could to buffet and shake the Atlantic off its singular mission but its tyres hugged each and every dip and rise in the road. The North Sea lay to her left and at times the waves lapped hungrily at the embankment supporting the steamrollered broken stone over which her car glided, its long low body dipping and clinging to each and every undulation in its path.

A north-bound car, which had appeared from nowhere, full beam headlights shining, sprayed a sheet of water onto her windscreen as they streaked past each other. It made Amelia jump with fright and her knuckles whitened as her grip on the steering wheel tightened. She wished that the Daimler would slow down and allow her some breathing space - she was tired and hungry and breakfast was but a distant memory. The Dingo was following signs for Berwick-on-Tweed and, as she looked left across another rugged bay, she instinctively knew that she had crossed the border into England again. She thought that she ought to be relieved to find herself back on familiar territory but then, of course, northern England was not familiar territory at all.

The wet road sucked the cars onwards, past signs for distant Holy Island, with its fairytale castle watching over its priory ruins, and Cuthberts's weather-beaten statue standing sentry nearby. They shot past Grey's Monument in Newcastle until, minutes later, the hillside of Durham came into blurry focus. An awe-inspiring vision was emerging from the wet greyness and, perched atop the low rain clouds, Amelia gasped as she took on the astonishing scale of the old Norman cathedral nestling above its ancient town. Amelia was reminded of Mont Saint-Michel, her favourite destination in all of France, its towering majesty dominating and feeding off the surrounding ring of village buildings, much like the queen bee and her busy minions. It was a sight to behold and she watched as the Daimler cut a path up into the city and onto the paved apron to the front of the monumental cathedral. Amelia had, as far as she was concerned, stayed largely out of sight of the blast-proof Dingo and she watched it from her less-than-blast-proof car as she pulled up in Owengate, parking a discreet distance from the cathedral with its courtyard and associated offices dotted around the Cathedral Square. She made her way on foot, stealthily manoeuvring through the old cut stone streets, closing in on the Great Western doorway. She stopped and she watched as Petrina emerged from the Daimler and made her way across to the cathedral entrance doors, towering high above her.

She lifted the masked face door knocker delicately and bounced it twice against the ancient oak. The thunderous raps inside the cathedral came to the attention of the curate and, seconds later, an impressively tall, grey-haired monk – why, he must have been seven feet tall and looking vaguely menacing in his black full length robes – pulled the door smoothly inwards. Her eye was distracted as he wore a single white cotton glove on his left hand, the one holding the enormous iron doorknob. This must be Peter, for that was the only name Petrina had mentioned in relation to Durham, and she decided that she somehow had to follow them into the cathedral as they disappeared behind the great cathedral doors.

She entered via the western doorway and glided quietly through the marbled square of the Gallilee Chapel, past Bede's venerable sarcophagus. Over the light tap of her footsteps, she was drawn towards the low drone of a female voice and a strangled male chuckle coming from somewhere beyond the altar screen of the chapel. They must be in the main body of the Cathedral proper, she decided, and she silently inched along the golden rail protecting the base of the screen, towards the sound. She reached the edge of the screen and stopped, her eyes focussing on a reflection of the pair in a highly polished brass memorial plaque riveted to the cold marble wall: the monk was stooped forward and it was clear to Amelia that he had Petrina in a loving embrace, their heads swivelling in time with each other as they were kissing and she could see Petrina's hands reach up to cup his chiselled features. "Well, well", she thought, "no wonder Petrina blushed so readily at the very thought of seeing Peter here". She herself felt a little aroused at the thought of this illicit liaison and she watched the reflection unabashed as Peter lifted the nun up, her arms locking around his neck as she wrapped her legs around his waist. They were kissing deeply and urgently, like long lost lovers, and she spotted bare skin and bodily contact amid the swirl of black and cream cassocks. Suddenly, the nun unfurled herself from the monk and her feet hit the floor with a muffled thud and the two began to speak in hushed tones: she heard "York", "Ampleforth", "Anselm", and she wondered if it meant that someone was going to pay a visit to these places soon, though she had not heard of "Anselm" before. At this point, she could see that she herself may well be visible in the reflective plaque and so she retreated out of view. And not a moment too soon because next thing she knew, the cathedral midday bells were being overshadowed by the air-raid siren sounding in the distance.

The sound of the siren was broken by the loud instructions of the ARP warden as he rounded up the Cathedral visitors into the more compact chapel. In fairness, it gave him better control of the incredibly stoical locals who, for the umpteenth time this week, found themselves following his familiar instructions to minimise their own panic and make the target that much smaller for the enemy. Amelia followed as she and her two charges joined the throng of visitors – a Women's Institute group from Harrogate on a brass-rubbing expedition; a knot of Anglican lay-readers visiting the relics of St Cuthbert; and a clutch of Northumbrian branch librarians visiting the underground Cathedral archives. The roar of the incoming fighter planes shook the cathedral walls and she could hear the engine screams as the first wave of Messerschmidts bombarded the vulnerable city from the south-east. Some of those incarcerated in the cathedral were seriously panicked all the same, and six of them ran out of the building through the courtyard to get away from the commotion. They were stopped dead in their tracks as bullets strafed the grassy square and Amelia realised too late that both Peter and Petrina had been part of this disparate group: it was as if, like convicts, they had all seen a chance to escape this congregation of sitting ducks and decided to make a bolt for it. Of course, uppermost in Petrina's mind was Peter's role to coordinate the response at the nearby searchlight station up the road at South Shields, so it was vital that he escape to do his duty.

Amelia darted forward to watch the escapees through an archway and was shocked when Petrina lost her footing as she ran. It was not such a surprise of course, given the extent of her recent injuries. She had lifted her robes at the side to reveal athletic legs, albeit one had been bandaged tightly and she ran as strongly as possible, somehow dodging the machine-gun fire. Her piercing, agonised scream was the first indication that she had been hit by a random bullet and she crumpled to the paving in the courtyard, her right leg again caught up behind her, blood streaming freely from another wound to the upper abdomen. Amelia was fascinated to see Peter stumble to a brief halt only to appear to continue with the ill-conceived "escape plan" after he had stooped to shake her shoulders gently. His face spoke to Amelia in its ashen pallor - it was clear at that moment that Petrina had been fatally wounded. Her head hung limply as Peter gently tried to stir her back to life but it was obvious there was little point trying. His face contorted as he realised the enormity of this loss – clearly, his friendship with the handsome nun was on another level – and he too was mortally wounded. The small white glove came up to meet the bare sinewy fingers of his other hand and he covered his distressed face as he bayed her name at the top of his voice, as if a powerful cry could revive her. It did no such thing, of course, and the horror was confounded when he took aim with his own revolver and fired a single shot into her chest – Amelia could only assume the nun had suffered a catastrophic injury, the machine gun bullet having torn straight through her back and exiting her body through her left breast. It had ripped through a lung as it did so and Fr Peter had decided there and then that the only humane thing to do was to finish the job. He sank to the ground, sobbing uncontrollably, the gun falling safely onto the grassy verge in the courtyard. He was cradling her uncovered head against his broken heart, the white glove stroking her hair tenderly, he cradling his nun in a macabre embrace. He pressed his lips against her unlined forehead, stared at the gun and tucked it up under his cassock.

All the while, Amelia was watching and wondering. Finally, he was on his way and, glancing around the silenced cathedral, he walked purposefully towards the main entrance and strode directly through the open side door of the armoured car.

Time was of the essence and Peter was torn now. There were three possible scenarios unfolding and he had a decision to make – to do his main duty at the searchlight station; to stay with the love of his life to make sure she received a happy repose; or to travel on to York to co-ordinate yet another attack.

Amelia waited until the Daimler moved off before making her escape back across the cobblestones to her little black roadster. Whatever route Peter chose, and he had no clue about it, Amelia was sure to follow.

Lightning Source UK Ltd.
Milton Keynes UK
UKHW04f2208150918
328943UK00008B/36/P